Bolan found himself in the middle of a firestorm

"There he is!" an angry voice screamed, a finger pointed accusingly.

The big man had no idea what was going on, but it spelled trouble in capital letters. A group of inmates was advancing on him, shaking their fists, yelling "Thief!"

The Executioner moved back to the wall, protecting himself from assault from behind. He was ringed by shouting prisoners, although they kept out of range of his iron fists.

On the fringes of the crowd, Bolan saw Raimondo's grinning face and knew that the prison boss was behind whatever was going down.

A rock sailed in from his left and delivered a solid blow to his shoulder, hard enough to bruise. A second whistled by his ear.

Suddenly he was surrounded by a black vortex, spinning wildly, staring into colored constellations of blinking lights. The lights faded with a roar as he fell over a cliff into total darkness.

MACK BOLAN®

The Executioner

DON PENDLETON's EXECUTIONER

MACK BOLAN.

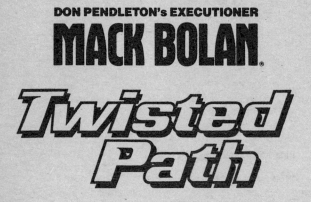

Twisted Path

A GOLD EAGLE BOOK FROM

WORLDWIDE.

TORONTO • NEW YORK • LONDON • PARIS
AMSTERDAM • STOCKHOLM • HAMBURG
ATHENS • MILAN • TOKYO • SYDNEY

First edition January 1989

ISBN 0-373-61121-8

Special thanks and acknowledgment to
Kirk Sanson for his contribution to this work.

The central task and the highest form of a revolution is to seize political power by armed force, to settle problems by war.

—Mao Tse-tung
Problems of War and Strategy

It's human nature to cut corners, look for easy answers—especially if it means a better way of life. But I take exception to someone promoting "social change" from the barrel of a gun. Wanting more from life is one thing. Terrorism is another.

—Mack Bolan

THE
MACK BOLAN®
LEGEND

Nothing less than a war could have fashioned the destiny of the man called Mack Bolan. Bolan earned the Executioner title in the jungle hell of Vietnam.

But this soldier also wore another name—Sergeant Mercy. He was so tagged because of the compassion he showed to wounded comrades-in-arms and Vietnamese civilians.

Mack Bolan's second tour of duty ended prematurely when he was given emergency leave to return home and bury his family, victims of the Mob. Then he declared a one-man war against the Mafia.

He confronted the Families head-on from coast to coast, and soon a hope of victory began to appear. But Bolan had broken society's every rule. That same society started gunning for this elusive warrior—to no avail.

So Bolan was offered amnesty to work within the system against terrorism. This time, as an employee of Uncle Sam, Bolan became Colonel John Phoenix. With a command center at Stony Man Farm in Virginia, he and his new allies—Able Team and Phoenix Force—waged relentless war on a new adversary: the KGB.

But when his one true love, April Rose, died at the hands of the Soviet terror machine, Bolan severed all ties with Establishment authority.

Now, after a lengthy lone-wolf struggle and much soul-searching, the Executioner has agreed to enter an "arm's-length" alliance with his government once more, reserving the right to pursue personal missions in his Everlasting War.

1

Cameron McIntyre barged into Jake Sharp's office, flinging the door back hard against the wall. He wore a Burberry topcoat and a deerstalker hat, affecting the manner of a Scottish laird from the moors of the old country.

"Get your coat, Sharp. We're taking a wee trip."

He turned on his heel and started down the hall, leaving the young man scrambling to catch up with him.

Sharp was accustomed to the brusque demands of his employer. During the past six months as director of Internal Audit he had often been summoned abruptly for a spur-of-the-moment meeting with managers and suppliers. Sharp always delivered perfect satisfaction. The FBI had worked hard to get him this position, and it would never do to be fired for incompetence.

The past few months had passed in silent, covert action as Sharp battled account books and computer files to force their secrets from them. On the surface the McIntyre Arms Corporation was perfectly legitimate. It manufactured assemblies for the M-16 and M-60 as well as acting as a certified arms dealer to foreign customers.

The FBI was convinced that below the veneer of corporate respectability, McIntyre was delving into the murky but profitable business of selling weapons to insurgents and terrorists worldwide.

Sharp had been following paper trails that led along twisted paths from one dummy company to another offshore subsidiary, then to yet more numbered fronts in a dozen countries. Every bit of corporate law in existence was being used to cloak sordid, cutthroat deals as legitimate business.

Months of digging had brought Sharp to the point where he was almost ready to tie the loose ends of a thousand unraveled deals together. Then he could truss McIntyre like a Christmas turkey and deliver him squawking to a grand jury.

It was early evening and the executive floor was deserted. Sharp would have left long before if McIntyre hadn't asked him to stay late to assist him at an important meeting. They took a private elevator thirty-six stories down to the reserved section of the garage that held McIntyre's armored limousine.

Kovack, a hard-looking bruiser who doubled as a bodyguard, held the rear door open. Sharp suspected that he was mute since he had never heard the man utter a single sound.

Sharp and his employer rode in silence in the back of the stretch limo, traveling eastward from the gleaming downtown Los Angeles office tower. McIntyre stared into the distance through the window, his chin propped on his hand. Sharp fidgeted, twisting his fingers together, forcing them apart by an act of will, only to have them join again almost of their own volition. The pressure of leading a double life was getting to him. Normally a talkative, outgoing man, he was uncomfortable with McIntyre's ability to remain endlessly silent.

Clearing his throat, he ventured a question. "Where are we going?"

McIntyre regarded him closely, but maintained his silence.

Sharp felt like a bug under a microscope. He had always been intimidated by his superior's reticence, which was combined with a ruthless and explosive temper locked behind a seemingly granite exterior. Employees who screwed up didn't last long before McIntyre fired them in a withering blast of sarcastic ire.

"I know you've been anxious to learn more about the business, so I'm taking you to see one of my best customers. It'll be quite a meeting." McIntyre's flat brown eyes held a hint of an unfathomable emotion, which left Sharp puzzled.

McIntyre reached for the built-in bar and spilled an inch of Scotch into two crystal glasses, passing one to Sharp. "Have a nip to ward off the chill and protect us from evil." He turned again to the window.

The limo angled into a decrepit industrial park, where weeds had enveloped the rusting remnants of railway spurs. Hunks of formless metal lay abandoned to the elements. As the black car pulled up to the third warehouse, twelve-foot-high doors slid back with a rumble. The big vehicle passed through, and came to a halt as the doors closed behind it.

A twin of McIntyre's car was parked twenty yards away. A pair of fourteen-foot Ryder trucks stood end on to the left. Two burly workmen leaned against the rear bumper of one truck, two more lounging by the warehouse doors. The old storehouse stretched the length of a football field, the far corners nearly invisible in the gloom. Supports for an overhead crane—long since removed—ran eighteen feet above. Shards of glass and scraps of wood and metal cluttered the floor, glittering in the headlights of the two stretch Lincolns.

McIntyre climbed out of the vehicle, motioning Sharp to follow. At the same time, four men in immaculate business suits poured from the other limo.

The shortest and roundest of the group advanced, his right hand outstretched, his left swinging a briefcase. "Ah, Señor McIntyre, a pleasure to do business with you again." The soft accent and the dark features placed the visitor from somewhere south of the Rio Grande.

"Good to see you, Mr. Carrillo," McIntyre responded, taking the proffered hand. "This is Mr. Sharp. I thought he might help convince you of the value of your purchase."

Carrillo looked blank for a moment and then roared with laughter.

"You are a good man to do business with, Señor McIntyre. You have such a wonderful sense of humor."

"I'm afraid that not everyone here will share it," McIntyre said, sending Carrillo into a fit once more.

Sharp wasn't sure what was going on. Obviously there was some joke at his expense, but he couldn't see what the point was. All he knew was that a sense of impending disaster was creeping down his spine, chilling his insides.

McIntyre gestured to the men by the truck, who promptly rolled up the tailgate. One reached inside to grab a coil of thick nylon rope before they advanced leisurely toward McIntyre and Sharp.

"Did you really think I was such a fool as to not notice what you were doing?" McIntyre remarked casually to Sharp. "You were poking your nose into things that were no business of yours. I keep track of who looks at my confidential files, you see."

Sharp stood openmouthed, shocked into inaction. He had known that there was a chance he'd be discovered, but now that it had actually happened, coping was beyond his power. His legs felt too weak to run.

"I can explain—" he began, but broke off when McIntyre held up a hand.

By now the two thugs had reached him. One produced a set of handcuffs and clipped the agent's hands together behind his back. The second tied a neat bowline around the cuffs and threw the other end over a support beam fifteen feet off the floor.

"When I started to suspect that you weren't what you appeared to be, I had you followed. I had your phone tapped. You were watched all the time. I knew who you met with and who you spoke to. I knew every time you went to the bathroom. And I found out that you were passing my secrets to the FBI."

McIntyre shook his head several times, as though he found what he was saying hard to believe. "I can never forgive an injury and certainly not treason against me. You took my money and sold my secrets."

"I'm an agent with the FBI. You will be in very serious trouble if any harm comes to me," Sharp retorted with more bravado than he felt. A sense of desperation washed over him, and his throat filled with bile. His boss at the Bureau had warned that he was pushing too hard, trying to crack the case too quickly.

McIntyre, stung by the opposition, exploded. "Damn you and your arrogance! Damn you and your sneaking, prying ways!" The arms merchant screamed into his captive's face, his twisted features mere inches from Sharp's. "I'll take that chance. But you can't be allowed to expose any more of my private business." McIntyre turned his back on Sharp and walked off, icy calm once more, as though a vault door had opened and then shut again on his temper. "He's yours, Carrillo," he called over his shoulder.

Carrillo turned to his waiting men. "Pick three."

He waved his hand to the two men from the truck. They pulled on the free end of the nylon, raising Sharp about eight feet above the cracked concrete surface, and secured the end to a ringbolt set in a girder. The agent grunted as his full weight pulled on his shoulders, stretched unnaturally behind him. The pain made him feel as though his shoulders were going to dislocate at any moment. One of the hardmen reached up and gave his foot a savage yank. The sudden agony forced a scream from Sharp's lips.

McIntyre joined Carrillo. "As we agreed. Twenty cases of M-16s, ten cases of M-60 GPMGs and a hundred fifty cases of 7.62 mm ammunition."

"And I have exactly what you want right here," Carrillo said, tapping the black leather briefcase he hefted in his left hand.

The three gunmen approached, two with M-16s and the third carrying an M-60 with a short length of ammo belt looped over his arm.

They took positions facing Sharp, about thirty feet from his heaving chest. The FBI agent began to kick his legs frantically, a last desperate attempt to somehow escape the fate that stared at him from three unblinking metal eyes.

Carrillo nodded, and the guns chattered just long enough to send two magazines and a short belt of slugs slamming into Special Agent Sharp. His body shuddered under the impact of the point-blank gunfire, shaking like a leaf in a gale as the rounds punched him.

When the last echoes of the drumming fire fell silent, Carrillo handed over the briefcase. "Thank you for an excellent demonstration. I shall have another, larger order for you shortly."

McIntyre grunted in reply, his attention fixed on the dripping remnants of Sharp.

The gunrunners took to their vehicles, speeding out of the darkened warehouse while one hitter paused to chain and padlock the door.

Inside, the flies were beginning to settle.

2

It was early afternoon, and the fierce southern sun drove the pampered residents of Lima from one air-conditioned oasis to another. The humidity sapped the energy of the few citizens who dared to venture out at that hour, temporarily slowing the heart of Peru's great metropolis.

Four men huddled nervously in a narrow side street close to the Plaza de Toros de Acho, Lima's famous bullring. At their backs, the foothills of the Andes rose abruptly, dominating the city sprawled at their base. The nearest peak was surmounted by a giant cross, testament to the Catholic heritage of Peru ever since the Spanish conquistador Francisco Pizarro had destroyed the Inca empire and founded Lima in 1535.

The four men had come from the squatters' settlements that covered the slopes of the hills. The tar-paper shanties were a world apart from the wealth of the city, far from the riches of Lima's Camino Real, the royal road, lined with shops where the price of one dress was more than a year's salary for the impoverished peasants.

The men were almost indistinguishable at first glance. High, prominent cheekbones, receding chins and leathery bronzed skin marked them as descendants of the Incas, who had ruled the country before the invasion of the Spaniards.

Now they were prepared to strike hard at their conquerors, to take a small step toward restoring Peru to its rightful owners and establishing a Marxist utopia.

Cautiously they crept onto the Avenida Abancay, a ten-lane artery that cut through the heart of the city. Brightly colored ponchos concealed their weapons, while broad woven hats sat like inverted dishes to ward off the sun. Each man carried a razor-sharp machete and three sticks of dynamite. Julio Nuñez, the leader, carried the prize, a cherished M-16 with a full clip and a spare, one of the few assault weapons his band possessed.

Julio didn't like the plan his unknown superiors had decreed. In theory it was to be a simple bank robbery to replenish the coffers of the organization. But in this enormous city he felt exposed, naked to the eyes of the many strangers who crowded the broad sidewalk. He would rather have been preparing to strike at some sleepy village in the high Andes, near to Ayacucho where he had friends and a safe retreat.

However, from what little he knew, he was only a small part of a larger plan to show that they could strike at the very heart of the government, to show that no one was safe, anywhere, at any time.

Like a good soldier, he would obey his orders.

He glanced at the cheap Taiwanese watch he wore.

It was time for action.

AT THE FOOT of Avenida Abancay, three men waited with growing excitement. They were parked in a battered olive-drab jeep across from the Ministry of Education, a modern twenty-two-story tower. For the past ten minutes limousines had been arriving at the ministry, each accompanied by a swarm of motorcycle police.

This marked the weekly cabinet session, which they had observed from a distance for the past two months. The order of arrival was nearly always the same, with the least secure ministers pulling in first to stake out their territory and to be on hand to greet each of the later arrivals. The president made his appearance three minutes before meeting time. The last to show was always the Minister of the Interior. Controlling the police and the intelligence services, he made a point of demonstrating that he was powerful enough to be independent.

"Here is the president. It won't be long now." The driver's words were unnecessary. His companions ignored him, eyes fixed on the activity across the street as the president was bundled into the ministry building, flanked by bodyguards.

"I still think that we should have gone for the president. Think of the stir that would have caused!"

"A lot of people inside and outside the government would have thanked us," the man in the passenger seat responded. "This will shake them just as much. Besides, we are not supposed to plan strategy, only carry out our orders. Now be quiet. Who knows if some spy is listening?"

As if to prove the superstition that naming an evil summoned it, a policeman wandered over to inspect the group of Indians he had noticed watching the arrivals so intently.

"What are you waiting for?" he demanded of the driver, a submachine gun cradled in his arms.

The driver's right hand crept to the machete hidden between the seats, preparing for a swift stroke, his dark eyes flickering between the policeman's eyes and the throbbing jugular vein where the machete would bite.

"We have never been to Lima before. We want to see everything."

The policeman hesitated. A nervous prickling tickled his neck. These three looked more surly than was usual. But the impassive Indians were so hard to read. This group looked as worthless and grubby as the rest of their kind. He was only surprised that they had enough money for a car. Finally he decided that there was nothing to be gained by hassling a few peasants and stalked off with a grunt.

All three tried to keep the relief they felt from showing on their faces.

Two minutes later, another limousine approached the Ministry of Education.

"Time," the driver said, as his two passengers reached for rough-woven sacks on the floor.

THINGS BEGAN TO GO WRONG the moment the four Indians pushed through the doors of a branch of the Banco Comercial del Peru.

Possibly some glint of metal showed through their ponchos. Perhaps it was the grim expressions on their faces. Or maybe the guard just didn't like Indians. Whatever the reason, the security man's eyes flickered to the four men, and he immediately reached for his holstered pistol.

The carefully prepared plan was abandoned on the spot. The closest man reacted instantly, launching himself at the guard. The two tumbled to the ground, the half-drawn gun skittering across the marble floor. The second man drew his machete from its sheath and arced a chopping blow at the guard's forehead, splitting it like a ripe coconut. The third intruder scooped up the dead man's pistol and stuck it in his belt.

Pandemonium exploded among the dozen or so customers and staff, and they stampeded toward the rear of the bank, pushing through the hinged opening in the barricade that separated the public and private sections of the branch. They retreated as far as possible from the Indians, and those who could, took shelter behind the few flimsy pressboard desks behind the counter.

Brandishing the M-16, Julio strode to the counter and ordered everyone to lie on the floor. The terrified hostages collapsed to the tile, kicking and clawing one another, trying to find a place where they would be protected from the robbers, even if only by another body.

A door slammed to Julio's right. He gestured to his men to start filling the sacks they had brought as he stormed to an office marked Loans. He kicked the door above the handle, shattering the soft wood and bouncing the door against the wall.

Inside a young man in a dark suit was shouting rapidly into a phone. It was a brave gesture, but foolish. A single round from the M-16 caught him in the neck, changing the shouts into an incoherent gurgle as the dark blood spilled from his shattered throat onto the receiver.

There was no time to lose. Julio rejoined his men, urging them to hurry. He glanced occasionally at the huddled prisoners but reserved most of his attention for the sidewalk outside.

One man had finished rifling the cash drawers and came to Julio's side, a bulging sack across his shoulder. The other two robbers were still cleaning out the vault.

Julio cursed loudly as two police cars pulled up outside, the officers springing from their vehicles to take positions on each side of the doors. The terrorist fired through the plate glass, sending shards flying as one of the doors exploded. Two quick rounds from the rifle drilled one policeman, sprawling him half in and half out of the passenger seat.

The remaining three cops took up positions behind their cars, spraying the bank interior with random gunfire. The glass in the second door tinkled to the floor, pulverized by flying metal. A hail of .38 slugs caught one of the terrorists as he hurried out of the vault, ripping into his belly and leaving him writhing from the pain of shredded intestines.

Julio and his companion were anxious to conserve their meager supply of ammo, and returned fire only sporadically. They knew they were certain to lose a waiting game, as reinforcements were probably only minutes away. They lay prone behind the body of the guard, which had already absorbed a couple of stray bullets. The third terrorist crouched slightly to their rear.

Julio turned to him and snapped a command. The man nodded, fished in the bottom of his money-filled sack and withdrew three sticks of dynamite. He cut a short fuse on one, lit it and tossed the explosive through the shattered door.

The nearest police car exploded into a pyramid of flame a moment later; the cop hiding behind the vehicle was blown into the air in the midst of the fireball. Hot debris rained in all directions.

This was the robbers' best chance for escape, maybe their only chance. Julio pointed to the right, back the way they had come. Neither the police nor the army could dig them out of the endless nest of rat holes and alleys that comprised the barrio.

"Now!" His two companions broke into a run, while Julio stood and blasted a 3-round burst at the only surviving cop. Luck, finally. The last uniform collapsed behind his protective door, his left temple streaming blood.

Julio poked his head into the blazing sunlight, with the ingrained caution learned from years of hit-and-run missions. His men were thirty yards down the sidewalk, picking up speed as they sprinted for safety. A sudden staccato hammering announced the arrival of the reinforcements.

Three more cruisers burst onto the scene, automatic weapons chattering 9 mm death from the open windows. The two terrorists stumbled and spun to the sidewalk, sliding in their own blood, which poured from a dozen punctures.

Julio dived frantically for the safety of the bank, just eluding a barrage of bullets that chipped away at the doorframe and the brickwork.

A flurry of slamming doors was followed by a moment of silence, presumably while the reinforcements crept into new firing positions. There would be no opportunity to surrender.

This was the end of the line.

The terrorist leader knew that he had one final task, one final action to make sure that the government remembered this day with horror, as a promise of what was to come until his people were free.

As he grabbed the two remaining sticks of dynamite and lit the fuses, he was proud that his hand shook only a little. Shots were peppering the doorway again as the police prepared for an all-out assault.

The hostages had remained on the floor, some sobbing, some wrapping their arms around their heads in futile protection. The fuses were burning down, with only seconds to go. One after the other, Julio flung the sticks among the prone captives. They shied away from the hissing objects as if they were deadly snakes, scrambling over one another on hands and knees, sobs turning to shrieks of terror.

Julio Nuñez grabbed the rifle and, shouting, "Gonzalo!" at the top of his lungs, he burst from the bank, firing from the hip. And ran straight into a wall of lead. Suddenly he found himself flat on his back, his lifeblood seeping from myriad wounds. He barely heard the explosion that detonated behind him.

THE THREE MEN in the jeep sprang into action. Fernando Montero unwrapped an M-60, with the ammunition threaded from a canister into the firing chamber. His brother, Raul, pulled out a futuristic-looking fifty-two-inch Kevlar-wound tube, a Stingshot, which was a shoulder-fired antitank weapon. Capable of penetrating tank armor or seven feet of concrete, it would slice through the minister's armored car like scissors through paper.

It was an anxious moment. None of the attackers had actually fired the weapon before. Stingshots were too expensive to waste on target practice. That was partly why the ambushers had chosen such a dangerously exposed position. From here, visible as they were, they were within forty yards of their target, well within the rocket launcher's effective range.

"Don't miss, Raul," the driver cautioned.

Raul didn't bother to reply; his attention was focused on keeping the target steady in his sights.

Just as the minister's limo rolled to a stop, he twisted the rocket's tail. The projectile streaked forward, covering the distance in the blink of an eye.

One and a half pounds of high explosive turned the minister's car—and the minister—into a blazing fireball. Fragments of disintegrated metal scythed like shrapnel through the surrounding crowd, transforming nearby police and government workers into shredded meat.

The terrorists watched, stupefied for a moment by the result. This was far better, much more horrific than they had hoped.

One policeman had recovered his wits more quickly than the rest. He scanned the vicinity, his eyes lighting on the three openmouthed Indians with a strange, smoking weapon in the back of their jeep. He rushed toward them, clawing at his pistol in its holster.

Fernando elbowed the driver in the side, urging him to get them out of there. He levered the M-60 onto the edge of the door and loosed a burst at the cop, stitching a line from groin to chin.

The jeep's gears engaged, throwing them against the cushions in a sudden surge of acceleration. The driver swung left, speeding for the outskirts of town and a waiting safehouse.

Fernando held down the trigger in a sustained burst, the M-60 chewing through the ammo belt at 550 rounds a minute. Death flew at the onlookers, smashing into flesh and bone.

The jeep powered down the broad avenue, weaving in and out of the traffic. Jewelry stores, furriers, expensive clothing shops and arcades lined the street. Whenever the machine gunner saw a small crowd of well-dressed strollers, he would squeeze off a burst, toppling the gaily dressed shoppers into ragged, oozing heaps. Raul had gotten into the act as well, throwing sticks of dynamite like firecrackers along both sides of the street, leaving a trail of devastation in his wake. This was the enemy, the privileged class. All wealth was theft, Marx had said, and as far as the Indians were concerned, there were no civilians and no truce in their war of liberation.

Almost as though they had crossed into another country, the character of the street changed, even as it narrowed to a mean little avenue. Now there were only small vendors and fruit sellers, tiny dress stores that sold rough woven shawls and ponchos.

The Indians housed their weapons. They were back among their people.

"TELL ME, General Palma, what would you have me do? Let me guess. You think that the time has come when I should give up my position and turn the country over to a military dictatorship—in other words, to you.''

President Alan Garcia sat back in his chair, idly tapping a pencil on his desktop. He knew that random noises irritated the general.

General Arturo Palma, chief commander of the Peruvian military police, didn't bother to protest. He was well-known as the strongest advocate of law and order in the country. His ferocity and outright brutality in suppressing political unrest had made him many powerful friends. There were enemies, of course, but the general dismissed them as either jealous or part of the bleeding left.

Palma had risen through the ranks rapidly, and now thought of himself as the best man to save his country from the increasing trend to violence of the warring political factions. He didn't trouble to conceal his good opinion of himself.

"Mr. President, these are difficult times, as we both know. The radical left is ready to cause trouble any time. Incidents of violence are escalating rapidly. Two days ago the Shining Path killed nearly fifty people and wounded five times as many in those two attacks. Now not even your own ministers are safe.

"There can be no accommodation with these terrorists. They seek only one thing: the overthrow of the state by force. Only a strong central government can prevent this, one that is prepared to meet violence on its own terms. National security cannot be compromised for the sake of personal freedoms, which would certainly disappear if the terrorists ever took power."

Palma paused, pleased with his own rhetoric.

"Very touching, General. Quite suitable for the presidential campaign. One might think that if the Shining Path did not exist, you would have to invent them." Garcia held up his hand at the stormy look clouding Palma's aristocratic face. "No disrespect intended, of course, General.

"But tell me, why are you sure that it was the Shining Path?"

"I am positive that they are behind this outrage. The four terrorists killed were Indians, who, as you know, comprise the majority of the group. Bloody, senseless attacks are their trademark. The only new feature was the use of some modern weapons."

"General, have you obtained any further information on those weapons they used? It would be catastrophic if the Shining Path was able to obtain that kind of firepower in quantity."

Palma consulted some notes stretched before him. "The M-16 we recovered was part of a shipment from the U.S. for Turkey that never arrived. It was diverted while en route. We believe that the attack on the minister of the interior involved a U.S.-made rocket called a Stingshot. How the Path got one is anyone's guess."

Garcia, disturbed by this information, got up from his desk and began to pace restlessly, hands clasped behind his back, chin thrust toward the floor.

"The CIA, General. Could they be behind this? I have never been very popular with the Americans, especially since I limited repayment to those damnable foreign banks and nationalized our own. Some say the Americans hate a man who costs them money more than one who disagrees with them over ideology. I have heard rumors that the American president calls me another Castro. Could he be supplying the Shining Path to oust me?"

Palma considered his answer before replying. Would it be better to play on the president's well-known paranoia? If he harped on this theme, possibly with some false evidence he could concoct, it might have the president seeking an American behind every bush. Could he turn that to his advantage? Or was Garcia just probing to see how far Palma would push his presidential ambitions? He decided to take the safer course at present.

"I don't think that is likely. What would they have to gain by replacing you with a group still farther to the left? Anyway, I don't think the CIA has much stomach for foreign intrigues of that kind these days. They are still hurting from the Nicaragua affair."

"I'm so glad that you agree with me, General Palma," Garcia said with ill-concealed sarcasm. "I have asked the Americans to look into this weapons matter as a personal favor. Nothing promised in return, of course, but just enough of a hint to send some very powerful people digging extremely hard. I think they might have some information for us very soon."

Palma was angry, a sudden blaze that showed in a stiffened jaw and carefully enunciated words. "I wish you had consulted me, Mr. President. I would have advised against it. This is a Peruvian problem, and it should be solved by Peruvians."

"I wish that was possible, General!" Garcia shouted, angered in turn by his subordinate. "I wish that you could solve the problem without assistance. Instead the Shining Path grows stronger, not weaker. You are the general in charge of the military police. There are thousands of troops and police scouring the highlands, and still you have not been able to crush this rebellion. Guzman, an old philosophy professor, and his ragtag band of Indians are crippling my government. And let me remind you that I am still president, and I will not have you questioning my decisions. Good day!"

Garcia studiously pretended to read a memo as Palma got up and stormed from the room, not bothering to close the door.

The president wondered for the thousandth time how best to remove the thorn in his side that was named Palma.

3

Mack Bolan crouched behind a palm tree at the edge of an open field forty-five minutes north of Miami.

Clad in a snug blacksuit, face and hands covered by combat camouflage cosmetics, the big man blended into the shadows. He held a sleek Beretta 93-R, the barrel fitted with a custom silencer, and a .44 Desert Eagle rode at his hip. Black military webbing held spare magazines and a wicked Ka-bar knife for close work. Fragmentation and thermite grenades completed the warrior's weaponry for the upcoming hit. NVD goggles covered his eyes, giving the field a spooky illusion of daylight.

Bolan was here to meet Delmar ''Big Deal'' Jones, one of the main distributors in the area. Jones ran roughshod over the street-level dealers and the shooting galleries of the roach-infested slums. He dealt whatever made money, everything from crack to smack. Anything a buyer could swallow, snort or shoot, Del's boys would be happy to provide. Del was becoming a very rich man.

A Justice Department informant had whispered that the dealer would be restocking tonight, receiving a shipment from a factory located somewhere in the Bahamas. Bolan's aim was to make sure that the chemical death never hit the streets. Delmar Jones was about to discover that he wasn't such a big deal after all.

This wouldn't be the first time he'd met Jones. Ten days ago the dealer had been in a courtroom, facing charges that ran the gamut from conspiracy to commit murder to possession of an unlicensed firearm. Bolan had been there at the invitation of Dale Givens, an acquaintance in the district attorney's office who was sympathetic to the warrior's objectives but skeptical of his methods.

"Come down for the trial. You'll enjoy it. Jones is going to go so far down that he'll be lucky to see the sunshine on alternate leap years." The prosecutor had been confident, obviously holding an ace.

The courtroom ritual was very impressive. The judge, a hard-jawed man in his fifties, retained an air of solid competence. His mouth was pursed in a sour expression, the product of years of trying to separate the half-truths from the outright lies, of dealing with an unending string of lowlifes and their sometimes equally criminal counselors.

The orderly progression of events, the American flag, the symbols of law and justice all gave Bolan pause. He wondered yet again about the lonely course he had chosen for himself. His enemies accused him of subverting the system he was trying to protect, saying that he was no better than the men he destroyed. They said that if more people did as he did and played the roles of judge, jury and executioner, the fragile fabric of society would collapse into a horror of vengeance and retribution.

Maybe they were right.

Occasionally Bolan worried that he might be on the wrong track; perhaps he should let the law take care of things in its own sweet time. Did his means justify the end?

He didn't have all the answers, but in the final analysis he did know this: he destroyed so that others might live. The people who had faced his judgment had lost any right to live long ago. Bolan was only carrying out the sentence they had written on their own foreheads with the blood of their victims.

The courtroom scene had had one disturbing detail: Delmar Jones hadn't acted like a man who expected to go to prison.

Jones was in his late twenties, and had an arrogant attitude that seeped from his pores. He hadn't bothered to dress to impress. Clothed from head to toes in flamboyant white, Jones dripped heavy gold, with multiple chains at his throat and wrists. A single large ruby shone in his left earlobe. He looked every inch the wealthy thug he was.

He paid no attention to the prosecutor's righteous denunciation of the many crimes he had committed, the sorrow he had sown, the lives he had ruined. Instead, Jones studied a racing form, doodled on a pad, turned around in his chair to ogle and smile at a couple of beauties among the spectators.

The reason for his confidence became apparent when the prosecution's star witness took the stand, a former lieutenant in Jones's ring. The D.A. expected that the man's testimony would put Jones away for life.

It didn't go down that way.

When on the stand, the pusher changed his story. In a voice almost too low to be heard, he denied everything. He claimed that the confession and the carefully transcribed testimony were lies of his own fabrication, made out of envy for his boss. Delmar Jones was an honest and good patriotic citizen who gave to charity and wouldn't hurt a fly.

A few sarcastic comments in reply from Jones's high-powered attorney and it was all over. The judge, looking as though he had swallowed a quart of lemon juice, had no option. Jones was a free man. His former lieutenant went to jail for perjury.

Before he left, Jones had a few parting words for Givens. "Don't look so surprised, dude. There's no lawyer yet been born who can keep Delmar Jones down. Hey, you want a real job? I can afford you. Why, I've got so many girlfriends that I spend more than your little salary on condoms. Come on, baby." Jones departed with a roar of laughter, his attorney in tow.

Bolan hit the streets to start digging.

Later, Bolan had a word with Givens over Jones's acquittal.

"I don't know what happened, Mack." The attorney had been angry and puzzled, his voice weary with the fatigue of endless sixteen-hour days spent in preparing a case that had vanished in minutes. "He was in a safehouse. He was watched every minute. No one could have gotten to him."

"Somebody obviously did. Anytime more than two people know something, it's only a matter of time before a man as rich and nasty as Jones finds out. The old carrot and stick. Offer some underpaid cop fifty grand to carry a message and threaten to tear off his children's heads if he doesn't. How many people can resist that kind of pressure?"

Givens didn't bother to answer. Bolan was right, and there was nothing he could do to change the facts. He pressed his fists into red-rimmed eyes, rubbing them to try to remove the sting. "My father-in-law has been asking me to join his civil law practice in Maryland. Easy money. Good clients. Short hours. I've said no. Until now."

Bolan didn't say anything. He couldn't give anyone else the motivation to fight when it looked as if it was against his own best interests. It had to come from inside, or all the coaxing and rationalizing in the world wasn't worth a damn. Shell shock didn't only happen in shooting wars. The trenches of downtown Miami had their casualties, too.

Bolan just rested a hand on Givens's shoulder, a salute from one soldier to another, and left.

He had business to take care of.

The business deal would go down any minute now, but Jones wasn't going to like the price the Executioner would make him pay.

A line of three cars was kicking up dust, traveling slowly down the dirt road that ended in the open field where Bolan crouched. The first and last vehicles were inconspicuous American sedans. The middle car was the Porsche 911 that Jones favored.

Three gunners got out of each sedan to establish a defense perimeter. Jones hadn't lived this long by taking chances. The guards spread out, four making a slow examination of the area around the cars, shining flashlights into the pockets of tangled underbrush. The other two men walked the length of the field, checking for any newly erected posts or wire. The authorities had been using drastic measures of late to try to discourage the dealers from using vacant fields as landing strips. This one was still clean.

Bolan tensed as one of the gunners approached his hiding place, thirty yards from Jones's car. He recognized the silhouette of an Ingram Model 10, a short-barreled machine pistol that could spray 1100 rounds a minute like water from a hose.

He held his breath, easing the Ka-bar from its sheath.

The hardguy played the beam to Bolan's left, as the rustling of some night creature attracted his attention. Then he disappeared into the bush as the warrior exhaled slowly.

After a shouted relay of all clears echoed from the end of the field, Jones and another bodyguard emerged from the Porsche. At the far end of the field, two red flares were placed forty yards apart to serve as guideposts.

A few minutes of silence passed, broken only by the croak of frogs and rustle of palm fronds in the light evening breeze. Bolan could smell the burning cigar that was clamped between Jones's lips. The warrior could have dropped him then, but the timing wasn't right.

Bolan, a master sniper, could've shot Jones's eyes out a dozen times during the past week. But he was waiting for the moment when he could not only take out Jones, but could also intercept the drug shipment. The informant had specified that the street value of the drugs would be between thirty and fifty million.

Several minutes passed before the droning of a small airplane engine became audible from the east. Bolan spotted the plane flying low above the treetops, hugging the ground to avoid radar detection. The Cessna skimmed the low palms at the end of the field and touched down in front of the flares.

Jones and five of his gunners converged on the aircraft, which had halted a hundred yards from the parked cars. The flares were abruptly doused.

Bolan moved out from the shadows, confident that any noise he made would be covered by what was taking place down by the plane, as the cargo was pitched onto the ground for Jones to inspect. The nearby guards were less than professional, paying more attention to the lights and action in front of them than to any potential threat from the rear.

The two gunners stood twenty feet apart, one about five feet closer to the plane than the other. Bolan decided to first take out the man who was casually leaning against the right fender of a Cutlass Ciera.

The Executioner padded forward, edging between the parked cars with all the stealth of a prowling jungle cat. The gunman never suspected Bolan's presence, until he felt a callused hand clamp over his mouth, muffling the scream that ended stillborn as six inches of cold steel sliced into his back. The tip pierced the heart in an instant, and the big muscle was torn to shreds. The enforcer died without a gasp.

Bolan eased the body to the ground between the cars, so that the man appeared to have abruptly vanished. The warrior went to the ground by the left door of the Porsche.

The second gunner, aware by some sixth sense that his partner was no longer listening to his chatter, turned to probe the darkness. "Hey, Dixie. Where are you, man? The boss is gonna skin you."

The gunman advanced slowly, the Ingram nosing the shadows ahead of him.

Bolan didn't want to give himself away but the problem was how to silence the alerted guard without giving him a chance to loose a warning burst. The warrior slid a magazine from a pouch and held it in his left hand. His right still grasped the Ka-bar, slick with Dixie's lifeblood.

The triggerman had reached the front of the Porsche. Another few feet, and he was sure to see the body of his companion. Bolan flung the magazine overhand above the roof of the car. When it bounced off the hood of the far sedan with a metallic ring, the gunner spun toward the sound.

Bolan catapulted into action.

The timing was split second. In a quick step he was behind the gunman, thrusting hard with the Ka-bar into the guy's left kidney. Bolan knew that this was supposed to be so painful that the victim wouldn't have the strength to cry out. The warrior's right hand flashed to the trigger guard, a strong forefinger pushing behind the gunman's trigger finger, jamming the trigger forward as a spasm jerked through the dying gunner.

The machine pistol slipped from the dead man's hand and into Bolan's as the gunner fell backward, his eyes and mouth open in a silent scream.

Bolan wiped the knife on the fallen man's shirt and sheathed it before starting off toward the knot of men clustered around the plane. Only a little more than a minute and a half had elapsed since Bolan started to make his move.

The warrior ran forward in a combat crouch, determined to make the most of his surprise visit now that he had secured his retreat.

When Bolan was still seventy feet away, he booted a stone that rustled through the low grass. The slight noise attracted the attention of the pilot, who was idling near the nose of the plane, thinking of how he would spend his bonus in the fleshpots of Miami.

Bolan let loose with the little subgun, spraying twenty manglers a second at the men unpacking the plane. The pilot went down first, four rounds churning his guts. Three more ripped into the chest of the nearest guard, who slid to the ground leaking blood. Two more collapsed by the door of the plane, one with half his skull missing.

Bolan flung away the empty Ingram and dived to ground, rolling to his left as he depressed the safety spoon of a thermite grenade. The remaining gunners opened up in short bursts, probing the area where Bolan had last been.

On a two count Bolan hurled the grenade, sending it tumbling under the fuselage of the Cessna. He hugged the ground as the bomb detonated, sending coals of thermite scorching into the backs of the gunmen. A few blazing chips penetrated the fuel tank, and a moment later the plane exploded, incinerating the remaining cargo. A foul stench of burning flesh combined with the reek of oxidizing chemicals.

Bolan unleathered the Beretta before moving forward to inspect the damage. Only one body was still twitching—a gunner whose left leg was nearly severed. The guy was screaming from the pain of thermite nodules scorching their way through his flesh. He wouldn't last long, but Bolan helped him on his way with a mercy round. The twitching stopped.

The big man swore under his breath. The one body he wanted to see most was missing. Jones must have run at the first shot, using the plane for cover and leaving his men to bear the brunt of the Executioner's wrath.

Delmar Jones had escaped judgment once. It wouldn't be as easy this time.

Bolan moved away from the killzone and edged through the undisturbed grass looking for the dealer's trail, using the combat skills that had kept him alive through dozens of campaigns.

The trail was clear for two hundred yards as Jones had blundered wildly through the field and bushes; clear, that is, to someone who knew how to read the signs. At one point a fresh gouge in the earth marked a spot where the drug dealer had missed his footing, coming down hard on a rock, which bore a drop of blood. A narrow, shallow stream put an end to the easy pursuit.

The possibilities ticked through Bolan's mind. Jones had three choices: one was to hide out and hope to remain undiscovered until the battle zone was clear; another was to cross the stream, strike out for the highway a half mile south and flag down a ride to the city; the last was to travel east or west along the stream, circle around back and try to make it to the car.

The last was clearly the most dangerous, since Jones had no way of knowing how strong the opposition might be. Someone might be lying in ambush just to prevent that

possibility. But remaining in hiding was almost as dangerous. The most reasonable thing for the dealer to have done
was to have continued south to the highway.

Bolan paused a moment to listen for the sound of
splashing. Negative. Jones wasn't trying to fool him by
following the stream. The warrior crossed the water,
searching the banks for clues.

Twenty yards to the left, a wet heel mark on a rock was
made visible by the NVD goggles. The Executioner was off
and running again. With the advantage of the goggles and
long practice in open-terrain pursuit, Bolan expected to run
Jones to ground before the guy could make the highway.

Every hundred yards he paused to listen. His diligence
paid off when he finally heard the faint sound of rubber on
concrete in the distance. Jones was approaching the relative safety of the highway. A couple of stops later, ears
cocked for the slightest unusual sound, he heard a muffled
thump and a curse only a few yards ahead as Jones tripped
over his own feet.

Bolan proceeded cautiously, knowing that Jones would
be armed.

The warrior poked his head around a low palm and saw
Jones on hands and knees, searching for something. His
night goggles showed him the butt of a pistol in the grass
ten feet to Jones's left.

"Time's up, Jones." Bolan stepped into the open.

"I give up, man!" The drug lord scrambled to his feet
and threw his arms over his head, all bravado gone, a sickly,
supplicating smile etched into his face. His clothes were
torn and dirty, and he was bleeding from multiple cuts and
scratches sustained on his wild flight through the underbrush. Still, Jones tried to brazen it out, using tactics that
had always worked before. "You want money? I got it,
man. You walk away, you can name your price, any

amount. A hundred thousand, a million, you just say the word. You just name your price. I've got gold, I've got diamonds. Whatever I've got, you can have if you just let me go."

"Jones, you've got nothing at all."

The Beretta coughed a 3-round burst, stitching a bloody triangle into Jones's heart.

BOLAN STOOD in the shower, enjoying the feeling of the water as it cascaded over his weary body. The warrior spent so much time wallowing in the gutters with the filth that made up the underworld that he sometimes felt he would never be able to get clean.

An insistent ringing pierced the sound of the pounding water. There were only two people who knew he was at this number: his brother, Johnny, and Hal Brognola. A call from either meant trouble.

Bolan climbed dripping from the shower and grabbed the phone. "Hello."

"Striker. How's it going down there?"

"You can read about it in the morning paper, Hal."

"That's good. Because I need you for something very special."

"What's the catch this time?"

"Striker, really." Brognola did his best to sound offended, but they both knew that the man from Justice never got in touch unless Bolan's involvement was strictly necessary. "Let's just say that this has an international flavor. When can you be here?"

"Is tomorrow soon enough?"

4

"You know I hate political games, Striker. They're usually worse than grubby—most often they're just plain stupid." Hal Brognola paced restlessly around his Justice Department office, eyes skipping rapidly over the cluttered surface of his desk. He didn't like being told what to do, especially when it meant calling in a favor from a man who not long ago had had a heavy price on his head, put there by the same people who now were pressuring Brognola to ask the guy for help. "But maybe this time there just might be some sense in those lamebrains."

Mack Bolan waited patiently for Brognola to come to the point, maintaining a still silence that would have spooked anyone but the man from Justice.

"It seems the President got a call from one Alan Garcia, president of Peru. Now this rather pleased the Man, since these two haven't exactly been on speaking terms for the past while. You know why?" Brognola jabbed out the question with an index finger as he sank into the chair behind his file-covered desk. He fixed Bolan with a flinty stare.

"Money."

"Give the man a cigar. Peru has been holding back payments on billions of dollars' worth of American loans. That has gotten a lot of people very hot under the collar."

Bolan knew it. A lot of people refused to see the evil that stood on nearly every street corner in the United States, a menace that was slowly making honest Americans prisoners in their own homes. The worst of the ostriches were the few who could afford the life-style that insulated them from the realities of the street. But touch a dollar that belonged to them, and those same people would scream as though someone had shot the family dog.

Brognola was a little uncomfortable. He'd asked Bolan here for something that amounted to a politically motivated request. In spite of their long association, Bolan set his own priorities. There was nothing to stop the big man from walking away for his own reasons. The Fed pushed ahead. "In a nutshell, Garcia hinted that Peru might rethink its position on the loans in return for one small favor. A favor that's a cry for help."

"So there's a catch, is there?" Bolan's tone was noncommittal. He had worked too closely with Brognola to believe that his friend would ever knowingly throw him a curve. Brognola had earned his respect and friendship long ago and had hung by Bolan when just knowing the Executioner was close to treason. But even Brognola couldn't see through a brick wall, so Bolan had to decide for himself if someone at a higher level was trying to pin something on him.

There were people in every country on the planet who would pay a small fortune to read his obituary. Some of them lived right here in Washington.

"Don't worry, Striker, this is right down your alley. You know much about the Shining Path?"

Bolan had a file-card memory, with an entry for most of the terrorist organizations in the world. Put on paper, it would practically make an encyclopedia, but the answer sprang immediately to mind.

He knew the Shining Path all right, and his interest quickened as he spoke. "They're a fanatical left-wing terrorist group trying to destabilize the Peruvian government. They're aggressive, primitive and violent, extremely secretive. A real problem on the home front."

"Absolutely right, except for one point. Now they're no longer primitive. They used to be a pretty low-budget revolutionary group. They carried on their war with a few hundred captured weapons, mostly without ammunition, and about 300,000 sticks of dynamite. But now they've changed tactics. The Shining Path has been hitting banks and using the money to buy black market arms. And the death toll looks like it's going through the roof."

"And this is where I come in?"

"Exactly. The latest information shows that they have an American source. The same M-16s and M-60s our Army uses are ending up in the hands of the Shining Path."

Bolan felt his stomach do a flip as a sudden anger coursed through him. Somewhere an arms dealer was turning armament made to keep the peace into weapons of terror. Innocent people were dying because another "businessman" was intent on making a buck.

And every bullet was stamped Made in the U.S.A.

Bolan shifted in his seat, the sudden urge to action becoming almost a physical force. "Why me, Hal, instead of the CIA? And where would I start?"

Brognola leaned back in his chair as the sudden power of the man across from him showed in the contained, catlike movements and blazing eyes. The big Fed experienced a momentary desire to follow Bolan into the field, such was the strength that Bolan radiated. But it was only a brief fantasy. Brognola knew his limitations—he'd be about as much use to the warrior as a rubber scalpel would be to a surgeon.

"Garcia is a little paranoid where the Agency is concerned. Having a bunch of spooks wandering around Peru would probably cause more problems than it would solve.

"As for the second question, you start out on the West Coast. The FBI has a lead that would be worth following. I hope it pans out, since right now it's the only one we've got. Officially the mission is to plug the arms pipeline from this end. If you find something that might send you on to the Peruvian connection, that's up to you. But I know that a lot of people would appreciate it. Unofficially, of course."

Brognola fished among a thick pile of files weighing down a corner of his desk before dropping one in front of Bolan. "That's what we know about the Shining Path. It'll make for some interesting reading. There's also a plane ticket and the names of your contacts on the coast."

Bolan grabbed the manila folder and rose to leave. Now that he had a target there wasn't a moment to lose.

Brognola's voice stopped him with his hand on the doorknob. "One more thing, Striker. The FBI recently lost a good man on this arms-dealing case. They're taking this one kind of personally. You'll keep that in mind, won't you?"

With a grunt that could have been an agreement, an acknowledgment or a snort of disgust, the big man slipped through the doorway, leaving Brognola staring at a room that suddenly felt cold and empty.

He shook his head and grabbed another file.

ABOARD A DIRECT FLIGHT to San Francisco, Bolan flipped open the file and began to absorb details.

The Shining Path, or Sendero Luminoso as they were known locally, had first appeared in 1980 with political communiqués tied to dogs hanged from lampposts in Lima.

Since then, a campaign of terror, including assassinations, small-town executions and blown-up railways and bridges, had taken more than ten thousand lives.

The founder was Abimael Guzman, an ex-professor of philosophy, a moon-faced idealist in his fifties who had a taste for classical music and violence.

An ardent Communist, Guzman had absorbed early Russian revolutionary writings and had kept marching to the left. Rejecting Russian Communism and Castroism, he had eventually settled on Chairman Mao as his model. Sickened by the new quasi-capitalist China, he now believed that the only true representatives of Communist ideology had been Marx, Lenin and Mao Tse-tung. Calling himself "The Fourth Sword of Marxism," he changed his name to Gonzalo and proclaimed himself president of the Republic of New Democracy.

Leaving the Western-funded university where he taught, he then launched a revolutionary movement aimed at overthrowing the democratic government and achieving an agrarian-based Communist utopia, dominated by the Indian descendants of the Incas.

Concentrated in the highlands along the spine of the Andes, Guzman and his disciples had proved impossible to run to ground. Three provinces were under direct military rule to try to halt the spread of "Gonzalo's" terror. So far, there were no clear winners in the hard-fought contest—only a lot of dead losers who would rather have remained on the sidelines.

The latest intelligence on Guzman was pure speculation. Some claimed that he had died of leukemia years before. No one outside the movement had seen the revolutionary leader for nearly ten years.

Dead or alive, Gonzalo had the ability to inspire a ruthless fanaticism in his followers. Organized into rigid cells, the group was impenetrable. The members knew very little apart from the names of their cell mates, and seldom broke even under rigorous interrogation by the Peruvian police.

Bolan sighed. There was much more in the bulging file, mostly accounts of various atrocities committed by the Shining Path, along with government excesses in trying to suppress them. He didn't need to read any more. He'd seen the same story written in blood in dozens of different countries, and from time to time he had written the final chapter himself.

Bolan looked out the window, resting his eyes on the purity of the sun-streaked cumulus clouds below. The warrior had seen firsthand how badly most of the impoverished masses of South America lived. He understood the almost hypnotic appeal of a few ringing phrases spoken by a magnetic personality or preached to uneducated peasants almost like a religious cult.

So many people were looking for easy answers, especially when they meant a better life. Bolan couldn't always blame them, particularly when there appeared to be so few choices that might lead them out of their crushing misery.

But Bolan drew the line when it came to promoting social change from the barrel of a gun or with a stick of dynamite. Working for the betterment of his fellow man was something he'd been doing in his own way ever since he'd decided to make a stand for what was right.

Blowing someone apart because he disagreed with your politics was terrorism.

The Executioner knew that there was only one reply to those tactics, only one answer that the terrorists would understand. Force must be met with counterforce, strong medicine in a dose that would leave the Shining Path choking on their own violent prescription.

Brognola was right, he was the ideal man for the job.

5

Special Agent Roger Kline was not a happy man, and the person sitting in the visitor's chair across from him was doing nothing to improve his mood. Kline spoke a little louder to try to conceal the growing sense of unease that had crept over him.

"Now, see here, Mr. Blanski, you aren't being very helpful."

Across the desk, Mack Bolan, traveling under his Michael Blanski alias, said nothing. It wasn't his job to be helpful to the FBI. Rather, it was up to the FBI to cooperate with him. Kline and he both knew it, and the special agent was clearly resentful. So far, this so-called briefing session had consisted of Kline trying to probe him for information on who his backers were. Bolan wasn't giving.

They were seated in a shabby second-floor walk-up in a run-down office building several blocks from the docks. The spacious, bare office had been transformed into a temporary mission headquarters for the duration. In a far corner, two other agents were poring over paperwork.

Bolan scrutinized the agent, eyes flickering from carefully sculptured hair to immaculate three-piece blue pin-striped suit to perfectly trimmed nails drumming sporadically on the desktop. Kline's gaze locked with Bolan's, then darted away.

"Cut the crap, Kline. I know you don't want me here, but you don't have a choice. Get on with what you're going to tell me."

The uncompromising growl jerked Kline's attention back to the big man. Blanski, a strong-jawed and solid-looking man who stood well over six feet, was dressed in a sport coat and casual trousers. Kline felt that there was something odd about the way his visitor was dressed. Not that there was anything wrong with the clothes themselves. It was more a sense that they were inappropriate to Blanski's whole being.

Sort of like a gorilla in a suit.

No, that was all wrong, Kline corrected himself. This man looked capable of dining with the President and being perfectly at home. It was more like seeing John Wayne in a tuxedo, he decided. No matter how Blanski dressed, he gave off an aura that didn't square with offices and ties. A sense of danger clung to the man like a second skin.

Kline had an uncanny intuition about people that he relied on heavily. Its accuracy was one of the things that had propelled him this far up the ladder in his eleven-year career with the Bureau. He would guess this man as former military, maybe an ex-commando, probably a fairly high-ranking officer from his self-possessed air of command. The agent meant to find out what he was up against.

He would start by betting his pension that this guy's real name wasn't Michael Blanski.

The problem, as Kline saw it, was to use Blanski—or whoever he was—to advance the case. And at the same time, Kline's career.

The best way, he decided, was to appear to capitulate, but to still pull the strings. The special agent had had plenty of practice in being the puppet master. He'd have Blanski dancing his tune in no time.

"Well, getting an urgent message from the Justice Department telling me to cooperate with someone from outside the Bureau isn't something that happens every day. Especially when the case involves the murder of an FBI agent. But I'll be happy to keep you fully informed."

In a pig's eye, Bolan thought. This guy was suddenly a shade too affable to be believable.

Kline settled back in his chair and clasped his hands behind his head, a pose he often adopted when he was in a lecturing mood. "Let me just run down what has happened so far. A young agent, Jake Sharp, infiltrated the operation of one Cameron McIntyre, a major arms manufacturer. We've had our suspicions about McIntyre for a while now, and Sharp was gathering evidence to nail him. Suddenly, about a month ago, Sharp disappeared. A couple of vagrants found the body about two weeks later. It wasn't a pretty sight." Kline forced away the image of the mangled, half-decayed body he'd had to identify at the county morgue. He'd been battling with the recurring nightmare vision every day since Sharp's body had been found hanging like a rejected haunch of beef.

"McIntyre denies everything." Kline nodded repeatedly for emphasis. "He has a pack of unimpeachable witnesses who swear that he had nothing to do with Sharp's death. There's no evidence to link Sharp and McIntyre together that night. End of case, so far. But we'll keep digging."

Bolan brooded momentarily, hands clasping the wooden arms of the well-padded executive chair. It was a shame about Sharp, but that wasn't his concern. If McIntyre was really dealing arms illegally, he was guilty of a lot worse than murder.

"Fill me in about McIntyre."

Kline had no trouble with that request. He made it a point to be on top of the facts of a case, a trait that impressed his superiors. "Cameron's grandfather founded the firm during World War I. His father expanded it enormously and made a fair-size fortune during World War II. Business has been pretty steady since then. Cameron took over about five years ago and has been pushing the export side of arms dealing. All very legitimate, of course. He's made sure to get the proper end-use certificates from foreign governments. Without these as an assurance that the arms are going to U.S.-approved states, he isn't allowed to export a Bowie knife."

Without being told, Bolan knew that this was only part of the story. A terrorist group could often find a way around the export restrictions. Sometimes an end-use certificate could be forged. More often, a few properly placed bribes in some Third World nation assured that once the arms that had been purchased through normal channels arrived, they went out on the next boat to some clandestine destination. A third common trick was simply to play-act a hijacking to divert some of the arms, with a little hard cash spread around to soothe guilty consciences.

"Why did you land on McIntyre's back? There must be dozens of equally likely suspects."

"More like hundreds, Blanski. But a little over a year ago McIntyre came to our attention when some Indian troops discovered an arms shipment en route to the Tamils in Sri Lanka. They were part of an order destined for Kenya that had never arrived. Another cargo was found when Spanish troops uncovered an arms cache belonging to Basque terrorists. That was a bit more than six months ago and prompted the current investigation. We've been following paper trails that end in brick walls ever since. Sharp thought that he was on to something, but . . ."

Bolan understood the problem. Following every trail, finding the necessary clues that would stand up in court was a difficult job, one that might require years of sorting, shuffling and examining boxcars of paper. In the meantime, McIntyre and others like him would be free to conduct their arms-for-millions deals, profiting from the sorrow and suffering of victims in every corner of the globe.

"As for McIntyre himself, there's no doubt that he could use the money. He owns a lot of the stock, but he has a board of directors to make sure that he doesn't do anything too funny. Certainly he has a lot of expenses, with three greedy ex-wives and a string of girlfriends. Also, he likes to play high-stakes poker. Unfortunately he doesn't play very well."

If McIntyre was having money problems, the arms black market would be an easy solution. Third World gangsters paid top dollar for reliable weapons, especially some of the more exotic ones suitable against military targets. And every dollar that McIntyre received would be tax free.

"That's it? That's all you've got?" Bolan figured that there was plenty more, but it suited him to play along.

Kline was more relaxed now, feeling that he was in control of the situation once again. "There are a lot of little details, of course." Kline rose and proceeded to a corner filing cabinet. Smiling to himself, he pulled a thick envelope from the third drawer. "These are transcripts of McIntyre's office phone calls for this month. This should keep you busy for a while."

Bolan understood that he was being diverted. Let Kline think that he had taken the bait.

Kline turned from the cabinet to find Bolan at his elbow. He hadn't even heard the chair creak. "Then I'll just take that and be on my way."

As the door closed softly behind Blanski, Kline began to wonder if he had made a mistake. The man was either a lot smarter than the agent gave him credit for, or else not very bright at all. Kline wouldn't want to bet on the latter.

"Elwell! Get over here!" he shouted over his shoulder.

The junior agent rushed forward.

"See that chair? I want it dusted for prints. Any that aren't ours I want routed back for identification, pronto." Kline held up his hand to check a half-formed question. "I want an answer in an hour. Get to it."

Kline decided to take a hike to the corner coffee shop. Bad as it was, it was better than the motor oil that Elwell brewed. In an hour, he would have a handle on Blanski. Whoever he was.

BOLAN STEERED AWAY from the curb, uncertain as to what his next move should be. He did know that he wasn't about to waste precious hours skimming through phone logs. He doubted McIntyre would be foolish enough to say anything in the clear over the phone. However, there might be something of value buried in that filing cabinet back at the Bureau office.

The warrior had always had a difficult time when forced to work with the FBI. If he had to work with the law, it was easier dealing with the local police rather than the touchy Feds. The Bureau meant well, but they had such a snooty, elitist attitude that they tended to rub other lawmen the wrong way.

Kline was typical. Probably a lawyer or a chartered accountant, he adopted a paternalistic attitude at the drop of a pin. The agent equated the good of the FBI with the good of the country. Kline liked to leave the dirty work to the street cops so that he wouldn't get his freshly pressed suit mussed.

Back in his hotel room, Bolan was fieldstripping his weapons when the telephone rang. "Hello."

"Striker, I'm glad to hear you've been getting along so well with the FBI."

"Hal. What's up?" Bolan knew that Brognola wasn't calling just to shoot the breeze.

"For openers, I've got a note on my desk from none other than the director of the FBI himself. If it was any hotter, this office would be cinders by now."

Bolan smiled. Brognola was able to make any memo-pushing pea brain sorry that writing had ever been invented. Especially since he had the heavy artillery behind him. "Calm down, Hal. I know how you love to play fireman."

Brognola was exasperated. "Easy for you to say, Striker. The second thing is that Kline has been trying to put the make on Michael Blanski. Your fingerprints came in for identification. I was informed by a friend in that section."

Kline would get a surprise, but it didn't make Bolan think any better of him. "The standard package is going back?"

"No worries. What Kline gets will make you look like apple pie personified. I just thought you might like to know who your friends are. Or aren't, as the case may be."

"Thanks for the news, Hal."

"So tell, Striker. What did you do to those guys out there?"

"Nothing . . . yet."

BOLAN MADE HIS MOVE an hour after midnight. He was dressed in street clothes with the Beretta in its custom shoulder holster. He wasn't expecting a gunfight with the FBI, but he couldn't discount a bold mugger. A sport bag held assorted goodies he had collected during the afternoon.

The door to the old office building gave up almost as soon as Bolan touched a pick to the lock.

The second-floor office represented a bit more of a challenge. Even though it was only a temporary field office, Bolan expected that some sort of alarm would be in place. A careful examination of the lock and doorframe failed to turn up any evidence. The picks went to work once more, and in seconds the door swung open.

The beam of a flashlight revealed a square metal frame an inch beyond the doorway. The right side held a three-by-six-inch control panel with a numeric keypad for code entry.

Bolan took an aerosol can of hair spray from the bag. Directing the mist between the metal uprights, he was able to see four detector beams spanning the artificial doorway. There wasn't enough space to safely squeeze between any two of the beams.

Undoubtedly an alarm would sound at some FBI post if he broke one of the beams, and he suspected there was a motion detector in the base that would do the same thing if he moved the frame away from the doorway. He didn't have the equipment to decipher the entry codes.

From a pouch inside the bag he withdrew a length of transparent, flexible cable, the same kind of fiber optics cable used to carry telephone messages in the more sophisticated networks. He quickly fixed one halfway over the transmission point of the lowest beam, then over the receptor. A moment of adjustment and the cable was in place, held by two suction cups. The lowest beam was now diverted through the cable, which rested partly on the ground, allowing plenty of room for Bolan to crawl through.

Once he was inside, the filing cabinet took only a moment to pop before he settled down to a leisurely examination.

Most of the files were worthless to him, including equipment receipts, expense statements, copies of weekly, monthly and quarterly reports and the other paperwork required by any large bureaucracy. One folder held a manual on "The Guardian Model II—The Latest in Anti-Intruder Technology." Very little of the data was even remotely connected to case work.

However, there was one grain of gold among the slag. A slim file held a list of all long-distance calls for the past six months, obtained from the telephone companies. The agents hadn't bothered to identify the people or corporations that had received the calls.

The numbers ranged through several dozen area codes on almost every continent. Three pages into the file, two of the calls leaped off the page. The numbers rang a phone somewhere in Lima, Peru. Bolan copied them and left the office.

Back at the hotel, he made an information call to Washington concerning the Peruvian number. A ring back a short while later informed him that the number belonged to the Lima Farm Import Company. There was no data whatsoever available on the company, its operations or its personnel.

Bolan smelled a front, a dummy company set up for one purpose only—to smuggle arms into Peru. He had to decide now how best to proceed so that he wouldn't spook the game before the hunt was truly in progress. One false move and the connection would be buried. Then it would be back to square one.

Lima was three hours ahead of San Francisco. A quick check of his watch told Bolan it would be 9:15 in Lima. He dialed the number and the phone rang once. A pause. And again.

A soft-spoken woman answered the phone. "Hello."

"Let me speak to Señor Estevan." Bolan planned to brazen it out. A little boldness sometimes worked wonders.

The woman at the other end was clearly puzzled. "There is no Señor Estevan here. You must have the wrong number."

Quickly, before she could hang up, Bolan took back the initiative. "This is the Lima Farm Import Company, is it not?"

"Why, yes, but—"

"Then I must have the right number but the wrong name. I'm really not very good at all with names. What is your boss's name, anyway?"

"Why, his name is Jorge Carrillo. But he is not in yet."

Bolan smiled to himself. He had been counting on it being a bit too early in the morning for the boss to show up. He could have handled Carrillo, but it simplified matters this way. "Never mind. I'll call back, Señorita..."

"Antonia de Vincenzo."

Bolan dialed again, this time to the McIntyre Arms Corporation. He asked for the shipping department. A bored male voice answered. "Shipping."

"I'm calling from the Lima Farm Import Company. My last order is overdue. Could you please verify the shipping details?"

"All right, hang on." The voice sounded dubious, and the line went dead as Bolan was placed on hold. "There's no order here for anywhere in Peru."

"Are you sure?"

"I checked twice, mister. That's why I took so long. Did you think I was having a coffee break or something?" Then the shipping clerk hung up.

Bolan would now have to try the front door. He sighed and called the arms company again. "May I please speak to Señor McIntyre? I'm calling long distance."

"Cameron McIntyre." The strong voice was brusque and clipped.

"Señor McIntyre, I'm calling from the Lima Farm Import Company in Peru. Señor Carrillo regrets that he is unable to call you himself but sends his greetings. I'm his assistant."

"Señor Carrillo is not well?"

"No, sir. He is fine, but unfortunately finds himself out of the country for several weeks. He has left me to attend to matters in his absence."

"You speak excellent English."

"I was fortunate enough to spend many years in your delightful country."

McIntyre didn't seem happy to talk to the supposed Peruvian. Things were balanced on a knife's edge. Any slip, and Bolan would have to go fishing again with stronger bait.

After a pause that indicated an inner struggle, McIntyre finally asked how he could be of help.

"We have had a small problem here and many of our records were destroyed. We no longer have the specifics of your next shipment to us. It would be most helpful if you could provide those details once again."

There was a long silence at the end of the line. "I think I should discuss this with Señor Carrillo," McIntyre responded slowly.

"I appreciate your position, *señor*, but we have customers to satisfy. Some very impatient customers, as I am sure you understand. They do not wish to wait for Señor Carrillo's return, or I would not trouble you."

"And your most efficient secretary, Miss..."

"Señorita de Vincenzo does not remember the specifics, I'm afraid."

McIntyre sighed and relented. "Have you got a piece of paper?"

The big guy smiled to himself. The easy part was over, now the real fun was about to begin.

6

Bolan lowered the 7 × 50 Zeiss field glasses from his stinging eyes. His vantage point in the upper reaches of the rusting hulk of a disused crane allowed him to observe the activity in the bustling Los Angeles dockyard without the possibility of detection.

His attention was focused on the *Pacific Rambler*, two hundred yards away. Badly in need of a paint job, the small freighter didn't look capable of sailing out of port, let alone braving the Pacific waters.

The cargo carrier had arrived earlier in the afternoon from San Francisco. According to McIntyre, it contained the munitions that tomorrow would be loaded onto the *Pride of Peru*, destined for Lima.

For once luck had been on the warrior's side. It was simple good fortune that the arms dealer had timed a delivery so conveniently for Bolan. Less than six hours had elapsed since their conversation, long enough for him to contact Kline, grab a commuter flight to Los Angeles, dress as a workman and choose his observation post.

Bolan had gotten all the information he needed from the arms merchant, except a list of the cargo itself. He had been sure that McIntyre would refuse to give specifics over the phone, and just asking the question might have caused the wary dealer to clam up.

The late-afternoon sun was creeping toward the horizon. The shadow of the crane where Bolan lay concealed stretched immense over the banks of warehouses below.

The sweating stevedores had unloaded several pallets of goods already, but nothing had triggered an alarm in Bolan's head as yet.

The workmen were waved off for a break as the last heavy barrels of a chemical shipment were stowed onto a stretched flatbed truck. The oversize rig moved laboriously toward the exit gate, diesels grunting under the load.

The white-hatted foreman and an assistant toting a clipboard loitered near the gangplank, glancing down the dockyard road as though on watch.

They were not disappointed, for ten minutes later a gray Ford arrived, followed by a canvas-topped two-and-a-half-ton truck. Three men in jeans and matching jackets spilled from the Ford, followed by a burly man with a full beard. Tubs appeared to be the leader, for the foreman singled him out and began to shout and point to his watch.

Bolan guessed that the crew boss was forcefully reminding the newcomers that it was nearly quitting time. The discussion ended when the bearded man pulled a brown envelope from an inside pocket and handed it to the foreman. Work resumed within moments.

One of the newcomers disappeared into the hold with the work crew. Two large men climbed from the truck to pull back the canvas top. One after another, three pyramided pallets swayed up from the bowels of the hold and were deposited in the rear of the truck. Each was covered by a tarpaulin, shielding the contents from Bolan's eyes.

After a ritual of form signing, the dockyard workmen sauntered away, bound for the nearest tavern to spend their bonus. The Ford and truck traveled in the opposite direction, deeper into the maze of warehouses that lined the docks.

Bolan watched the truck take the fourth left and then the second right before it disappeared from his binoculars. He waited until the activity had subsided, then cautiously climbed down from his perch, making a last-minute weapons check. His stained blue workman's coveralls concealed the holstered thunder. He was ready to start plugging the pipeline of death. This was one weapons deal that was going to go down hard.

Damn hard.

Bolan wandered the lanes between the warehouses, hoping to spot the truck and guard crew. It had been a calculated risk to remain so far from the dock that he couldn't follow the cargo when it was unloaded. But he had expected that the armament wouldn't be moved farther than necessary before being reloaded in the morning. Now it was only a matter of time before he ran the men to ground.

This remote area of the dock seemed to be deserted. Early-evening shadows filled the spaces between the neglected warehouses. The faint scuffing of Bolan's shoes on the cracked asphalt seemed magnified.

A sporadic hammering resounded from somewhere dead ahead. Bolan edged closer, ears cocked to pinpoint the source.

The hammering seemed to emanate from the next warehouse ahead on the left, a ramshackle structure with traces of faded blue paint peeping through the peeling battleship-gray overcoat. As the warrior approached, the sound increased in volume. As Bolan halted outside towering double doors, the erratic noise ended and was followed by a few inaudible shouts. No light penetrated the doors, so Bolan had no idea of what was going on inside.

He continued on, looking for a way to do a reconnaissance of the situation before plunging in. He had no intention of dropping—guns blazing—into unknown territory, particularly when he was unsure that this was even the right spot. The strategy and tactics of staying alive had taught the warrior to know his enemies and their dispositions.

He had learned the lessons well.

Around the far corner, the warrior found a window that looked into an office. He chanced a quick glance and recognized the bearded leader of the work detail stooped over a battered desk, facing away from the dirt-encrusted panes. The leather of a shoulder holster crisscrossed his back. Peering through the grimy window, Bolan could see right across the office and into the main area of the warehouse. He spotted the squat deuce-and-a-half bathed under roof lights. The rest of the work crew was outside his line of vision.

Bolan circled the warehouse, looking for an unobtrusive way in.

On the side opposite the office, a medium-size window stood twelve feet aboveground. There was no way up the side of the warehouse without a grappling hook, an item that Bolan didn't possess at the moment.

An idea flashed to mind. He retraced his steps down the lane and along to the next warehouse. Ranged by a platform were ten fifty-five-gallon drums labeled Acetic Acid. Bolan tipped each one in turn. Nine were full, and probably weighed five hundred pounds apiece. Fortunately one was more than half empty.

Bolan heaved on the last in line, easing it onto the heavy metal rim. He then carefully wheeled it down the lane, balancing the drum on an angle such that he had only to guide it. A few minutes' work saw two full drums below the window, with the half-empty one beside them. With a muscle-straining effort, Bolan lifted the third canister into place, creating a secure pyramid.

He scrambled to the top. The window ledge was now just above waist height. The window was locked, but when the hammering inside reached a momentary crescendo, Bolan rapped a small pane with the butt of the Beretta, shattering the glass. He reached through to flick open the catch.

In seconds, Bolan lay prone on the edge of an upper-level loft, peering at the activity below.

Four men were working in pairs around the pallets that had been removed from the back of the truck. As Bolan watched, two of the men picked up a long crate and carried it to a separate area. They dropped it into a slightly larger and deeper crate, so that the original container was completely concealed. The two men added a precut sheet of plywood, which rested on the edge of the box inside. Gathering several spades from a supply in a corner, they covered the crate of guns with a layer of farm implements. A few more minutes' work with a hammer and a paintbrush, and the load of guns was transformed into an innocuous shipment of rakes, hoes and tractor parts from the California Machinery Company.

It would take a very suspicious customs inspector to discover anything unusual about an apparently ordinary delivery of farm tools.

Very neat, Bolan had to admit. No doubt the paperwork was just as efficiently done. In some foreign capital, a less than honest official would be pocketing the bribe necessary to sign the papers showing that the arms had really arrived. Payment would be made to the McIntyre Arms Corporation in the normal manner but siphoned back to the phony customer through a dozen tortuous legal and accounting tricks. With the documentation complete, no one would suspect that anything was out of the ordinary.

Until these guns were used to kill people in Peru.

The Executioner wasn't going to let that happen this time. Payment was due in full for what had gone down already, and he was going to collect.

Starting now.

Bolan had seen what looked like an Uzi resting against a box between the workers. No doubt more firepower lay around the area within easy reach. Five to one odds. Not bad, particularly with the advantage of surprise. However, he didn't want to chance that the guy in the office might signal McIntyre before Bolan arrived to deliver his own personal greeting. He decided to be patient a short while longer and see if a better opportunity presented itself.

Bolan's moves were restricted as long as he was on the upper level, so his first problem was to find a way down without alerting the crew. Discarding the coveralls to increase his mobility, he crept to a rear corner stairway that led to the lower level. The ground floor was littered with old packing materials and drums, so it would be easy to conceal himself once he got there. But he'd have to wait for a distraction, since the stairwell was in plain sight of everyone below.

He resumed his watch, steeled to the waiting by long hours of suspense on a thousand battlefields. Hurry-up-and-wait was an experience familiar to every soldier, and Bolan had learned to master the boredom without sacrificing his alertness.

Sometimes the numbers counted down fast, and when he had to Bolan could move with the speed of a striking cobra. But he believed that when time allowed it was better to let the other guy make the mistake, the momentary inattention or bad move that made the difference between life or death. It was always a gamble when the Executioner went into battle. One stray bullet by a panicked gunner could obliterate the best-laid plans. War was sometimes a matter of luck, and you had to take your chance and roll the dice with your life bet on the outcome.

But the secret was knowing how much to leave to chance.

In half an hour the workmen had finished packing the illegal arms. The bearded guy emerged from the office to inspect the handiwork, and after a cursory check, he gave his okay. One of the crew jumped aboard a parked forklift, revved it up and loaded the truck.

Bolan decided that this was the best opportunity he'd have. Unleathering the Beretta, he padded down the stairs, eyes fixed on the chatting group. He was conscious of the stairs creaking under his feet, although the noise couldn't penetrate far above the roar of machinery.

He found an ideal spotting post behind a large old boiler, which afforded a clear view of the office and the single exit, as well as the area around the truck.

When the last crate was stowed, the driver switched off the lift and joined his friends. Bits of conversation drifted to Bolan's hideout, informing him that the guard was to be relieved in eight hours.

Three of the workmen departed while the remaining two made themselves comfortable for the long watch ahead. One pulled a holstered pistol and a small radio from a cloth bag and settled them on a box. He lit a cigarette and tuned in to an L.A. Kings game. The other gunman sat beside his Uzi and pulled a comic book from a shopping bag.

The two gunners were on the opposite side of the warehouse, near the office entrance. Both were facing the door, although "watching" was too strong a word for the minimal attention they were paying to their job.

Bolan waited another few minutes to be sure that one of the other three wouldn't return for some reason, then began his stalk.

Circling wide to the far end, he eased his way through the dimly lit edges of the warehouse. Part of his attention was focused on the lazy guards and part was required to make sure that he didn't slip on any of the abundant oil slicks or walk into cast-off bits of garbage.

It would be so easy to just pick off the thugs, seize the weapons and turn them over to an openmouthed Kline. But the agent had been adamant that the big guy keep his hands clean and leave the muscle to the Bureau.

Bolan had to smile as he recalled his brief conversation with Special Agent Kline from a telephone booth at the commuter terminal of San Francisco International.

"Kline? Blanski. I want you to get your team together and be ready to move at my signal. I've got a few things to check out first, and then we should have McIntyre in the bag." The announcement for the flight to L.A. interrupted him as he was about to sign off, giving the Fed an opening.

"What the hell are you talking about, Blanski? Where are you? I didn't authorize any of this." Bolan could almost feel the receiver heat up in his hand as Kline's anger was transmitted across the connection. "Blanski, I want an explanation and full details."

"You'll get what I give you, and that's all you're getting now."

"Who the hell do you think you are? There are procedures that must be followed, and I'm not about to blow this case on account of some undisciplined renegade, even if you are connected." The sarcastic emphasis on the last word was not lost to Bolan.

Kline clearly had no appreciation of Bolan's take-charge way of doing things. He obviously hadn't learned that procedure was of little value when the top-ranked crime mongers were involved. The criminal elite were rats, clever and wary, and if you gave them even a second's head start, they would take advantage of the delay and scramble back into the gutters and garbage piles where they'd come from.

Still, a little PR wouldn't hurt, but he had better be fast. The last call for Flight 602 to L.A. rang through the busy terminal. Bolan softened his tone slightly. "Don't worry, Kline. I'm just going to recce the situation and relay back. Then you can swoop in for the kill."

The agent seemed slightly mollified; either that or he recognized when he was outmatched.

"Listen up, Blanski, and listen good. I want this reconnaissance of yours clean." Here it comes, Bolan reflected, the FBI by-the-book lecture. He knew it by heart and had to restrain himself from just dropping the receiver and letting Kline ramble on to himself.

"In other words, look but don't touch. The minute, and I mean the very minute that you have anything, I expect this phone to ring.

"Make no mistake, if you so much as muss the hair of any of the suspects your ass will be wrapped so tight in interagency paperwork that you'll be lucky if you ever get out from under. And I don't care *who* you're working for. You got that?"

"I heard you, Kline." Bolan hung up and ran for the plane.

He shoved Kline's warning into his mental file under C, for crap, then coiled for action.

Fifteen feet away from the two guards, Bolan let loose with the Beretta, one silenced round exploding the radio into chips of circuit board and flying plastic.

"Don't even think about it," Bolan growled as the two men spun to face him. The man on the left, the older of the two, settled back with an expression of anger written across his face as he slowly raised his hands above his head. He didn't spare a glance for the holstered pistol three feet in front of him.

The second guard was young, long-haired and muscular. Eyes flickering back and forth between Bolan and the Uzi just beyond arm's reach telegraphed the kid's foolish impulse.

"Get your—" Bolan barked, but the kid made his move anyway, falling to his left. Battle-trained reflexes gave the proper response, and the Beretta spit a 3-round burst as the guy dived for the Uzi.

All three rounds grouped around the gunner's left ear, blowing his brains in a red hail over his bag of superhero comics. Bolan felt no remorse. The kid's own stupidity in making a suicide play had killed him. That's what happened when comic-book fantasy was confused with real life.

The surviving gunner raised his hands a little higher, eyes bulging as his companion collapsed across the Uzi.

Bolan knotted the other man's hands behind his back and rapped him behind the ear with the Beretta. He collapsed onto the floor, without a sound.

The Executioner looked down at the two bodies.

"Sorry, Kline."

He then padded into the office and rifled the drawers. The only item of note was a clipboard containing the manifest of the shipment. Bingo!

Bolan rolled back the warehouse doors and drove the deuce-and-a-half into the night, pausing to shut the doors behind him. He gunned the rig toward the gate, fingering the FBI badge in the name of Michael Blanski that he would use if the gatekeeper gave him any trouble. He still had a lot of ground to cover before morning.

As the warrior roared away, the office phone began to ring.

BOLAN HAD PLENTY of time for thought on the lonely drive up the coast. This end of the pipeline was closed—or would be when he caught up with McIntyre—so the mission was just about wrapped up.

Or was it?

The load he carried convinced Bolan that this was only a part of the mission he had set for himself, a mission that didn't confine itself to borders or briefings or favors for the Justice Department.

If these weapons didn't arrive, it would only be a matter of time before some other greedy vermin passed a cargo of death into the hands of the Shining Path.

Bolan wasn't so naive as to believe that only he could make a difference, or that he could settle a problem that had an entire country teetering on the brink of civil war.

The big man had known of the Shining Path for some time now, and he had despised their fanaticism, a mania that led to murder in the name of freedom. Holding the truths of justice and equality as their banner, the Shining Path had become a twisted path leading to destruction.

The ideals they once stood for had become corrupt in the withered, skeleton hands that reached out to the oppressed peasants, a knife clasped to slit the throats of anyone who didn't want their particular brand of comradeship. Justice and freedom had been forgotten long ago, reduced to meaningless phrases mouthed by crazies whose only reality was a smoking gun.

The names changed, from Red Brigades to Black September to Shining Path. But the hand holding the knife pointed at the heart of innocent pawns of political terror tactics always stayed the same.

Bolan had planned to visit the Shining Path in their mountain retreats one day, but it was a big world, with violence exploding in what seemed like every corner. It was hard to know where to begin, which was the current priority, since at every turn a hundred targets abounded for the Executioner's fury.

But this mission had tied him to the Shining Path, even if the string was thin and insubstantial. He wasn't about to walk away.

Several hours later, Bolan eased the rig to a stop in the San Francisco dockyard. The arms had come back full circle to where they had departed from a few days ago.

Kline and his men were waiting as Bolan had instructed during a quick call from a truck stop along the route. To say the agent was angry was an understatement. His ego was bruised from losing control of what had been his case, and he was hell-bent on making the big guy pay for the "minor, but necessary casualties" that had been left in the warehouse.

While Kline was steaming, waiting for Blanski's call, the ID report on the guy had come in. Surprisingly it had shown that the man was really Michael Blanski, a war hero with a biography that made him the next thing to Michael the Archangel. One thing that jumped from between the lines of the rundown was that Blanski had some very powerful political connections, so potent that Kline, who had the nose of a bloodhound for politics, could smell the touch of the White House.

To make matters worse, a few hours later he had been awakened at 4:00 a.m. by an assistant to the director, calling from Washington. Kline was informed that he had come to the director's attention. The director had been admonished for questioning the Justice Department's direct involvement in this affair. Needless to say, the director didn't relish being admonished, nor did he look favorably on subordinates who involved him in such a predicament. Kline was urged to cooperate fully with Mr. Blanski in future. The director wished to be kept informed of the progress of the case. With that the phone went dead.

Kline got the message. One more screwup and he might find himself teaching fingerprint identification in Montana. Or worse.

He had resolved to maintain a very low profile where Michael Blanski was involved, but to keep lots of notes—just in case. Now, remembering the conversation with Washington, Kline suppressed an urge to quiz the man on how he had acquired the truck.

Bolan spoke first. "McIntyre is in it up to his neck. Just check this." Bolan tossed over a clipboard. He didn't bother to explain the circumstances behind the body in the warehouse. He hoped to keep his distance and didn't want any complications with the police.

Kline flipped through the invoices, a low whistle escaping from between tightly pursed lips. Listed on the yellow sheets were enough deadly toys to supply a small army. Apart from a couple of cases of small arms and ammunition, the shipment contained fragmentation and thermite grenades, rifle grenades, antipersonnel and antiarmor mines and two cases of Stingshot antitank rockets. A real surprise was the load of Jackhammer combat shotguns. Able to fire four 12-gauge shotgun blasts per second from a preloaded ammo cassette, the Jackhammer was a deadly close-assault weapon.

Kline was excited by the captured arms, practically dancing with anticipation. "This will make excellent evidence. I have no doubt that we can tie it back to McIntyre. He should get ten years. Although, of course, I was hoping to get him for Sharp's murder. But I suppose we can hope for a confession. Or maybe further evidence will surface when we raid the plant. I'll be able to get a search warrant with this."

"No."

Kline's jubilation turned to anger as Bolan halted him in full flight. "No? What do you mean, no? This is evidence!"

Bolan's eyes bored into the agent's. "It won't be evidence, Kline, because I'm taking it with me. Why do you think I had you meet me at the docks? That ship behind us sails in a day for Central and South America. And those weapons are going to be on that ship. Is that clear enough? And one more thing. About that body in the warehouse—don't even fantasize about pinning anything on me."

He didn't enjoy playing the heavy when it involved coming down hard on people in the law-enforcement community. But sometimes there was only one way to deal with guys like Kline, who were used to running things their own way—you stepped on their toes until they apologized to you for getting their feet in your way.

"But if you take the stuff away, how will we make the case against McIntyre? Are you going to let him get away with this whole business?" Kline didn't bother to hide how annoyed he was at the possibility that McIntyre might escape punishment. Bolan liked him for the first time since they had met.

"Don't worry, Kline. Just make sure that you handle your end properly. I want all of this forwarded to Lima and stored in a warehouse. I've left written instructions with the invoices. Handle the paperwork and leave the rest to me. McIntyre won't get away with anything. I'll see to it personally."

Bolan grinned, a tight humorless smile that reminded Kline of the toothy snarl of some feral cat.

Kline didn't ask any more questions.

7

Cameron McIntyre was beginning to wonder if he might have made a fatal blunder.

He sat alone in a paneled library in the heart of his sprawling estate. It was a warm room, lined floor to ceiling with hundreds of books representing the best of modern writing and the classics. McIntyre had read none of them, and had no interest in doing so. His father had told him that every civilized man owned a well-stocked library. Consequently he had a standing order with a bookseller for every book on the *New York Times* bestseller lists, which the butler rearranged as required.

McIntyre was in the library for a reason unconnected with books. A cherry corner cabinet held the private stock of Scotch, imported directly from a small Highland distillery, that he reserved exclusively for himself.

The businessman had canceled a previously arranged rendezvous with one of his girlfriends. He wanted the evening to think, something that would be impossible with the woman's vacant chattering.

Not that she would miss him terribly, he acknowledged in a rare moment of self-honesty. He recognized that all the heaving and moaning during their couplings had more to do with the expensive, glittering baubles he brought than any genuine feeling she had for him.

Her rival was no different, and both were exactly the same as the three grasping, avaricious harpies he had married. All of them wanted a piece of the McIntyre fortune rather than a piece of McIntyre himself. Neither of them was any better than a well-paid hooker.

McIntyre realized that he was verging on self-pity. Much better to think about his problems—the quarter-million he owed Davis from his incredible run of bad luck at poker last weekend; his second wife's petition for an increase in alimony payments; that puzzling call from Peru.

The more McIntyre thought about the telephone call, the less he liked it, and the more afraid he became that he had said too much. He should have waited to speak to Carrillo after all, but the assistant had been quite convincing.

As McIntyre stewed, he decided that he could easily dispel any doubts. He refreshed his drink and strolled to the end of the left bookcase. He withdrew a thick history book from the end of the second shelf and depressed a knot in the paneling. A six-inch piece of the bookcase upright popped out from a seemingly solid panel and swung back on a hinge. McIntyre reached in and withdrew a thin black book.

The first page contained a list of numbers. Moving to an antique model telephone on a low table, McIntyre dialed Peru.

"*Buenas noches.*" The telephone was answered on the third ring.

McIntyre took a moment to compose himself. He had been counting on Carrillo being absent. "Señor Carrillo, what a pleasure. I thought that you were out of town."

"No. I have not been out of town for some weeks. But why are you calling me?" Carrillo sounded puzzled at the arms dealer's call.

McIntyre's stomach sank. Now he was almost afraid to hear the answers to his other questions, although there was no doubt he had to get to the bottom of whatever scheme was being played out. "I spoke with your assistant this afternoon. I merely wanted to confirm that you now have all the information you need."

"My assistant? Do you mean Señorita Vincenzo?" The Peruvian's voice revealed a tremulous note, and it was obvious that McIntyre's inquiries were making him nervous.

"No, the gentleman. The one who speaks such good English. I don't know his name."

"I have no such assistant. There is only myself and Señorita de Vincenzo. Is something wrong, Señor McIntyre?"

McIntyre was becoming alarmed at Carrillo's responses, but he fought to keep his voice casual. "My mistake, *señor*. I am sorry to have bothered you. I see that the gentleman that I am speaking of is an associate of a Mr. Capistro, an Italian business contact of mine. You see, I am in error and have simply called you through a mistake of my own. Please forgive me. Good night." His explanation was weak and he knew it, concocted on the spot so as not to alert Carrillo to any trouble. McIntyre quickly hung up before the Peruvian could question him about his mistake.

He stared at the phone, half expecting it to ring.

When it hadn't rung in ten minutes, McIntyre began to regain his composure. After all, there was nothing concerning the arms shipments that could be tied directly to him. He had made damn sure of that. If the facts ever came out, there were going to be some very unhappy and unpleasantly surprised executives at McIntyre Arms Corporation. One of the advantages of being the boss, particularly one with a reputation for being harsh and unapproachable, was that subordinates didn't look too closely when they were made to sign piles of forms and contracts.

By the time his high-priced legal beagles got through suing everyone in sight and firing off every writ, stay and affidavit in the legal dictionary, he doubted if he would ever see the inside of a courtroom, let alone a jail.

His only real worry concerned the Sharp killing. He realized now that Carrillo had maneuvered him into that rash act, with grand speeches about "honor," "treason" and "just vengeance." Mistake or not, there had been a certain horrible satisfaction at the killing. He had been astonished at how calmly he had watched Sharp die.

But now Carrillo had a hammer over him that the Peruvian could use as he chose. Carrillo had begun by insisting on the hasty and rather insecure delivery of the order that was now en route. McIntyre would bet that this was only a sample of a long and increasingly difficult association with the Latin arms smuggler.

McIntyre began to wonder if he could arrange an accident for Carrillo the next time the two of them met.

The arms dealer pushed the thought aside. Carrillo lived in the dark underworld, while McIntyre had barely put a toe in. Whatever he thought of that might be devious or treacherous, he would bet that Carrillo would have planned a countermove.

He couldn't beat Carrillo at his own game.

McIntyre's anxiety began to return as he reflected on his precarious position.

Finally, turning his attention to the problem at hand, he picked up the phone once more, intending to verify the status of the cargo in San Francisco. He let the phone ring for three minutes.

McIntyre slammed the receiver down and threw himself into an easy chair. Even though the crew guarding the arms shipment were morons, they weren't stupid enough to leave it unattended. If no one was answering the phone, it was because no one was able to do so.

That could only mean serious trouble.

In spite of how well he had distanced himself from his covert deals, McIntyre began to wonder if he was as secure as he imagined. He could only surmise that it was the FBI that was interfering with his secret arms shipment. If the Bureau felt confident enough to seize the arms, it must have some very solid evidence, something that might link him to Sharp's death. Almost as bad, he would have to repay Carrillo the advance for the weapons, and he had already spent the cash.

It was time to cut his losses and get out of the country before the ax fell.

McIntyre had no confidence in the rent-a-cops manning the front gate. They were fine for scaring delinquent kids and shooing away curious strangers. If there was real trouble they would be as useful as straw scarecrows. He phoned a shady contact of his who had helped him out with the mechanics of the arms deals. They agreed on twenty of the roughest, meanest ex-cons on the streets, every one packing his own hardware. Any one of them would knife you for a U.S. Grant, let alone the Grover Cleveland they were promised for a six-hour shift. His three personal bodyguards would make sure that the hired help didn't get out of hand.

McIntyre then phoned his pilot to get him to warm up the company jet and file a flight plan for Argentina. It wasn't exactly his favorite spot in the whole world, but it would be safe. Besides, someone with solid American currency could live like a king, if the water didn't kill him first.

Fortunately the arms dealer had retained enough self-restraint to preserve a little nest egg in a Swiss account, safe from the eagle eyes of his ex-wives' lawyers. With about five million, he could live reasonably well in the impoverished southern country.

In the meantime, he would gather a few little trinkets to take along with him, starting with the contents of the wall safe downstairs.

McIntyre drained his Scotch and got to work.

BOLAN EASED through the woods, gliding through the trees as easily as the chill western breeze.

The night stalker had an eerie sense of déjà vu; it was only a week ago that he had put the hit on Jones under similar conditions. The foliage was a bit different, and there was a quarter moon peeping above the treetops, but he wore the same blacksuit, and the Beretta and Desert Eagle rode in their usual spots.

This time the Executioner carried a second Beretta with him to provide a little rapid firepower. It was the Model 12-S submachine gun, a deadly minigrease gun that featured exceptionally little vibration and no muzzle climb on full-auto. It could spit 9 mm parabellums at 500 rounds per minute. For this hit, Bolan carried a liberal supply of 40-round clips jammed into pouch pockets.

He crawled on elbows and knees into the grass at the edge of the tree line to inspect the main house. Earlier, he had driven to the front gate under the pretext of asking for directions. The gate guards were unlike any he had ever seen on an upper-crust estate—three toughs who made no attempt to hide their hardware. The smallest came to the car brandishing a Remington shotgun, a Colt Python stuck in his belt. He made no pretense of civility as he roughly told Bolan to get the hell out of there. From the intent way his two companions watched Bolan, the warrior had no doubt he wouldn't have gotten off so lightly had he looked like an easier mark.

McIntyre must be scared witless, Bolan reasoned, to even have that kind of scum on his property. It looked as if the arms dealer had dived into some sewer to find a bunch of goons to replace his regular security staff. That implied that he was planning a break sometime soon, which meant that Bolan didn't have any time to waste.

Bolan had an edge-on view of the two-story Georgian house about two hundred yards away across a vast and carefully manicured lawn. A series of outbuildings lay beyond the main house, and clustered around the front door were four guards, with a case of beer at their feet. Two more chatted idly by the wall around the corner.

So far he had counted nine hardmen, and he would bet that there were at least as many more hanging around other areas of the estate. However, they weren't taking their assignment seriously, and were paying almost no attention to what was going down. They were obviously relying on safety in numbers, trusting to bulk and brawn rather than brains to keep them safe.

That hadn't worked for the dinosaurs, and it wouldn't work for these guys.

There was almost no cover between Bolan and the house, just a few trees and shrubs cut and trained into ornamental patterns. But he took advantage of what was available, making the approach to the front door on an angle, weaving from cover to cover. At each bush he paused to observe the guards, but saw no sign that they were aware of his presence. They were content to chat, rifles and stubby machine guns slung over their shoulders. The glow of cigarettes flared from time to time.

One more silent rush brought him to an evergreen carved like a perfect pyramid. Bolan had heard a superstition once that pyramids brought good luck. So much for old wives' tales.

Time to do it.

Bolan unsheathed the 93-R and sighted on the two hardguys laughing by the side of the house. The Beretta coughed out three rounds, sending one gunman staggering, his belly chewed into ribbons. His buddy gaped openmouthed until the Beretta spit again and the Executioner sent him reeling to the soft grass.

He replaced the magazine with a full clip and switched to the submachine gun, bringing it to bear on the little party by the doorway. The Beretta had been so quiet that they were still unaware of Bolan's arrival. He squeezed the trigger, hammering a stream of 9 mm death at the unsuspecting gunmen.

Bolan fired low, stitching a fat man in his ample belly as his last beer can went flying from between twitching fingers. One man caught a full load in the groin and collapsed screaming for the few seconds it took for a severed femoral artery to bleed his corpse dry over the marble stairway. A spray of steel-jacketed stingers ripped into the faces and throats of the two remaining hired killers.

The man in black inserted a fresh clip on the run, pausing by the blood-drenched stairs, listening for reinforcements. From the sounds of running feet he guessed the gunplay had attracted at least two groups.

The three hardmen by the gate were charging up the driveway, seeking a target for their half-drunken fury. The Beretta SMG stuttered its one-note death chant as Bolan drew figure eights of blood on each of the running gunmen. Three rapid bursts sent the hoods tripping over the doorstep to hell.

Flying mortar chipped from the heavy balustrades as two more gunners made their appearance from around the corner. One was blasting away with a large-caliber handgun, sighting carefully, pistol leveled in a two-handed grip. A long-haired and mustached giant of a man was spraying Bolan's cover with an Uzi assault pistol grasped in one oversize ham of a fist.

The Executioner swiveled and dropped onto the blood-stained stairs. Target acquisition took only an instant, and the Uzi flew into the darkness as Bolan riddled the gunner with half a magazine. The giant flopped hard onto his back, empty eyes staring at the quarter moon, as his chest seemed to dissolve into one large, red spot.

The stuttergun clicked on empty as the second man turned to flee, all thoughts of resistance and his easy pay vanished from his mind. Bolan drew the big .44 and sighted over the long barrel at the retreating gunner. The cannon roared and sent its prey sliding into the dirt.

The warrior listened a moment for the sounds of more reinforcements. From the gate came the metallic thump of slamming doors, followed by the squeals of tires from what sounded like two cars.

The hired muscle were abandoning their position—those that still could.

That reduced the odds a little more in Bolan's favor. But the soldier would have bet that there were at least a few hitters left who had gone to ground to wait him out in ambush.

The Executioner still had a few surprises in store.

Bolan reloaded, then ripped two fragmentation grenades from his belt and depressed the safety spoons. He smashed one through the window on each side of the main door and dived for cover behind a large plant stand at the base of the stairs. A terrified shout erupted from a window as the two grenades exploded within heartbeats of each other, showering the lawn with glass and rubble.

The soldier bounded up the refuse-strewed steps and halted by the oak door. A solid smash from his booted foot above the brass door handle drove it back on well-oiled hinges as Bolan ducked away from the opening.

A storm of angry lead whistled through the opening from somewhere inside, expecting to find a body flying through the entrance.

Bolan wound up and tossed off another grenade, throwing it overhand with an easy motion around the edge of the doorway. He heard it strike a wall before bouncing away like a lead billiard ball.

In a second, a blast of scorching flame erupted through the doorway. Bolan made his move, diving through the floating plaster dust and landing in a roll. The Beretta nosed in the gloom, seeking a target.

All Bolan found was destruction. Shredded ancestors hung in tatters from the hall walls. Fine antiques looked as though they had been chewed by a marching army of termites. In a dining room to the left, the floor was covered in crystal and china fragments, hurled from glass cabinets lining the room.

The killers had set a trap for Bolan, with cross fire coming from the doorway on the left of the hall and from a second man hidden behind an overturned mahogany dresser at the end of the hall. One of them lay crumpled halfway through the door leading into the dining room. A second killer lay behind the dresser, leaking onto the Persian carpet in the hall, twisted into an unnatural position by the blast. He was partially concealed by the remnants of a crystal chandelier jerked from its mooring by the explosion.

After a moment of study, Bolan eased to his right to peer into the opposite room. Feathers and flecks of padding floated in the air, torn from the insides of assorted kid-leather furniture. Two empty frames stared like sightless eyes from each side of a massive fieldstone fireplace. Bolan surmised that McIntyre was making his break, and was taking what he could with him.

Not a chance.

Bolan got to his feet and started up the broad carpeted staircase to the second floor. This was the type of situation he didn't like—pushing ahead into enemy territory where the foe knew the ground and made the rules was nerve-racking work, like clearing a village in house-to-house fighting. Still, it had to be done, and the soldier would do whatever it took to get to McIntyre.

Or die trying.

Bolan shut that thought away. Death was something that he lived with, a force as close to him as the air he breathed. There was nothing new about facing death; and he had delivered too many enemies into cold, wet graves to fear his own passing. Conquering fear was the challenge, fighting down the icy panic that clawed at a man's chest when he had to lay everything on the line, especially his life.

He had faced down that fear long ago. Now death and fear were merely other weapons in his arsenal. Quieter than a Ka-bar, they slowed the enemy's hand and clouded his judgment, giving the Executioner the fighting edge that sometimes made the difference.

Ahead of him, someone was loaded down with a lot of fear. He could feel it streaming out to meet him.

A long hall at the top of the stairs stretched to the right and left, half a dozen closed doors ranged along each length.

Bolan eased the 93-R out of its holster and turned left. Creeping along noiselessly, he paused by the first door and placed his ear against the wood, watching the opposite door intently. Silence.

He repeated the maneuver at each of the remaining doors. At the last on the right, he heard muffled, ragged breathing on the other side. Bolan edged away from the door slightly and flattened himself against the wall, the Beretta extended in his grasp.

The fear got to the man inside. He couldn't bear the waiting any longer. Bolan saw the door handle turn infinitely slowly. Tugging gently on the door, the gunner opened it a crack, peered down the hallway—and found himself looking down the cavern of the Beretta's barrel.

Bolan squeezed, and the back of the thug's head flew into the room behind as a red star appeared above his right eye. The corpse slid out of sight with a thump, an astonished expression etched permanently on its face.

The Executioner catfooted back down the hall, aware that the noise, slight as it had been, was more than enough to alert any other tense watchers to his presence.

At the first door in the other section of the hall, Bolan paused again, pressing his ear to the dark wood.

The door flew open with a jerk, as the man inside decided to go for a quick kill, planning to get the drop on Bolan as he eased along the hall. Caught off guard, Bolan fell forward, striking the gunman in the knees. The two collapsed in a tangle, with the other man momentarily on top, and Bolan on his stomach.

Bolan flipped over like a five-star wrestler, bringing the Beretta around quickly to bear on the guy. His left hand automatically clutched for the killer's throat. But the other guy wasn't about to give up. He swung his .22 in an arc that connected solidly with Bolan's wrist, knocking the Beretta from the warrior's hand.

Grinning in triumph, the gunner poked the .22 into Bolan's side and jerked the trigger.

8

The professional gunner's look of satisfaction changed to consternation as he realized he had forgotten to release the safety. Chalk up another victory for the fear factor, Bolan thought, relief washing over him as his knee exploded into the other man's groin.

The killer collapsed on his side, all interest in Bolan lost as he struggled with the agony. Bolan solved that problem for him as he sprang to his feet, retrieved the Beretta and knocked the guy into unconsciousness.

Bolan paused a minute to flex his hand. Fortunately, nothing seemed to be broken, and the fingers responded to his commands. His wrist was protesting, but Bolan didn't have time for the pain. There would be an ugly bruise up and down his arm in a few hours, but he was still sound enough for combat.

The big man proceeded down the hall, listening at each door, barely conscious of his throbbing wrist. McIntyre was nearby, as proved by the stiffening resistance. The last guy had been dressed as a professional bodyguard might be, not like the collection of local toughs Bolan had previously encountered.

Pausing at the fourth door he checked, he thought he heard the sound of something scuffing on carpet. He listened more intently, but the sound was not repeated.

He listened at the last two doors to make sure that he wouldn't be gunned down from behind.

The problem was getting through that door unscathed. It was one of the hardest challenges that any military man had to face without backup. Sure, he could pop the door and clear the room with a double load of grenades.

But he wanted McIntyre alive to answer a few questions.

Bolan had been in similar situations before, and he had learned from experience that the first man through a doorway often ran into a barrage from waiting gunners, living only long enough to distract the targets for the backup troops. It was a method often used by suicide terrorist squads, or by self-confident thugs who didn't know the odds.

There had to be a better way. Bolan opened the door nearest to the stairwell to test out a theory. Inside, he found a deserted bedroom, with faint moonlight pouring through floor-to-ceiling windows. The large windows swung open wide—like French doors—after he released the catch.

Sticking his head out the window, he observed the next window some eight feet away. There was no ledge that he could use as a support to creep along, nor were there any irregularities in the wall to give him enough hand holds to climb up the side of the house.

The warrior unwound a length of webbing with a hook at the end and fastened the hook to his belt. He tied the other end to the center bar of the window and gave a strong yank. It held. Stepping carefully on the windowsill, he leaned back out the window at a forty-five-degree angle to inspect the roof.

The eaves trough above looked old and fractured, barely strong enough to support the water it carried. A large stone chimney protruded halfway down the roof, just a few feet beyond where the next window ended.

Bolan pulled a length of black nylon cord from around his waist and tied on a grappling hook that he extracted from one of the many pockets of the blacksuit. Trying to compensate for the awkward angle he was forced to assume, he whirled the hook around his head in a widening circle before letting fly.

It missed, and Bolan remained motionless as it scraped along the roof and bounced off the eaves trough with a sound he imagined could be heard in the next county. This was not the best position to be caught in.

One more try, but this time the hook disappeared near the chimney. A couple of heaves on the line, as though he were trying to land a marlin, failed to dislodge the hook.

Bolan untied himself from the webbing and checked his weapons once again, then put on a pair of goggles to shield his eyes. He eased out the window, grasping the nylon rope as tightly as possible, and began to work his way toward the next window. He edged along in crablike fashion, fighting against the torque of the angle, which would flip him over and over if he lost his footing. Several times he had to raise himself on the rope as the angle decreased.

In about three minutes he was by the window, his feet planted on the concrete two feet from the glass. He risked a peek to the side. Even though there were no lights on in the room, from the illumination from the moon and the lamps around the grounds, he spotted two gunmen near the doorway. One was crouched behind a large desk, the other behind a solid wingback chair. Both appeared to be sighting submachine guns on the doorway, ready to shred the first person through. He could see someone else sitting in a corner by the base of the bookcases, who he supposed was McIntyre staying out of the line of fire.

Bolan eased the SMG into his hand and pushed off slightly to the side, with as much force as if he were going for the winning basket in the NBA championship. He came down with just as much force, shattering the window into a thousand shards that drove into the room like sleet in a gale. Bolan dropped to his feet, the SMG up and ready.

The three occupants were caught by surprise, their attention fixed on the door to the hall, which they had assumed was the only way in.

It was a fatal mistake for the two henchmen. As they turned to meet the threat, Bolan held down the trigger in a sustained burst, crunching flesh and bone, flinging one man to the floor in an untidy heap. The second man half rose to his feet, squeezing off a burst, tracking bullets through the rows of books lining the room. The stream of lead climbed to the ceiling and ended abruptly as Bolan cored the guy's chest with a group of parabellum manglers, staining the gunner's crisp blue suit with dark red blood.

Bolan swiveled the smoking gun toward McIntyre, who seemed to crouch farther into the corner.

The Executioner walked over to the one remaining lamp and snapped it on, the sudden illumination making the curls of gun smoke visible in its rays. The room reeked of blood, gunfire and fear.

"Get up, McIntyre. I'm not going to kill you. Not if you cooperate." Bolan shoved his goggles onto his forehead. He was suddenly weary as the adrenaline rush of battle faded, tired of the killing that had happened this evening, yet knowing that there was more to come, much more, before he had put an end to this particular mission.

McIntyre slowly rose to his feet as the fact that he wasn't dead yet registered. With any luck, he thought, he might still live to die in bed. If he played his cards very, very carefully.

The arms dealer glanced briefly at his dead bodyguards. It was an unpleasant sight, but they were fools who deserved what they had gotten. He hadn't paid them nearly enough for them to die for him.

"What's the matter, McIntyre, don't you like the sight of what guns can do? It's exactly the same as what they're doing in Peru now. Your guns." Bolan had watched McIntyre carefully, had seen how he had glanced at the guards and away, as if they were only so much offal. Apparently a harder man than he had at first given him credit for.

"I'll cooperate, all right. What is it that you want?" McIntyre studied the big man carefully, noting the bloodstains on his clothing. Obviously a very capable man, able to fight and think, who would be of great value against Carrillo or anyone else. McIntyre was a pragmatist, and wouldn't let a few dead thugs prevent a possibly advantageous arrangement. Right now the only question was price, and so the businessman prepared to make a deal.

"I want information. Tell me what you know about Carrillo and his operation."

"Very little, really. He approached me several months ago with a business proposition that seemed advantageous. I admit that I needed the money badly. But it was a very simple arrangement. I sent the cargo as he directed, making the necessary contacts in other countries to ensure a valid end-use certificate. There were a number of different ways to divert the cargo into Carrillo's hands. In return, I was paid very handsomely. Who his customers were I have no idea. Before we began to conduct business, I had him investigated thoroughly. There was nothing suspicious in the way of police or military connections, although he was reported as someone not to trifle with. It was also rumored that he was an agent for another person or persons, but that was never substantiated."

"You have never met any of his associates or dealt with anyone other than Carrillo?" Bolan, adept at detecting lies and misrepresentations, believed that McIntyre was telling the truth.

"Not unless you count yourself, whoever you are." McIntyre smiled a bitter grin. "I recognize your voice as the man I spoke with this morning. I suppose you have the shipment?" Bolan nodded. "Well, I'm certain that we can come to some arrangement. I could certainly use a man like you in my organization."

To McIntyre's chagrin, Bolan merely smiled, as though the arms dealer had said something exceedingly funny. "Come now, I'm very reasonable, even generous. I'll make you an offer you can't refuse."

Bolan said nothing. He didn't bother to refuse.

McIntyre found it difficult to restrain his annoyance. Everything was for sale. Companies, women, friends.

Even himself.

He had gotten what he had thought was a very fair price at the time, although right now the deal didn't look so attractive. He refused to believe that this man didn't have a price. If he was holding out for more than he was worth, McIntyre would agree to it to get him off his back—he really wasn't in a position to argue. There would be plenty of time to settle the score later.

"Look," he said, trying to sound conciliatory. "There's a briefcase by that desk. Open it."

Bolan did so, keeping his weapon fixed on McIntyre's heart. He found piles of bills wrapped into packages of ten thousand dollars each.

"There are fifty bundles there, man. That's five hundred thousand dollars! And that will just be your signing bonus. When you've finished working for me you will never want for anything again in this life. There'll be plenty more, I assure you. So what do you say, do we have a deal?"

"Not enough, McIntyre, not nearly enough. You're going to make me a partner."

McIntyre steamed, trying to keep the lava from boiling over. He was Cameron McIntyre, a descendant of one of the most successful business families in America. As if he would actually take this man in as a partner, this upstart madman whose only asset was a fast gun. McIntyre would see him dead and damned first. Repressing the anger, he said, "I suppose that would be possible. We can see my lawyers tomorrow to work out some arrangement."

With an effort, Bolan prevented the contempt from registering on his face. "We'll start right now, then. Get Carrillo on the phone. I'll be handling the Peruvian connection in future."

The arms merchant retrieved his address book from his coat pocket, placed there in preparation for escape. He moved to the phone, stepping over the body of the gunman sprawled by the armchair.

McIntyre dialed a couple of numbers, then waited for the call to go through. "Señor Carrillo. Sorry to disturb you at this hour. However, there have been some new developments at this end that may concern some mutual friends. There is a man here I'd like you to speak with, a close personal friend of mine for more than ten years. I'll put him on now." He held out the phone for Bolan, a mocking smile flickering over his lips.

Bolan grabbed the receiver, a little nodule of worry sending a warning down his spine. McIntyre seemed a shade too confident. "This is Michael Blanski, Señor Carrillo. It's a pleasure to speak with you."

Carrillo's voice drifted over the phone lines, placid and undisturbed. "It is my pleasure as well, Mr. Blanski. A friend of Mr. McIntyre's is someone I am happy to welcome as a friend. How may I be of service?"

There was no trace of unease in Carrillo's voice. Bolan wondered if he was starting to jump at shadows. "Mr. McIntyre and I have come to a business arrangement whereby I will be taking over the South American operations. I would like to come to Lima and discuss future arrangements with you personally. Say in two days' time?"

"That would be convenient. Please call me when you arrive and I will arrange to be your most attentive guide to beautiful Lima. I will look forward to seeing you. Good evening."

Bolan replaced the receiver. "Well, McIntyre, it's time to pay for Sharp's murder."

McIntyre was stunned as he read his death in Bolan's cold eyes. "What about our partnership, the money you'll make? You need me to deal with Carrillo. You need my company and my connections. You need me!"

Bolan shook his head and drew the Desert Eagle.

"I...I... But you said if I cooperated..." McIntyre stammered, his eyes fixed on the huge silver pistol.

"That was then. This is now." A slug from the .44 cored McIntyre's forehead, blowing a fist-size exit wound in the back of his skull. The arms dealer crumpled to the floor.

JORGE CARRILLO TURNED from his code book and sighed. He had known from the conversation that something was wrong, but the past few minutes had confirmed it. It was fortunate that he and McIntyre had worked out an emergency code in case of trouble.

"Concern some mutual friends" had signaled the trouble, while "close personal friend" had meant that there was a specific enemy involved. "Ten years" told Carrillo that this enemy was considered ten out of ten on a danger scale.

He would have an opportunity to deal with this Michael Blanski in two days. In the meantime, he must inform his superior.

Carrillo sighed again, a mournful sound like wind whistling through a canyon, and reached for the phone. His boss would be very displeased.

9

Mack Bolan arrived in Lima feeling a little on the naked side. Airport security being as strict as it was these days, it was seldom worth the risk to try to smuggle a gun aboard. It didn't fit in with the big man's plans to spend the next few years in jail.

His second task would be to get hold of a weapon. The first was to make sure that he wasn't followed to his hotel.

Bolan scanned the waiting crowd at the airport as the bored customs officer checked him through, approving Michael Blanski's passport without question.

He had left a storm brewing when he departed from San Francisco. Kline had been distressed, to put it mildly, when he learned of the carnage that Bolan had left in his wake. The agent had been strongly inclined to have Bolan locked away for murder. It had taken some arm twisting by Brognola to convince Kline that this was something he had better keep his nose out of.

The Bureau man had agreed reluctantly, but Bolan wasn't entirely sure that he trusted Kline's word. It was possible that Michael Blanski might have to be retired as a viable alias.

In the meantime, Bolan had no intention of worrying about things that he couldn't control. Right now staying alive in Peru required all of his attention. He would operate as though he were in a hostile environment until circumstances proved otherwise.

He walked to the string of cabs ranged outside the terminal and picked the third one in line, ignoring the shouts from the first two drivers. He waved an American five-dollar bill at the startled cabbie. "Go. Now."

The cab shot from its position in line to a crescendo of horns. Given that the average annual wage in Peru was only about seven hundred dollars, as a free-spending American Bolan held an immediate advantage. Almost everything was for sale if an agreement could be reached without offending Latin machismo.

He had the driver head toward the city, instructing him to turn right and left aimlessly as he watched through the rear window for signs of surveillance. At random he changed taxis twice more before he gave instructions to drive to a hotel not far from the Plaza de Armas.

The hotel itself was nondescript, the sort frequented by budget-conscious travelers with North American tastes. He checked in as David Bowes, not wishing the name Blanski to be traceable to a hotel in case anyone was looking. When the clerk asked for his passport, Bolan deflected the request with a subtly proffered twenty, explaining that he seemed to have dropped his identification at the airport and would have to go to the American embassy for a replacement. But of course that would take some time. The clerk graciously accepted the explanation—and the money.

Bolan hit the streets after stowing what little gear he had brought. He crossed the Plaza de Armas, where guards strutted in front of the Palace of Government, also known as Pizarro's House. The guards glittered in silver helmets, crisp, snow-white jackets, red pantaloons and polished jackboots, uniforms inspired by Napoléonic splendor. But very modern rifles were slung over their shoulders.

At the second intersection Bolan angled away from the plaza, delving farther into the narrow streets that lined the core of the city.

The side streets were jammed with *ambulantes*, the sidewalk vendors who crowded the city peddling food and goods. The big man, easily recognizable as a tourist, was offered alpaca ponchos, skewers of beef heart and ewers of murky red "iguana blood," and even what were supposed to be genuine pre-Columbian artifacts. Bolan brushed by the outstretched hands of the vendors, intent on following the directions Brognola had given him for the prearranged meeting.

Apart from the street merchants in their rough clothes, shoeshine boys, wandering minstrels and tour guides competed incessantly for his attention and his funds. Once, as Bolan dodged around a girl who suddenly appeared in his path, he felt a skinny hand snake into his pants pocket. Bolan's hand darted out to grab the invader. A frightened, ragged boy of about eight stared wide-eyed at the tall man, afraid that the American would drag him to the police.

Bolan stared back for a moment and released the thin wrist. The child was lost in the crowd in seconds.

He continued on for another few blocks before stopping at a small shop called the Lore of the Incas. Inside, the tiny store was jammed to the ceiling with books, postcards and plaster replicas of Inca treasures. A glass case that supported a battered cash register held a scale model of Machu Picchu, the lost city of the Incas. A grinning proprietor stood behind the case.

"Do you have any Nazca pottery?" Bolan asked.

"Any particular era?" the shopkeeper inquired.

Bolan shook his head. "It's for a friend."

"Is this a Washington friend?"

"That's right." Bolan hated the question-and-answer games, but Brognola had insisted on the contact procedure.

The owner drew a six-inch pottery statue from a cupboard behind the cash. The idol examined Bolan from wide owl eyes on either side of a flat nose. "This should be to your satisfaction." He slipped it into a plastic bag. Bolan left a fifty-dollar bill on the cash register and departed with his purchase.

Back in his hotel room, Bolan examined the statue more closely, failing to find an imperfection in the glazed surface. He dropped the statue, turning it into rubble. Picking through the fragments, Bolan extracted a flat key.

He took a taxi to the main shopping area, absorbed in the passing scenery. It was surprising how little of the past had survived the modernization of Lima. Although it was older than any North American city, few reminders existed of its ancient heritage. The only signs of the long-forgotten Incas were advertisements for Inca cigarettes and Inca cola. The relatively recent Spanish influence showed in the multiplicity of churches. The cathedral held the remains of Francisco Pizarro, the soldier-adventurer who had humbled the last of the proud Inca kings.

Bolan got out of the cab at a mall in the ritzy shopping area frequented by the Peruvian elite, the Camino Real. Stepping inside under the eyes of vigilant security guards, he turned to a bank of yellow lockers lining a far wall. The key rewarded him with a solid black bag in a bottom locker.

In the privacy of his hotel room once again, Bolan smiled as he unpacked the bag. Some embassy staffer must have gotten a thrill out of delivering this particular package.

Brognola had come through as he had promised. A diplomatic pouch had forwarded a Beretta 93-R and a machine pistol, as well as fifteen clips for each and a shoulder holster for the pistol. Twenty-thousand dollars in crisp new bills provided pad money, hush money and pocket change for his stay.

Bolan felt a lot better with the weight of the Beretta under his arm as he dialed Carrillo. After exchanging pleasantries, they arranged to meet at a restaurant south of the Camino Real.

He arrived early, taking a seat in a corner near a fire exit. His eyes scanned the doorway and the plate-glass window that looked onto the wealthy streets of the suburb of San Isidro.

The crowds streaming by weren't much different from similar crowds in Paris or Madrid. For the most part, the women were fair-skinned *criollas,* dark haired and flashing eyed, of nearly pure Spanish descent. Others were marked as mestizas, the issue of the Spaniards and the native Indians. Many of these displayed dark red good looks that attracted the eyes of the men striding along as imperiously as conquistadores. Occasionally a native Indian would walk by, eyes downcast, garbed in a colorful poncho and a felt hat, looking as out of place among the stylish shoppers as an elephant at a horse show.

Bolan glanced at his watch. Carrillo was late. Bolan wasn't entirely sure what to expect from this meeting. He knew that he had a powerful bargaining chip in the captured weapons, and he hoped to press Carrillo for an introduction to the Shining Path connection. He was flying solo on this one and almost as blind as a bat. He would have to count on his own internal radar to steer him clear of danger, knowing that Carrillo had a reputation for treachery.

The shipment would be in port within a day or two, disguised as farm machinery, to be stored in a local warehouse. Unless he contacted the shippers with other instructions, the cargo would be sent to Ayacucho a week later. High in the Andes, the arms would wait safely for his disposal.

The headwaiter was speaking with a lovely young woman at the door who was looking beyond him to the patrons inside. She smiled and stepped through the door, approaching a tall dark man four tables away from Bolan. The warrior paid her no more attention than he would give any pretty woman until he heard "Michael Blanski" mentioned.

Bolan raised a hand to get her attention, motioning her to his table. He stood as she approached, conscious of Latin manners. Besides, it would improve his draw if required, although the woman appeared to be an unlikely candidate as an assassin.

"You are Mr. Michael Blanski?" Her voice was soft and musical.

"Yes. Please sit down." Bolan was already charmed, although his eyes flickered past her face from time to time, maintaining his watch on the street and the other patrons.

"I am Antonia de Vincenzo, Señor Carrillo's secretary. He sends his apologies, but regrets that he will not be able to come this afternoon. However, if it is convenient to come by his office at ten tomorrow morning, he promises that it will be worth your while."

"That will be fine, Miss de Vincenzo. I'll see you then, if you leave me the address."

"Certainly." She dug in her purse momentarily for a business card. "Señor Carrillo is most disturbed that he will not be able to show you around Lima personally this evening as he had promised, but if you like, I will be happy to be your guide."

Bolan was sorely tempted. The woman was exquisite, with cascading dark red hair and a glowing cinnamon complexion. Rich, full lips held a sensuous promise. The only clue to her mixed ancestry was a nose that was slightly too broad at the nostrils. A clinging garment much like a silk tube top exposed strong shoulders above a high bosom and a tiny waist. A single strand of pearls hung around her neck.

However, he had no wish to compromise his position by revealing anything inadvertently. The "honey pot" was one of the oldest tricks in the book for obtaining information, and Antonia was certainly a tempting dish.

"Thank you for your kind offer, but I'm otherwise engaged. Perhaps some other time."

"I shall hope so," she replied. Flashing Bolan a dazzling smile, she left, hips swaying gently.

IN THE MORNING Bolan took a taxi to one of the new downtown high-rise office buildings, part of the growing urban sprawl of the metropolis.

He disembarked a few blocks from Carrillo's office, preferring to walk the rest of the way. He paused several times to stare into the glass shop windows. The reflection served almost as effectively as a mirror, allowing Bolan to examine the surrounding pedestrians in case he had been followed. If he had, then his hotel might not be secure for another night.

Having satisfied himself that no one was trailing him, Bolan continued on his way.

Antonia de Vincenzo sat behind a mahogany secretarial desk in the sumptuous eighteenth-floor office. She looked much less relaxed than she had the day before. A flicker of some emotion that Bolan couldn't place flashed across her face at his arrival.

"Please go right in, Mr. Blanski," she said, rising and following him to the closed door on the other side of the room.

Bolan paused, hand on the doorknob. There was something wrong with the setup. He couldn't put his finger on it, but a tiny alarm told him that he was walking into danger.

He reached into his jacket to grasp the butt of the Beretta and turned the door handle. One step inside revealed nothing. At first glance the office appeared empty. He drew the Beretta and walked cautiously forward.

The Executioner felt someone looming behind him. He raised his left arm as he turned, attempting to ward off whatever was coming.

The world exploded into twinkling lights, and he fell heavily to the floor.

WHEN BOLAN AWOKE, the first thing he was conscious of was the pounding pain in the back of his head, as if a little man was trying to break his way out with a sledgehammer. The next thing he noticed was that he was lying on the floor. He couldn't move his arms or legs. His arms seemed immobilized behind his back. Finally, a few inches in front of his face, he saw the large black boots that had "policeman" written all over them.

There was only one conclusion—he was under arrest.

"What the hell is going on?" Bolan was mad, and his headache wasn't making his temper any sweeter.

"Be quiet, American." One of the cops nudged him in the ribs, none too gently.

Cameras were flashing in the office, and several people were speaking at the same time. Bolan's Spanish was fair, but the unusual accent made it difficult to follow what was being said. Another language was being spoken as well, probably the Quechua used by the Indian population.

A sudden chill indicated the arrival of a superior. Bolan had a snail's-eye view at this point, but could identify the newcomer by his gleaming knee-high boots. The officer walked around the room in absolute silence.

"Take him away. I will deal with him later."

Four policemen grabbed Bolan by the arms and feet and carried him from the office.

Bolan was thoroughly confused about what was going on, but two things were clear: he had been framed for something, and somebody was going to pay.

An hour later Bolan was lodged in a filthy cell in an underground Lima jail. He still hadn't been told why he was there. It was pretty clear that human rights and justice had a different meaning in Peru than they did in the United States. No one had bothered to remove the manacles or to bring him water, although he had asked for both.

Some initial exploration of his bonds had revealed that he could break them with a little effort. However, that would be wasted if he didn't have a method of escape or a place to go to ground.

At the moment he was completely on his own.

Footsteps echoed down the dank hall as someone came his way. Two guards halted outside the bars, machine guns leveled. A third man unlocked the door and stepped aside to allow entrance to a tall and burly officer in his early fifties, gaudily dressed in a perfectly fitted military uniform. He carried a leather crop that he tapped against one sparkling boot.

"I am General Palma. I take a special interest in terrorist cases."

Bolan was momentarily dumbstruck. It was ironic beyond belief to find himself accused of terrorism when much of his life had been devoted to crushing that hydra-headed demon in all its apparitions.

"You think I'm a terrorist?"

"I do not think it, I know it. It only remains for you to confess your crime."

"What have I supposedly done?"

Palma grinned, cutting the air with his crop. "You Americans astonish me. No matter what the evidence, you seem to think that we Peruvians must believe your 'sincere' denials and instantly allow you to walk away on the strength of your sterling character. No, sir. Peru is a just country, and I will see justice done in your case."

Bolan decided to play it straight. Without information he was helpless. "What am I charged with?"

"Well, Mr. Blanski, since you wish to continue this charade of innocence, I will play along for the time being. You are charged with the murder of Señor Jorge Carrillo, performed as a terrorist assassination."

"I never even met the man. The office was empty when I got there, and then I was struck from behind by someone, probably the same person who murdered Carrillo. You've got the wrong man." Bolan had a sinking feeling that all his arguments were in vain. There was an air about Palma that suggested the case was closed.

Palma shook his head and flashed a toothy grin. "How do you explain the pistol shot in Carrillo's heart? I am sure that ballistic tests will show that it came from your gun. Not that they are necessary, since we found the gun beside you. A Beretta, I believe. As well, we found the knife in your hand that you used to slit Carrillo's throat and carve the *S* on his chest to indicate the work of the Sendero Luminoso. We also found that you had checked into your hotel under a phony name, and that a machine pistol had been hidden in a false-bottomed suitcase."

The evidence was damning, certainly. The machine pistol was going to be hard to reconcile with his cover as a tourist.

"Carrillo had to have been killed by the person who slugged me and then left me to take the fall."

"Mr. Blanski, I do not know why you persist in these obvious lies." Palma turned away and ran the crop along the row of bars. "Señorita de Vincenzo swears that she conducted you into the office. She heard you and Carrillo talking, then a shot. She hesitated a few moments, but then, brave as she is, she rushed into the room and felled you with a blow to your head with a statue. She is a hero, Mr. Blanski."

"She is a liar."

Palma whipped around and with a practiced flick of the wrist cracked the crop into Bolan's jawline, raising an ugly red welt. "In Peru it is not our custom to speak of women the way you do in the United States. I trust that you will remember that in future."

Palma signaled to the guard to reopen the door. Before he made his exit, he stopped to confront Bolan one more time. "I suppose that you have heard stories about Peruvian prisoners, how they are beaten regularly and how confessions are extracted through torture." He looked at Bolan expectantly.

Bolan said nothing.

"Yes, it is said that we use cattle prods, electric torture, water torture, starvation, any number of tactics. Well, Mr. Blanski, it is true. I shall leave you now to compose your confession. I will be back tomorrow to assist you."

Palma strode down the hall, laughing loudly.

Bolan lapsed into a gloomy study of his options.

None of them looked worth a damn.

10

Bolan waited three more hours before another armed party arrived to remove his shackles. He recognized that he was being treated like an extremely dangerous man. Fortunately they brought water and some food—purple-fleshed potatoes in a thin soup. It was a long time since he had eaten, and he was parched.

The policemen ignored his requests to make a telephone call, and left him to rub his arms and legs to restore the circulation. Bolan paced around his narrow cell, ignoring the pricks of pins and needles as he moved. He gingerly touched the egg-size lump on the back of his skull. The hair around it was matted with blood, but at least his headache was abating.

He reviewed his options. He could break out as soon as possible and hide somewhere. Through Brognola he could arrange for a new identity and some cash. The down side would mean giving up on the mission.

A second possibility was to hang tough and roll with the punches for now. His chance of escape would probably not be much worse in future than it was at the moment. It was apparent that he'd been set up, but the reason why was unclear. The de Vincenzo woman was deeply involved, but he had no idea why she would kill her boss.

Bolan lacked facts to string together. All he had was a thousand nagging questions.

His thoughts were interrupted by the arrival of more police. This time they opened the cell and motioned him outside. Two guards led Bolan along, while two more brought up the rear, pistols drawn, ready for any sudden moves the prisoner might make. They walked through a doorway at the end of the dark corridor.

The section beyond was lined with larger cells, packed with wretched humanity from Lima's slums. By comparison, Bolan's tiny cell was first-class accommodation.

The warrior was hustled to a processing area where his clothes were taken from him in exchange for a rough-woven blue jail uniform. His wallet and watch had vanished long ago, before he had regained consciousness in Carrillo's office. The police continued to ignore his questions.

The next stop was a lineup. The procedure was a farce, since none of the other four suspects came within five inches of the big man. Although the others were as dark haired as Bolan, none of them was Caucasian. While he responded to the loudspeaker commands to turn right and left, he guessed that whoever was observing the ritual would have no difficulty in picking out the "guilty" party.

When Bolan was back in his cell, he cast himself onto the lumpy cot, staring at the low-watt bulb above him. Someone had ordered Carrillo killed, although the reason was murky. Blanski was obviously blown, somehow identified as a threat to the Peruvian operation, and his arrival had triggered a chain of events that had caught Bolan by the throat. He suspected that Carrillo's death served a dual purpose in plugging a possible leak and at the same time eliminating a potential danger.

Bolan recognized the trap he had fallen into. He couldn't call on Brognola for any official assistance. His mission to Peru was intended to halt a situation embarrassing to the

United States. No one in Justice, State or the White House would thank him if he involved the government.

The soldier had been in tighter jams on many occasions. He was used to biting the bullet and forcing the issue, making the big play alone, with nothing but his brains and guts to carry him through the hellfire. This would be no different.

Since there was nothing else he could do, Bolan slept.

BOLAN WAS AWAKENED by the sound of a heavy door down the hall creaking open. Two silent guards brought another dish of potato soup and a metal tin of water. He was beginning to loathe the sight of the repetitious jail house food.

He spent the next couple of hours doing some calisthenics, although barely able to support his weight on his still-aching right wrist. When it came time to make his break, his survival might depend on remaining in top condition. Besides, the hours moved slowly in a five-by-eight cell.

The thump of the door and the clump of police boots signaled a break in the monotony. This time Bolan was led to an interview room where a short young man was already seated. Two guards remained by the door, their hands resting on their pistol butts.

"Mr. Blanski, I'm Donald Creighton, a lawyer with the U.S. Embassy. General Palma informed us of your arrest. I apologize for not seeing you earlier, but I wanted to take some time to familiarize myself with your case."

Bolan was favorably impressed. The blond man seemed very straightforward for a lawyer. But then, he was still young.

"Good. When can I get out of here? I was set up. Can I post bail?" Bolan was anxious to get moving again.

"Mr. Blanski, I'm afraid that it isn't that simple." The lawyer removed his wire-rimmed glasses and began to polish the lenses with a silk handkerchief that had been neatly folded in the breast pocket of his suit jacket. He looked through them at the fluorescent light overhead and then placed them back on his nose.

"There is a great deal of evidence against you. You were found in Carrillo's office after he had been shot with your gun. A bloody knife was in your hand. Another weapon was found in your hotel room. Witnesses have identified you as being on the scene. A sworn statement testifies that you argued with Carrillo and then shot him. The case for your guilt appears to be airtight."

"What motive would I have to kill a man I had never met?"

"Money, or so the authorities say. Twenty thousand dollars was found in your room, money that you did not bring into the country. More than enough to persuade a hired gun to perform a political assassination. General Palma tells me that Carrillo was well-known in government circles as a fierce opponent of the Shining Path, and that an attempt on his life had been made once before."

Bolan contemplated the news in silence. It didn't ring true to identify Carrillo with the anti-Communists. Knowing the arms dealer's business connections, he found it hard to accept that Carrillo would pass himself off as a strident friend of the government. A low profile would have suited the merchant far better.

"So what happens now? A hearing, a trial?" Bolan was not very optimistic about the outcome of a trial. He knew a stacked deck when he saw one.

Creighton looked pained as he stared over the big man's shoulder at a barred window. "I'm afraid that there won't be a trial. Because you have been connected to a terrorist organization, a joint police and military commission has reviewed your case. Based on the facts as they have been presented, you have been sentenced by an administrative order in council. The sentence is life imprisonment."

For a moment Bolan was stunned to silence. He had had a pretty low expectation of the treatment he might get from the local judiciary. But this was beyond his worst nightmare. The only question now was when and how to make his break.

For the sake of appearances, he made the required protests, feeling as though he were playacting with a part of his mind, while the bulk of it evaluated possible escape scenarios. "You've got to be kidding. No one could think that I'd be stupid enough to murder Carrillo in his office in front of witnesses?"

"Yes, I thought of that. It doesn't make any sense. However, General Palma thinks that you would have killed Señorita de Vincenzo as well to prevent identification. It was plausible enough to convince the other council members."

"Palma was a witness against me?"

"No, he's a member of the administrative council. He is well-known as a hard-liner against the terrorists. If there is ever another military coup in Peru, a lot of people expect that Palma may be installed as president to wage war on the Path."

A knock on the door announced that the interview was being terminated.

"That's all the time we have right now. I'll visit you later at the prison to see how you are doing."

"Prison?"

"The Lurigancho. I'm afraid that it doesn't have a very good reputation."

Bolan turned to the door. The police certainly weren't wasting any time getting him out of the way. He noticed that Creighton hadn't said anything about diplomatic channels, protests or appeals. From the uncomfortable look on the young lawyer's face, he suspected that specific instructions had been given to dissociate the United States from Bolan to every extent possible.

Creighton's voice called him back. "Mr. Blanski, good luck." The lawyer extended his hand. Bolan reached for it, feeling a wad of paper slip into his palm. "Take this," he whispered. "It will make life a little easier inside."

"Thanks, Creighton." Bolan slipped his hand into his pocket as the guards led him away.

Palma lounged by the rear door of a paddy wagon. "Ah, Mr. Blanski. I'm sorry that we will not have an opportunity to become better acquainted." He tapped his crop against the spot where he had previously cut Bolan. "However, it was decided that the evidence was so overwhelming that we really did not need a confession. A pity. I would have enjoyed breaking you."

"Do you really think you could have?" Bolan's voice was low and menacing.

"You are too proud, Mr. Blanski. There are no heroes in the interrogation room, only broken men and corpses. You would have been one or the other. But I reluctantly bid you goodbye."

Palma signed with his crop, and the soldiers shoved Bolan inside. Examining the slip of paper Creighton had passed him, Bolan discovered that it was a carefully folded fifty-dollar bill. The warrior often found that at the most unexpected times and in the tightest corners some simple act of human kindness surprised and impressed him. People like Creighton were the reason that Bolan kept up the long, usually thankless and unknown struggle when other men would have built themselves a fortress and resigned from a brutal world, sparing themselves the pain of the fight.

GENERAL PALMA RETREATED to his private office, indicating to his secretary that he did not wish to be disturbed. He dialed a number from memory.

"Hello," a soft contralto said.

"I wish to congratulate you on your good work. Blanski will not trouble us again." Palma paused for a reply, and obtaining none, continued. "I have my men looking hard for the shipment. When it is found, I will contact you. In the meantime, stay where I can reach you. Do you understand?"

"Yes, I understand."

Palma found himself holding a buzzing phone. As he replaced the receiver, the general reflected on the curious chain of events that had led to this point.

Two years ago he had arrested Antonia de Vincenzo on suspicion of terrorist acts. He had soon discovered that she was guilty all right, but her fanatical ruthlessness combined with her beauty and intelligence had made him realize that the cinnamon-colored terrorist represented a special opportunity.

His goal was absolute power within the country, and Antonia and the Shining Path were a means to that end. The more violence they engendered, the more support there would be for a military coup to restore order.

With General Arturo Palma as the savior.

Striking a suspicion-filled and fragile truce between Antonia and himself, he had installed her as secretary to Carrillo, a man known to operate on the fringes of every shady deal that originated in Lima. Shortly afterward, Palma had approached Carrillo with the promise of a hands-off opportunity to make some money smuggling arms to the Shining Path. More powerful weapons in their hands meant an increasingly bloody and savage conflict, with severe casualties and stern repression.

All of which only increased Palma's power.

Carrillo had been shocked, of course, but had agreed for the right price. Antonia had served the role of intermediary between the arms dealer and the Path, since they refused to deal directly for security reasons. Unknown to Carrillo, she also served as a watchdog for Palma.

Unfortunately Carrillo had not been very wise in his choice of suppliers. When the weapons merchant had phoned Palma to inform him that the supply line had been blown, it had been necessary to arrange for Antonia to murder him.

All they needed was a fall guy, a role Blanski had conveniently filled. A neat solution that eliminated two of the potential dangers of exposing the general, Carrillo and Blanski.

He wondered if he should have Antonia killed, as well.

BOLAN WAS JOSTLED in the featureless box for nearly an hour before it screeched to a halt. As the paddy wagon started up again, he could see through the narrow rear window that it had cleared a checkpoint at the head of a one-lane road.

Two minutes later the police wagon passed under the overhang of the main wall of Lurigancho prison.

Once inside, Bolan was given a lecture by the prison warden on the need to obey the rules exactly, then was led through the decaying halls of the prison. Although he saw armed soldiers here and there, there was more of a sense of communal living than of the strict prison regimentation Bolan had experienced from time to time in the United States.

As opposed to the small cells with barred doors that he had anticipated, there were fairly open areas that housed two to four men in relative comfort. None of the cells was the same, and each had been improved with blankets, furniture, small cook stoves, books and pornographic magazines according to the occupants' taste. The tall man attracted fixed, unfathomable stares from the other residents as he was guided deeper into the maze that formed the residential barracks. None of the quarters had doors, although each could be made private by a thick curtain drawn across the front. Some were closed even now.

The lead guard stopped beside one of the openings and motioned Bolan inside. He stepped in to find another occupant reading, the book placed under a ray of sunshine streaming through a high, narrow window.

"I don't suppose you brought any books with you?"

Bolan shook his head.

"Oh, well, it doesn't matter. English books are the hardest things to get in this hole. I'm Jason Stone." Stone extended a skinny hand.

They shook hands as Bolan scrutinized his cell mate. He appeared to be in his late forties, slight, with round glasses and a straggling mass of brown hair streaked with gray, which tumbled over a long, mournful face. Stone looked as though he had been cooked over a slow fire, which had rendered out all the fat, leaving a sinewy frame and leathery skin.

Almost by way of contrast, a round face poked past the edge of the curtain. Not much taller than Stone, the fat, bald man must have carried twice his weight. A guard's uniform was plastered to the round tub, although he didn't carry a weapon.

"Here is Cristobal to greet you and welcome you to our happy establishment. He is responsible for order in this section of the barracks. And this is..."

"Michael Blanski."

Cristobal was delighted and promised to perform any service at a reasonable rate. He backed out, waving and grinning, hoping to see Blanski very soon after he was settled in case he needed any small thing.

"Welcome to Lurigancho, Blanski. You are a very lucky man, you know. Have a seat over there. That will be your bed." Stone gestured to a wide bed in the corner, tucked beside a tall dresser. Several blankets covered the bunk, which was topped by a feather pillow.

"I hadn't expected the conditions to be so luxurious." Bolan was surprised at the furnishings Stone possessed, including a small library, some solid furniture and a modern radio and cassette player with a selection of tapes that leaned toward the classical.

"That's one of the reasons why you are so lucky to be here. I've had three other cell mates since I arrived. The first one went mad and was sent to the asylum. The second one was killed in a fight. In both those cases their belongings were split among their friends. Fair is fair, you know. But the last fellow hanged himself one afternoon just above where you're sitting. It seems he had been getting anonymous letters—something about his wife fooling around. Well, most of the people here don't want to have anything to do with unhappy ghosts, so most of his belongings have been left for you. A very superstitious lot, in general. Even though they are Catholics, they seem to believe much more deeply in the devil than in God. You aren't afraid of ghosts, are you?"

Bolan shook his head. In his profession he couldn't afford to be.

"Cristobal seemed like a friendly sort of fellow."

"He is. It's a peculiar arrangement. In a strange way he is almost like our servant. But he can be vicious if you cross him or make him look foolish to the other guards. As long as you pay him off regularly and use his services, with a cut for his trouble, of course, he'll be a very happy man. And so will you. You can buy nearly anything you want here. Except your freedom. The whole thing still seems funny to me, but then this is the only prison that I've ever been in. What about you?''

"I've seen the inside of a prison before. But this seems strange to me, too." Bolan was already making plans. If Cristobal was accommodating, there might be a way to obtain the tools necessary to stage a breakout. Comfortable as this was, for a prison, Bolan had no intention of remaining here any longer than was strictly necessary.

"What are you in for?"

"Not yet, not yet. We'll be together for a very long time. There's plenty of time to get personal and exchange stories in the future. But not too soon. The best friendships are forged slowly and crawl together at a snail's pace. I'll be here for another twelve years. You?"

"Life."

Stone gave a low whistle. "You must be a bad character, although you don't look it. I wonder if I'll be safe in my bed with you around." Stone laughed to take away any possible sting. "Come along and I'll show you around. But wait, wait. Do you have any money?"

Bolan drew out the fifty. He didn't imagine for an instant that Stone would be the sort of man to steal it. Although in prison, Stone had a wise and educated air that made it impossible for the warrior to consider him a hardened criminal. Bolan expected that Stone, who obviously knew the ropes, might be a valuable ally and would take pains not to offend him.

Again Stone whistled, this time sounding a note of amazement. "You're as rich as a bloody prince! You're worth a Peru, as they used to say. That will keep you for almost a year in this place. Cristobal only gets a quarter a week, and that's your main expense. Let me show you my former cell mate's hideout.''

Stone drew the curtain and moved the dresser a foot from the irregular stone and mortar wall. He pulled a small rock from near the base of the wall, revealing a depression about six inches deep. At his direction, Bolan placed the fifty in the hiding hole. With the small stone back in place, a very careful scrutiny would have been required to detect the treasure trove.

"It will be safe now. You really don't have to worry about the other prisoners. Stealing is one of the things that can get you killed. Looking inside a cell when someone has the curtain drawn is another, since you might find someone hiding their stash. This is mostly to keep it hidden from Cristobal and the others. As it is, one member of a cell usually is pretty close by at all times, or you carry your valuables with you.''

"What else can get you killed in here?" Bolan had to adapt as quickly as possible so that he could devote his attention to getting out, not to avoiding being killed.

"Do you like men?"

"Not to date," he replied dryly.

"Good. Looking at someone's queen the wrong way may get you carved up pretty badly. Some people here like men quite a lot. Apart from that, don't give the guards a hard time, especially the ones with guns. But they won't shoot you unless you try to make a break.''

Stone drew back the curtain and took Bolan on a short tour. A washroom lay a little farther down the hall, with a grinning Cristobal in attendance, engrossed in a girlie magazine. Water for showers was available on Wednesday and Saturday. Food was delivered three times a day, but it was only bread, cheese and water, serving to encourage the prisoners to patronize the services of the guards.

The main gathering place of the prison was the court-yard, which was the exercise area, conversation pit, soccer field, outdoor barbecue center—in short, the focus of prison life. About two hundred prisoners crowded the yard, singly and in small groups. Two soccer teams occupied the central portion, with an interested group of supporters cheering both sides.

The only jarring note was the ring of guard tower around the high wall enclosing the yard, each manned by two men with long-barreled rifles equipped with sniper scopes.

Complacency was the word that sprang to Bolan's mind to describe his surroundings. As long as the prisoners and guards all played by the rules, life was as easy and profit able as it ever could be in this environment. He suspected that most of the prisoners were here for long terms and were intent on doing their time as comfortably as possible.

Bolan could never live that way. Echoing New Hampshire's motto, he believed in the words Live Free or Die Spending one dreary day after another within four prison walls was bare existence. He would break through these forbidding concrete walls or die trying.

11

Bolan and Stone stood near a wall of the prison yard. Stone continued to chatter, explaining the intricacies of life in Lurigancho. Cigarettes were the standard medium of exchange, except for certain of the guards who demanded cash on a regular basis. There was a set fee for various services within the prison, from laundry to sexual favors. Food, clothing, furniture, even prostitutes could be obtained from the outside for a small amount of hard currency.

"It's livable, Blanski, as long as you keep your wits and can get hold of a little cash. The guards will beat you badly if you can't afford to pay off. I've seen prisoners beaten to death, the rifle butts rising and falling as though the guards were pounding corn. The corruption goes right to the top, so no one lifts a finger.

"Of course, there are rats among the prisoners here like anywhere else. Not real ones. Those are considered quite a delicacy when lightly fried, so you don't see too many, barring a few in breeding colonies that some prisoners keep. I mean the two-legged kind. And it looks like we're going to get a visit from King Rat right now."

Five men were ambling along the edge of the yard in their direction. The prisoners lining the wall and soccer field moved to let the group pass freely. Anyone who was a little

slow was shoved aside by two toughs who were the point
men for the small party.

"That's Raimondo," Stone explained. "He controls the
drug trade within the prison, and as such he's rich and
powerful among our little community. Don't try to inter-
fere with his operations. That's another way to get killed in
here. A couple of other cons have been knifed or had their
necks broken this year, either because they were dealing
themselves, or just because Raimondo didn't like them.
People try to stay on his good side."

"Don't the prison guards maintain any sort of control?"

Stone snorted his contempt. "Violence and kickbacks are
the way of life here. Sure, you can have whatever comforts
you can pay for, but only the strong survive to enjoy them.
If madness doesn't get you, disease or violence will. As for
the guards, as long as they get their payments, they don't
care if we beat or kill one another right under their noses.
They seem to regard us as a separate species, not really human at all. If you get into trouble, you'll get no help from
them. If you cause trouble with another prisoner, they
won't intervene, either."

Bolan stored away the data for later use. Stone was
proving to be a gold mine of information, just as he had
hoped. Some of that information might prove handy right
now.

The advancing party bore down on Bolan. Three of the
men were clearly the muscle, mottled with scars and broken teeth that showed long histories of hand-to-hand combat. The leader was dressed in a freshly washed and pressed
prison uniform, with a silver cigarette case protruding from
the shirt pocket. Gold flashed from wrist and throat. Slim
and self-confident, he seemed oblivious to his surround-

ngs, acting as though he were strolling the grounds of his own private garden.

Bolan had to look hard at the fifth member of the party. Small, delicate features had been enhanced with makeup and a blond wig, transforming a male prisoner into a very convincing simulation of a woman. A flower-patterned dress and high heels completed the illusion. The transvestite smiled broadly at Bolan.

Raimondo halted by Stone and Bolan, his henchmen forming a protective circle. Smaller than the hardmen who ringed him, the drug lord radiated a sinister menace that a lesser man would have found intimidating. Flat black eyes sparkled under heavy brows as Raimondo examined Bolan, trying to stare him down.

Bolan wasn't budging an inch and returned the thug's gaze, the warrior's steely look skewering the crime boss until the guy looked away.

"So, you are Blanski, the new prisoner." Raimondo's tone was icy, although a quaver betrayed his annoyance at losing face in his first confrontation with the new inmate. Raimondo struggled to regain the initiative.

Word traveled fast in the prison community, Bolan thought. Either that or Raimondo had had advance warning of his arrival.

Raimondo ignored Stone as he addressed Bolan. He waved a hand casually, encompassing the entire massive structure. "All this you see about you is mine."

With a pompous opening line like that, Bolan figured the drug boss was preparing a lecture about how great and powerful he was. Bolan was in no mood to listen to the guy rant about his own self-importance.

"I thought it belonged to the government of Peru," Bolan drawled.

Raimondo halted, his mouth open, as he was preparing to continue delivering his speech. His eyes glittered with a cold, reptilian dislike. He took a pace closer to Bolan, eyeballing the big man as he snarled, "The outside may belong to the government, but what happens inside, I control. The other convicts obey me, Raimondo." He thumped himself on the chest for emphasis. "You are as much my prisoner as the government's."

Bolan wasn't about to take any crap from a petty criminal. He rocketed his fist into the vermin's jaw, sending Raimondo sprawling onto his backside.

Sitting up in the dust and holding his chin, Raimondo shook his fist in Bolan's face, rattling the gold chains at wrist and throat. "Listen, you smart ass gringo, I run this prison. And I'll make sure that you don't forget it." He barked a command at the three hardmen.

The two nearest hitters charged, while the third held back to look for opportunities.

Bolan knew that a single man, properly trained, was more effective than any two or three hoodlums in a brawl. He stepped to his left as Stone scrambled out of the way of the bruisers.

As one of the men rocketed by, Bolan stuck out a foot and tripped him. As the guy fell to the ground, Bolan crunched a power-packed blow to the point of his chin, dropping the enforcer like a stunned ox.

The second man halted with a shout of rage as he found his outstretched arms empty of prey. The guy weighed about three hundred pounds, and Bolan guessed that his method of fighting was to flop on top of his opponents to crush resistance with his massive bulk.

The pig eyes focused on Bolan, and with another shout the fat man trundled forward like a maddened bull, heavy arms seeking to lay a bear hug on Bolan.

The soldier waited impassively by the prison wall as the other man built up speed. At the last instant, Bolan dodged under a flailing arm and reappeared behind the thug. With a mighty shove the Executioner propelled the tub of lard into the wall.

The hitter dropped on his belly, leaving a red streak down the rough stone from where his head had made contact.

A crowd of prisoners had gathered to watch the brawl. They were silent, which told Bolan that Raimondo and his men were not liked enough for the other prisoners to cheer them on. At the same time, the drug lord was obviously feared, since nobody had the guts to root openly for Bolan.

The last tough advanced to take his turn. He reminded Bolan of a gorilla, of medium height but broad and deep chested, with long arms and shoulders as thick as small tree trunks. He grinned through chipped teeth as he pulled a switchblade from his pocket. Raimondo stood impassively behind, a tight smile on his face, anticipating the sight of Bolan's blood.

The knife flashed in the morning sunlight. The crowd murmured, the excited sound that a mob gets when violence is on display, a diversion to pass the weary time.

This player knew his business, advancing slowly with the knife held loosely and pointed upward. Careful, restrained movements tested Bolan's reactions without allowing a countermove.

The warrior backed around the circle of prisoners, staying well away from the crowd, his main worry that someone might extend a foot to trip him up. If Bolan slipped, he wouldn't just be beaten, he'd be carved up like a jigsaw puzzle. He feinted to the side, but the knifeman turned in response, his lightning speed belying his squat bulk. Bolan

kept his eyes on the knife, knowing that it was possible to
fake an opponent out with the eyes or hands.

Bolan pretended to miss his footing, his left foot sliding
along the dirt. The knifeman stepped in, his blade flashing
toward his opponent's exposed throat.

The Executioner shot forward, his left arm grabbing for
the knife hand, while his right balled into a fist for a shattering blow to the larynx.

But this guy was no fool. He hadn't committed himself
as much as Bolan had thought, and he danced back out of
reach. As Bolan's fingers closed on air, the knife slashed
through his left sleeve, the point carving a small trickle of
blood along his forearm.

The knifeman was grinning, thinking that he had won.
Bolan knew it was time to try some tricks of his own.

He recognized the grin for what it was, and decided to let
the guy think that he controlled the situation. It might make
him sloppy next time and give the warrior a split-second
advantage, which would be enough.

The bulky Peruvian danced back and forth, performing
a little ballet as he edged Bolan around the ring of faces. He
feinted twice, flashing the knife at Bolan's eyes. The knife
flashed a third time, but as the warrior jerked his head
away, he saw the killer flip the knife into his left hand with
a flick of the wrist. This time, instead of pulling back, the
hardman stretched forward, his right hand still waving as
a decoy, the left hand guiding the blade to Bolan's heart.

The Executioner struck hard, his right arm smashing the
knife hand aside as he stepped into the advancing con. His
left arm shot forward, palm outward. The heel of his hand
connected with the tough's oversize nose, flattening the
flesh and driving the nose bone like a projectile back into
the brain case.

The knife went spinning as the dead fingers relaxed and the hardguy crashed into the dirt.

The crowd exploded into clapping and roared its approval. Almost everyone then drifted back to the entertainment of the soccer game, which had continued uninterrupted. One inmate placed the knife in Bolan's hand before he wandered off, the spoils given to the victor. Bolan folded it away after wiping it on the dead man's pants, pleased to not be empty-handed any longer.

Raimondo shook his fist at Bolan, although he had retreated well out of the Executioner's range. "Don't think that this is over, Blanski. You're a dead man." The two other enforcers had recovered and were backing him up, one of them with a sticky red bloodstain on the crown of his head.

"Listen, Raimondo. If I have any trouble, I'll see you about it. Personally."

With a last glare, Raimondo turned away and led his shrunken party back to their quarters. As they moved off, the transvestite looked back and winked at Bolan.

Stone approached Bolan, his admiration showing on his face. "Well, Blanski, I'm glad to see that you're still alive. You certainly have a remarkable way with people. I bet you took that course 'How to win friends and influence people'!"

Bolan chuckled, and he and Stone wandered off to explore the rest of the prison. Two guards arrived to remove the remains of the con, like a dead gladiator being dragged from the arena. Neither paid Bolan any attention.

One area that Stone pointed out interested Bolan a great deal. It was a set of barracks around a second small yard, almost a separate wing, which Stone explained held prisoners associated with the Shining Path. At present there were about three dozen of the terrorists in the compound.

"They keep to themselves almost exclusively," Stone explained, "maintaining an almost monastic kind of existence. They spend the days in silence, except for what are like prayer meetings when they sing revolutionary songs and chant political slogans. The guards leave them pretty much alone. In 1986 there were about 125 of them before they staged a mutiny. The government attacked with rockets and antitank missiles and killed every one. That was a very bad time. The prison ran with blood."

An idea popped into Bolan's head, a way of getting out and yet accomplishing what he had set out to do. "Do you have any contacts among them?"

"Well, yes, as a matter of fact I do. But they are very secretive and have little to do with anyone who is not a member of their group, so I wouldn't expect much."

"Do what you can to arrange a meeting between me and their headman, will you?"

Stone considered the matter. He had only known this man for a few hours, but something in Blanski's gruff but straightforward manner had impressed him. Blanski was the sort of man who inspired confidence, a natural leader. He appeared to be one of the strong silent types that Stone had admired in the movies, another Gary Cooper or Clint Eastwood. He was falling under the big man's spell.

"Sure thing, Blanski. I'll see what I can do."

THE NEXT TWO DAYS passed slowly as Bolan waited for a response from the leader of the Shining Path, an Indian who called himself Libertad.

Bolan pressed Stone to find out what was happening, and why there was a delay. Stone urged Bolan to leave matters to their own time. Any further inquiries would only arouse the suspicions of the terrorists, never a very trusting group at the best of times.

Steeling himself to wait, Bolan examined the possible avenues of escape. The direct route over the wall didn't seem very promising. Eight towers perched atop a thirty-foot wall, each manned with two alert guards with machine guns. Razor wire ran along the wall between the towers. At night, spotlights traversed the yard, while lights illuminated the walls. It would require a full-scale assault to break out against heavy opposition. For one man alone, an attempt to go over the wall would probably be suicidal.

A second possibility would be to get out the main door. As a start, that would mean getting into the administrative area from the prison compound. There was only one way in, down a long corridor heavily guarded at both ends. Except for unusual circumstances, only the older and more trusted prisoners went in there to work as servants to the guards and in areas such as the laundry. It would be a long time, if ever, before Bolan received that "privilege."

An honor that Bolan would gladly do without.

There were variations on the plans that involved more subtle approaches—a little sleight of hand, a few heavily greased palms, a sudden break under lucky circumstances. All of those possibilities involved more time, luck and money than he had available.

The heat of midday had ended the soccer game temporarily as prisoners scrambled to find a small patch of cool earth. Bolan and Stone had taken a choice spot in a corner of the prison yard. Other prisoners moved away at the big man's advance. As the two prisoners discussed methods of escape, Stone was pessimistic about the outcome. Bribery was out. One prisoner had escaped seven years ago by paying off several of the guards. In the aftermath, those who had been directly involved found themselves prisoners in other jails. Many of the remaining guards had been fired.

No one at Lurigancho was anxious for a repeat performance.

"What about feigning death and being smuggled out as a corpse?" Bolan was willing to consider any option at this point.

"Impossible." Stone shook his head in discouragement. "Some clever prisoner tried that years ago. Now they make sure that a corpse is really dead by cutting off its head before they bury it outside the prison. No one tries to escape that way any longer."

Bolan was beginning to regret not trying a break earlier, before he arrived at the prison. It looked as if he was in for a longer stay than he had anticipated. The whole Peruvian mission was turning into a disaster. Someone had been a step ahead of him every inch of the way.

The warrior was going to find out who the mystery person was. As soon as he got out of this hole.

Raimondo held court on the opposite side of the compound. The kingpin had avoided Bolan for the past two days, carefully placing as much distance as possible between them. The occasional hate-filled glares Bolan intercepted told him that Raimondo certainly held a grudge. The dealer's pride couldn't stomach being defeated, and Bolan guessed that he burned with anger when the other prisoners snickered at his bruised enforcers.

The soldier was way ahead of Raimondo on points, and everyone in the prison knew it. But Bolan read the guy as the kind who would always use a pawn to make the dangerous moves. The big man kept an eye on every move the other prisoners made, watched his back at all times. Except for Stone, Bolan distrusted the other inmates.

The warrior suspected there would be another confrontation soon, but in the meantime he was willing to lie low and not attract attention from the guards. He didn't want to be particularly noticeable as he tried to figure a way out of the pen.

Stone was an enigma still. The old prisoner had refused to share his background. But Bolan noticed that in spite of his seeming weakness, the other prisoners treated the aging con with a courtesy that bordered on fear. This reaction was particularly noticeable in the Indians, who often refused even to look him in the eye.

Just then a man approached, giving the news that Libertad would see Bolan in an hour.

Bolan sat back to review his plans for the meeting, just as he would have checked his firepower before a hit. This might be his only chance to score some information from the Shining Path, and the only weapon he could use was his brain.

He had better make sure it was loaded.

12

Bolan strode between two brawny Indians, who stood, arms crossed, at the head of the corridor that led deep into the prison, into the pavilion controlled by the Shining Path. They pretended not to notice his passage. He marched down a corridor similar to those in the main section of the prison. However, here each of the cells held only a bare cot, a small chest, a desk and a lamp. None was screened, and all were empty. Several were scored with bullet holes.

The residents were gathered in an inner courtyard, facing toward a massive thirty-foot banner, which showed a bespectacled, round-faced man in a jacket and open shirt towering above a vast army of peasants carrying rifles and pitchforks. In his left hand he grasped a book written by Marx, while the right held a red banner inscribed with the Communist crossed hammer and sickle.

Below the banner a tall man with a hatchet nose conducted the other captured guerrillas in revolutionary songs. "The masses roar, the Andes shake," burst from three dozen throats. "We will transform the dingy dungeons into shining trenches of combat."

Bolan noticed that there were no guards in sight. Blackened walls pockmarked with hundreds of large and small craters in the stone confirmed that this area had seen some heavy combat.

He waited, watching the crowd as they shouted their slogans. There was no lack of fanaticism among these terrorists. Their eyes glowed with the burning light of true believers. In the name of twisted principles, these men justified every crime conceivable. For every objection, there was a ready answer to be found in the writings of their leader, Gonzalo. These men no longer needed a conscience, no longer had room for one. Killing and dying had been reduced to a simple rule: follow orders for the greater good of the cause.

This fanaticism made them extremely dangerous. Killers hired for a paycheck would run if there was a way out. The Shining Path would embrace the chance to die as a noble sacrifice.

Bolan planned to give a lot of them that chance.

He had never understood this willingness to suspend thinking and judgment, to live by a formula. He lived large, and if he broke some of society's rules, well so be it. Bolan answered to no other man, and he had no need to be forgiven. He lived by a stiff moral code, but it was his own, not something that he had read in a book, or that someone else had told him to believe in.

The Executioner was prepared to kill or to die. For his own reasons.

The chanting ended, and the leader hopped off the platform and walked across the hard-packed earth to Bolan. The followers dispersed in silence.

"I am Libertad. Why did you wish to see me?"

A hard man, Bolan judged, as he scrutinized the Peruvian. Libertad seemed accustomed to giving orders and not wasting time on small talk.

"I have something for the Shining Path. Weapons. Cases and cases of American arms."

"What concern are weapons to us here, inside this prison? I can do nothing about anything you might have for sale." Bolan recognized interest in the tall Indian by the way in which the other man stiffened slightly at the mention of the arms.

Bolan continued, adopting the manner he thought would be appropriate to a tough death dealer interested in profit alone. "I'm sure you have some means of communicating back and forth with your superiors outside. You can tell them that I can supply all their needs in future. The down payment is a load that another merchant called Carrillo was going to deliver. His plans have changed, and he won't be doing any further business with you. So I'll deliver in his place, and as a special introductory offer, it will only be half the normal price."

"That does not sound reasonable, a capitalist such as yourself taking a low price. What is this shipment? What do you have to gain?" Libertad was testing him, wary of entrapment.

"Your boss will know all about the delivery, and I'll bet he's already made plans for it. I'm sure there will be some disappointed faces if it doesn't turn up. And it won't without me."

The soldier watched Libertad for any sign of reaction, but the man was inscrutable. "As for the price, let's just say I got the merchandise at a very big discount. Besides, there's one catch I haven't mentioned. You have to find some way to get me out of here. Either I deliver the arms personally or you don't get them at all."

Bolan tried to look nonchalant as Libertad considered. This was the trickiest part of his sell job. If the Shining Path balked at this, he was on his own, and no further ahead than he had been before.

Libertad had no intention of handing Bolan an easy victory. "Why should we deal with you at all? There must be hundreds of other possible suppliers anxious to sell us what we wish. Anyway, getting you out is impossible."

The warrior was sure he had the terrorist hooked. The only problem was to haggle over the price. "In case you think otherwise, you don't find black market arms dealers in the telephone book. Besides, you've already paid for part of the shipment in advance."

"Still, getting you out would be a service worth a reward."

"Now that you mention it, I'm prepared to agree. Two cases of SAW machine guns as a bonus."

"Ten. With ammunition."

Bolan rubbed his chin as though mulling over the terms. He was willing to promise anything, since he didn't intend to deliver a single bullet.

"Agreed." Bolan sighed.

Libertad still tried to sound as if he wasn't buying any of it. "How do I know that you have the weapons at all?"

"Simple," Bolan said, reaching for a piece of paper in his back pocket. "Go to this address and follow these instructions. In return you will get a case of M-16s. Besides, when I go with them to pick up the remainder, if I'm fooling you, then you can have me killed."

Bolan could imagine what Libertad was thinking. A perfect opportunity to grab the guns without paying. No trouble. And no witnesses. Right now Bolan was hoping that Kline had followed his instructions to the letter. If he had, there would be a specially prepared case of M-16s waiting and everything would be cool. Otherwise...

"I cannot decide this alone. Your information must be verified and a decision made by other parties. It may take several days." Libertad took the paper.

Bolan smiled to himself. He had no doubt what the answer would be. Trapped in prison, these Shining Path guerrillas were of no value. If anything they were an embarrassment and a liability as a potential source of information leaks. Dead, they were martyrs. Bolan believed that their leaders would sacrifice them all if there was the slightest possible benefit to be gained.

He would know soon enough.

The Executioner left, content with the seeds of self-destruction he had sown among the Shining Path.

Now all he had to do was wait for them to ripen.

BOLAN REENTERED the main prison courtyard and found himself in the middle of a firestorm.

"There he is!" an angry voice screamed, pointing an accusing finger at Bolan.

The big man had no idea what was going on, but it spelled trouble in capital letters. A group of inmates was advancing on him, shaking their fists. Several cons were yelling "thief" as they approached.

Bolan moved back to the wall, protecting himself from assault from the rear. Now he was ringed by shouting prisoners, although they all kept beyond the range of a lightning strike from the big man's fists, remembering the fight of a few days ago.

Bolan saw Raimondo's grinning face on the outer fringes of the crowd. He would bet that the prison boss was behind what was going down. A score to be settled later.

Right now he could either try to break through the rowdy mob, or wait it out and fight off attacks where he stood. He couldn't afford to lose his cool, not when he was outnumbered forty to one.

A rock sailed in from his left, delivering a solid blow to his shoulder, hard enough to bruise. A second from another quarter whistled by his ear.

That settled it. If he stayed where he was, he would be cut to pieces by flying stone.

Bolan charged, and Raimondo's grin vanished as the Executioner parted the crowd and headed right for him, menace blazing from his eyes. The kingpin scrambled like a pursued quarterback as Bolan plowed into his enforcers with the force of a defensive tackle.

He put his head down and aimed between two toughs, a shoulder taking each one in the chest. They dropped beside him as Bolan's hands stretched for Raimondo's throat.

They came up a few inches short as grasping hands pulled his legs out from under him and Bolan crashed on top of a con. He kicked viciously, feeling the satisfying snap of bone under his boot, and the clutching paws relaxed.

Bolan scrambled to his knees, searching for Raimondo, who had evidently left the yard while he was able.

A foot caught Bolan in the stomach, and the air whooshed out of him. The milling mob had regained its courage now that the big man was downed, and jostled around him, raining kicks indiscriminately while they chanted, "Thief, thief."

Bolan tried to rise once, twice, but each time a savage blow toppled him to the ground. He ached everywhere, but attempted as best he could to protect his head from the brutal assault.

Through the gathering fog in his brain, he heard what sounded like Stone shouting. The words rang faintly in his ears as if they were coming from deep underground. The black vortex around him began to spin wildly, breaking into fantastically colored constellations of blinking lights that extinguished themselves with a roar as he fell over a cliff into total darkness.

BOLAN AWOKE WITH A START, a stifled scream emerging as a gasp.

"Nasty dreams, Blanski? Well, have some of this." Stone gave the weakened man a cup of something hot that smelled and looked like boiled cow dung, while he wiped the beaded sweat from Bolan's forehead. Bolan was too tired to resist, downing the foul mixture while he held his breath.

"I expect it'll be a day or two before you're up and around again. You'll be sore for a lot longer than that, though. It's a good thing that you're all muscle, or those ruffians would have done you some serious damage. As it is, the worst you got was two cracked ribs, a mass of bruises and a severe bump on the head, probably with a mild concussion."

"What happened?"

"While you were in with Libertad, I was called in for a chat with the warden. Meaningless, really. He didn't have anything to say. When I got back to the yard, I saw that you were in need of some assistance. So I helped out and got you back here. That was a few hours ago."

Even in his fuzzy condition, Bolan recognized that Stone was leaving out something. While he thought about what question to ask next, he fell asleep again.

"GOOD MORNING, Blanski. Time for your potion again." Stone held out another cup of his noxious brew.

"What is that stuff?" Bolan was feeling less agreeable this time about drinking the evil-smelling liquid, although he certainly felt no ill effects.

"I don't want to explain it, and I'm sure that you would rather not know. Just take my word for it, it will do you good."

Bolan downed the mixture reluctantly, trying not to taste it.

"For your information, Blanski, this is a very potent native medicine known only to the natives of the altiplano, the high Andes regions."

"I can see why it never caught on."

"Ah, Blanski, somehow I had expected you to have a more open mind. The natives know remarkable things, if we would let them teach us."

"How is it that you are familiar with native medicines?" Bolan had been curious about Stone since they had met. His manners and bearing didn't identify him as one of the criminals or lowlifes whom Bolan was acquainted with.

"I was a university professor in the States, specializing in native medicine and witchcraft. Before I came to Peru, of course."

That explained a lot to Bolan, but not why his companion was in prison.

Almost as though he read Bolan's thought, Stone continued to fill in his background. "I was doing some field work in the province of Ayacucho about eight years ago. Rather foolishly, as it turned out, because that is the primary base of the Shining Path. They were just starting to make a nuisance of themselves back then. The region was placed under a state of emergency. Because I was educated, American and in the wrong place, I was connected to the left-wing revolutionaries, and so here I am. There were protests and appeals ongoing, but the last I heard of those was about four years ago. Looking on the bright side, I only have another twelve years on my sentence." Stone couldn't hide the bitterness in his voice. Bolan recognized that he wasn't the only victim of a bad conviction. "I'll never forget the man who sent me here. A Lieutenant Colonel Palma.

"That's where I met Libertad and many of his people, although he had another name then. I developed a certain sympathy for their cause, if not for their methods, while I lived in the region. We have maintained a loose contact since he arrived in the prison."

"So that's how you were able to get me a meeting with him." Bolan hadn't realized how fortunate he had been being paired with Stone.

"I have treated him and his men since they arrived. He was pleased to be able to return a favor."

Bolan turned to a more immediate question. The aches and pains that plagued him were a continuous reminder of yesterday's beating.

"What was all that about yesterday? I think they were accusing me of being a thief."

"Absolutely right. While you were away and I was diverted, someone, probably one of Raimondo's men, sneaked in and planted a stolen lighter under your mattress. Clumsy, but effective, since the prisoners despise a thief. Then, when the loss was discovered, another helpful prisoner claimed to have noticed you in the vicinity of the robbed man's quarters. A search turned up the evidence, and you were convicted in absentia."

It had been effective, all right. It had almost gotten him killed. Next time he might not be so lucky. There was more to the situation than first met the eye, Bolan was sure. It was no coincidence that Stone had been in the warden's office and away from his cell. The only puzzle was whether Raimondo had enough influence to get the warden to cooperate, or whether someone else was pulling the strings.

With the way the dice had been tumbling, Bolan would have bet on the latter.

"I'm curious about one thing, Stone. How did you stop them from killing me? I can't see you fighting them off single-handedly." Bolan smiled, to take the edge off in case Stone felt insulted.

"Blanski, you are looking at one of the very few *brujos* in Peru. A *brujo* is a caster of spells and can work almost unimaginable evil. He can cause melancholy, blindness, sickness and death. I told you once that the Peruvians were a very superstitious people. When I first arrived, one of the other prisoners gave me some trouble. I cursed him, using my knowledge of witchcraft. He was so terrified that he missed his footing running away from me, fell down some stairs and broke his neck. Since then, the Peruvians have taken it into their heads that I am a sorcerer, and none of them wish to cross me. So when I intervened, they let me have you. Now that it's clear that you are under my protection, I don't think there will be a repetition of yesterday's incident."

Bolan had already decided that. As soon as he was back in fighting form, he would hand Raimondo his head.

"As for the vile elixirs that I have been preparing for you, the Indians have a great deal of knowledge concerning herbs and roots and their medicinal properties. Thanks to a few pungent roots, you'll be as good as new."

Bolan vowed that Raimondo would need more than a few roots by the time he was finished with him.

13

Bolan spent one more tedious day under Stone's vigilant care. The former professor treated his charge with the bullying attitude of a drill sergeant combined with the protective demeanor of a fussy old hen. He exercised the dominance over his sick patient that was a prerogative of the well.

A splitting headache was the least of Bolan's worries, as he discovered when he tried to push his way out of bed and grab his clothes. The room reeled and his stomach churned, threatening to send the big man to his knees. Instead, he sat down hard on the bed once again before lying back against the lumpy pillows.

"Satisfied, Blanski? Maybe now you'll listen to me and let yourself rest." Stone looked at the now supine man more closely. He was already asleep. "Damned if I know why you're so anxious to get out of that bed. Raimondo and his goons will be waiting, no matter how long you stay here." With a sigh, Stone returned to his reading.

The next morning, Bolan awoke refreshed from a dreamless sleep. He felt clear-eyed and alert for the first time since the battering, without a trace of the nausea that had plagued him as a result of the concussion. The pain of the bruises and cracked ribs had retreated to a dull ache. Through determined concentration, Bolan forced the sen-

ations from his conscious mind into an area of awareness
hat was present, but unimportant.

He stood and began to stretch, performing a long ritual
of exercises designed to restore his fighting flexibility. He
gnored the protests of knotted, inactive deltoids and pec-
orals.

Stone watched silently from his bed, then said, "Well, I
can see you don't need my services any longer. All that's left
s to send you the butcher's bill."

Bolan turned to the older man and fixed him with a penetrating stare. "Stone. Thank you." The big man vanished
hrough the door in the direction of the shower.

Under the weak stream of tepid water, Bolan considered
his next move. It wouldn't be long before Raimondo
earned that his enemy was up and about. Whatever Bolan
did next would have to be done fast. Obviously inclined to
treachery, it was only a matter of time before the dealer arranged for Bolan to be poisoned, shot by a guard or killed
in some other underhanded way that minimized the danger to the crime boss.

A waiting game would be the best strategy he could
adopt—if he wanted to play into Raimondo's hands.

Bolan didn't plan to wait around. He had no intention of
being a target, either moving or sitting. Only the superstitious fear that the simpleminded inmates had of Stone had
protected Bolan as he lay injured and recovering. Once he
began mingling with the others, it would be open season on
him once again.

Strike first, strike hard—that old military dogma used by
everyone from Alexander the Great to the Israeli air force
would serve Bolan as well.

Cutting off the water jet and grabbing his towel, Bolan
returned to the cell. Equipping himself was a simple chore,

since his only weapons were the captured knife and a length of rough hemp rope that he wrapped around his waist.

"I don't suppose that you can be reasoned with, can you, Blanski? This isn't *High Noon*, you know, and the cowboys in the white hats don't always win in the final reel. You'll be safe enough if you remain here."

Bolan shook his head. True, being on the right side didn't make you invulnerable. The Executioner had buried too many good comrades in arms to think any differently. But he wasn't about to make himself a prisoner in his cell, even if it might be only a few days until he could make a break. He had never been afraid to meet danger eyeball to eyeball, and he wasn't about to change now.

"This was Raimondo's choice. He's made it clear with his 'This place ain't big enough for the both of us' attitude." With a short laugh, Bolan strode toward the courtyard.

Raimondo would be dying to see him.

Soon.

Bolan pushed into the prison yard, the fierce southern sun already giving promise of the blistering heat yet to come. The interminable soccer game was in progress, to be interrupted only by the scorching midday sun.

The big man powered across the yard toward Raimondo's cell block, half-conscious of the trail of murmuring he left in his wake. A few of the more intrepid followed like sharks after the scent of blood, while the timid crept away to safety—when elephants fight, it's the ants who take a beating.

The Executioner guessed that Raimondo would be expecting his visit. The Peruvian would see no reason to fear one man against whatever army he had assembled.

On the other side of the yard, Raimondo stood by a second-story window. He smiled tightly as he saw Bolan ushing toward his territory. He welcomed a rematch between his men and the American tough guy. The sight of he troublemaker's mangled body in the dust would retore his injured pride and reestablish his authority over the inruly and dangerous inmates.

The prison was a caldron that seethed with men anxious o gain a little power and a measure of safety by dominatng the weaker inmates. For more than five years, Raimondo had succeeded in being the number-one badman by liminating anyone who posed a challenge. If he showed veakness toward this single opponent and failed to detroy him shortly, the other inmates would begin to think hat he didn't have the grit to rule the prison. Rivals would gather around like buzzards circling a dying man.

That was how Raimondo had achieved control many ears ago. The boss at that time had underestimated Raimondo, while the new player put together a secret challenge. Within a month, the old guy was six feet deep in the prison cemetery.

Raimondo wasn't about to make the same mistake. Since hen he had fought off every upstart who thought he could become king of the castle. None of them lived long enough o do more than dream of taking his place.

Everybody loved a winner, even in the dunghill named Lurigancho. He had protected his position by sharing his drug profits generously with the prison guards and offiials, but their cooperation was a fickle commodity. They vould back anyone who could outwit him. The other prisners were the same. Right now they feared him, and that ear made his life safe. But if he fell, even his own paid men vould trample his bleeding corpse in their haste to switch ides.

It was dog eat dog all right, and Raimondo was the wolfhound, the champion killer who had trained himself to rip the life from whomever he set out to annihilate.

No matter that Blanski still lived. It would be a very temporary condition. This tough-guy American would be his next victim.

Blanski was out and on the hunt, but he was obviously a fool to come to Raimondo without a gang of his own. This time Blanski would be joining his predecessors in a moldy grave outside the prison wall.

The drug lord knew that this would be a great day in his life. And the last in the American's.

Bolan felt a little uneasy as he approached Raimondo's lair. It wasn't fear—he had faced death too many times for the prospect of dying to worry him. Partly it was because he hated to enter a situation where he didn't know the odds or the opposition or the ground. In this case he had no idea if he would be facing five men or fifty, or how they would be armed. He had done it before when he had to—that was one of the elements of living large, throwing yourself at something one hundred percent when you had decided that it was the only alternative. But he still didn't have to like it.

Partly it was the senselessness of the whole position he was in, stuck in a prison, dependent on a bunch of terrorists to spring him.

If his imprisonment weren't so infuriating, the irony would be almost comical.

Mostly there was an anger building inside him, a bit of which was directed at himself for being caught so easily. The large part was reserved for the Shining Path, who had caused his predicament and had somehow maneuvered him behind these prison walls.

The anger would be released soon, a tidal wave of blood that would wash over the Shining Path. But Bolan's rage would start lapping at the feet of Raimondo and his men first.

Seven men filed out of the doorway leading into the kingpin's block and ranged themselves across the entrance. Six of them held knives, while the seventh flexed a length of thick chain.

Bolan drew his own knife and broke into a run.

Events seemed to move in slow motion, as though his mind were racing faster than his senses could keep up with. First Bolan feinted to his right but broke left, heading for a small gap between the last two bruisers.

The Executioner's left arm brushed aside the wavering knife his smaller opponent held. His hand continued in a sweeping chop, the stiffened palm landing across the jugular. The Peruvian dropped like a sawed-through tree.

Bolan's right hand evaded a twisting stab by his second adversary, the warrior's double-edged knife plunging into and through the soft tissue below the ribs. The hardguy collapsed without a word, hands vainly trying to stem the blood spilling between his fingers onto the gravel.

The Executioner exploded into the remaining five, giving them no opportunity to regroup. He plunged his heavy boot forward, crashing it into one thug's chest like a stamping machine into sheet metal. The victim's ribs burst inward, punching through heart and lungs. The body plunged backward, dead on his feet, throwing the toughs behind into confusion.

Bolan took advantage of the tangle of bodies to step forward, his red-spattered knife flashing, once, twice.

Two bodies dropped to the ground, throats slashed ear to ear.

Now it was two to one, but only momentarily. One of the remaining hitters took to his heels, hoping to put as much distance as possible between himself and the American demon, oblivious to the jeers of the other inmates.

The last guy was nearly as big as Bolan, and swung a long, heavy piece of chain above his head. The warrior ducked as the flying metal whistled toward his face, then leaped into the air as the return stroke came back knee high.

Bolan stepped in fast, spearing the knife at the chainman's eyes. The big Peruvian reacted too quickly for an easy kill, retreating beyond the blade with surprising speed. The warrior lunged forward like a fencer.

This time the savage was ready. He held his ground and replied with a quick flip of the chain. Bolan pulled back instantly, but not rapidly enough to prevent the chain from catching the knife and sending it flying end over end into the watching crowd.

The Peruvian laughed, exposing cracked, stained teeth. He advanced slowly toward the Executioner, the chain singing through the air in glittering figure eights.

Bolan waited calmly, as his adversary approached. Then, when the chain was just beyond striking distance, he launched himself forward, diving at the man's knees. As Bolan's shoulder connected, the flying chain touched the edge of his shirt.

The two men rolled, Bolan in a practiced curl, the hardman landing heavily on his back. As the other guy lay momentarily stunned, the Executioner spun, grabbed the chain and looped it around the Peruvian's thick, muscular neck. Settling back on the ground, he placed a foot on each of the thug's shoulders and tugged. The hood's heels drummed on the ground as his hands clawed at the chain biting into his flesh. With a grunt, the Executioner heaved again, muscles bulging on his forearms. A vertebra popped with an audible crack, and the Peruvian lay still.

Bolan grabbed two knives from the scattered bodies, placing one in his belt. He edged through the door, expecting more trouble. A roar crescendoed outside as the other inmates fought for the privilege of stripping Raimondo's dead guards of anything of value.

The warrior paused a moment as his eyes adjusted to the gloom of the interior hallway. A long hall stretched before him, similar to his own area. Farther along, several curious but wary heads peeked from their cells. To the left, a stairway stretched to a landing and doubled back. The stairs were grooved beside each banister, silent testimony to the thousands of prisoners who had trudged their lives away inside the prison walls.

Taking time was to the big guy's advantage at this point. Whoever was up there knew that Bolan had carved his way through the main line of defense. He started up the steps, knowing that Raimondo was lurking somewhere above, gathering his remaining forces for a last-ditch stand.

He paused at the landing. A window at the top of the stairs poured sunshine almost directly into his eyes, making it impossible to see if anyone waited in ambush.

He crept forward more warily, conscious of his footing, and the sound of his breathing. His combat sense warned of danger ahead.

A step moved under his foot with a small sound that resounded like thunder in his ears.

A hitter popped from each side of the stairs and let fly, sending a razor-edged missile winging toward the Executioner before retreating for cover.

Their caution would cost them.

Catlike, Bolan ducked to stair level and the knives bounced harmlessly against the rough rock walls.

In the same instant, the warrior rushed forward, legs powering him up the stairs, eyes focused on the top.

A killer stepped right in front of him, arm raised to throw. Fright and surprise etched themselves briefly on the guy's face. He had obviously been expecting that Bolan would retreat and look for another way in.

No way.

Bolan punched his body forward, his head connecting with the hardman's chest as he plunged his knife deep into soft stomach tissue.

The Peruvian staggered back with a shriek, hands clutched to his streaming belly. The backs of his legs connected with the windowsill and he disappeared backward through the opening with a piercing scream.

The second criminal made his move, clumsily trying to take Bolan in the side. The warrior danced out of the way easily and launched a power-packed kick that got the knifeman in the side.

The thug took a dive down the stairs, rolling over the smooth steps until he came to rest in an untidy heap.

Bolan didn't bother to check if the guy was dead. His mind was focused on reaching his prey.

Raimondo saved him the trouble of searching by casually stepping from his quarters, a thin cigar clenched between his teeth.

A snub-nosed .38 stared at Bolan.

The warrior halted, gauging the distance and considering his options. If he tried a rush, Raimondo would riddle him before he could make it five feet from where he stood. If he stayed where he was, he was a dead man. Forward backward or stand where he was, Raimondo had him dead to rights.

Like hell he did.

"Congratulations, Blanski. I expected you would be dead long before this. But never mind. Now I shall have the pleasure myself."

"A gun, Raimondo? Hardly fair. Wouldn't you like to try this man to man? If you aren't too scared of me, that is."

The drug merchant laughed mirthlessly, although the gun never wavered from Bolan's chest. "Do not think that you can trick me into something as foolish as that. I will not fall prey to your amateur psychology. This is not your American West, and I am certainly not some John Wayne. I do not care how I win, as long as I win. This gun is a favor that I have had to pay the prison officials very dearly for. Now it will repay my investment. I have buried many other strong fools before you, and I shall crush many more.

"Now, go to hell, Blanski."

Bolan watched Raimondo's eyes for the faint tensing he knew would precede the tightening of the trigger finger.

At that instant the Executioner dived forward.

A red-hot pencil traced a line along Bolan's back, as the bullet carved a groove through the hard flesh topping his ribs, but luckily missing bones and vital muscles.

Bolan hit the stone floor hard, rolling onto his shoulder. As he completed the roll, he flung the knife at Raimondo. Bolan mentally crossed his fingers, for if Raimondo were sharp, this might be his only chance.

The warrior finished his roll in a half crouch, tensed to dodge another shot. There was none.

Raimondo sprawled in the corridor, one eye staring at the ceiling. Bolan's knife lay buried to the hilt in his other ruined eye.

When Bolan emerged into the sunlight, he was engulfed by prisoners cautiously but hastily edging their way past him into the prison block. Each was in a frenzy to raid Raimondo's area, to loot what they could before the guards came and took what remained.

As he traced his way back across the yard, Bolan became aware of the new wound. He could feel his shirt sticking to his flesh, captured there by the congealing blood. Everything else hurt, too, and now that the adrenaline rush had worn off, Bolan thought that he could count every bruise on his body with his clothes still on.

Things were rotten, but at least they were starting to improve. Raimondo was out of the way, a minor annoyance settled, another savage who could never prey on anyone else.

One down, and how many million to go?

Bolan wrenched his mind away from the futile speculation. Sure, there would be someone else jockeying for the fallen drug lord's throne, but one down was better than nothing. One step at a time.

One less obstacle to keep him from his primary objective, his date with the Shining Path.

Stone was waiting, still reading, when Bolan returned to the cell block.

"You need a keeper, Blanski," the older man observed as he gingerly pulled the shirt from the clotted wound. "Not very pretty, but not deep, either. Another scar to add to your numerous collection. Lurigancho hasn't been very hospitable to you so far, has it?"

"I'll live," Bolan replied between tightly clenched teeth, as Stone poured what seem like liquid fire along his back.

"I have no doubt about that. You're a survivor type and Raimondo wasn't. He was a weak man, as most bullies are, who ruled through fear."

"What's a survivor type?"

"That's easy. Survivors survive."

Bolan laughed in spite of himself, regretting it immediately as his aching body protested.

A few minutes later, they had a visitor. Libertad stood in the doorway, looking grim. Four of his men filled the corridor behind him.

"I did as you suggested, Blanski," Libertad spit. "We got the guns exactly as you said we would. But they are useless! The breechblocks are missing, so they might as well be scrap metal. Is this how you will deal with us? I want an explanation before I order my men to kill you, slowly."

Bolan acted unimpressed by the other man's anger. "Of course the breechblocks are missing. I wanted to demonstrate that I could deliver on the weapons, not to make you a gift with no guarantees from your people. Once we're out of here, you'll get your breechblocks, your rockets and your ammo. But you won't get a damn thing more until I can take you to it personally."

Bolan realized that he was taking a calculated risk. If the Path refused the bargain, then he didn't have any more chips to play with. He certainly wasn't about to deliver working weapons to the very people he had come here to destroy. And if he had to get out of here on his own...well, he might be spending more time here than he'd planned.

"Why shouldn't I just make you tell me where the weapons cache is," Libertad sneered at Bolan.

Bolan knew that he had won. The terrorist leader was acting a part now, as much for his own men as for Bolan. The moment of danger had passed. "In the first place, you need me, or someone like me, and we both know it. I've got what you want, and I'm prepared to deliver as soon as we get out of here and to keep on supplying your little war until you run out of targets.

"And in the second place, you couldn't make me talk if I didn't want to, and you know that, too." Bolan held Libertad's eyes until the terrorist turned back to his men, gesturing them away with a wave of his hand.

He paused in the doorway as he was leaving, and said, almost as an afterthought, ''Be ready tomorrow. At sundown.''

Bolan settled carefully facedown in his cot. He'd be ready for the Shining Path, all right.

But would they be ready for him?

14

Antonia de Vincenzo paused outside the door leading into the Revolutionary Council chamber, rehearsing the answers to questions she was most likely to be asked.

She had left Lima two days ago for the mountain hideout near Ayacucho, high in the Andes. Her great beauty and apparent membership within the Peruvian upper strata had made her journey an easy one.

How strange that the very qualities the wealthy establishment admired in her were the ones that alienated her from her true people, the Indians.

Her arrival unannounced at the Shining Path's secret headquarters was bound to raise the suspicions of some of the party commissars. With a last deep breath she pushed into the meeting room.

The council members were ranged on hard-backed chairs around a simple trestle table. The aged and worn men looked more like farm workers discussing a harvest than the leaders of a secret terrorist movement.

"Tell us why you have returned, Antonia." How typical of the chairman. He didn't bother to waste time on pleasantries, and yet concealed a merciless ruthlessness behind a mild, almost fatherly manner.

Antonia was not fooled, having known the chairman since she was a child. Her father had been an academic along with Gonzalo when their glorious leader had only been a humble university professor, and had been one of the first to join the new movement. Her father was long dead, killed in an early skirmish, but the chairman had prospered.

"My employer was murdered by an American over some business matter. With the police conducting an investigation, it hardly seemed prudent to remain in Lima." She couldn't very well tell the council that she had been in secret communication with the notorious General Palma, the self-styled "Scourge of the Shining Path." Or that she had fled for her life, fearing that his smooth compliments were meant to lull her while he arranged for her death. To admit knowing him would be to invite the council to flay her alive for information, a fate she preferred not to think about.

The council believed that their weapons were funneled through Carrillo because of an arrangement she had made after she discovered the extent of his contacts. She would let them remain ignorant of the true situation, now and forever.

"We hear, Antonia, that you and several of our comrades have been very busy. Many of the most spectacular bombings and shootings have been conducted by your small band, without our authority. Is that so?"

Antonia nodded, startled and suddenly frightened at the abrupt change of topic, searching her mind for clues as to who might have informed the council about her clandestine activities.

"It must stop!" The chairman suddenly flared into one of his violent rages. Antonia knew that they often terminated in the execution of the object of his volcanic wrath.

"Do you have any idea how badly our people in this area have suffered? The government has stepped up its repression tenfold. Hundreds have been murdered at random in reprisal. The result has been that our forces find it more difficult to secure the cooperation of the peasants and more difficult to obtain the supplies we require. All as a consequence of your unparalleled stupidity. I order you to cease at once!''

Antonia's own anger lashed out at the chairman, stung beyond fear for her own safety. ''What do you mean stop? Violence and death are the road to freedom for our nation, the path to a new and wondrous utopian state. A river of blood will wash away the money grubbers and dictators and bring power to the people. The ever-increasing savagery of the government is the whole point of our actions! The more we kill, the more they kill in return. Every peasant they martyr is another nail in the coffin that the capitalists build for themselves. The wheel of violence spirals upward, coating the country with a carpet of dead until, finally, the masses will bear it no longer and tear away the chains of their oppressors. So Gonzalo teaches, and so I believe!''

''This will be a long war, not won in a single violent campaign. It is up to the council to determine the strategy, and every loyal member is required to obey.'' The chairman stressed the word *loyal* faintly, but it was more than sufficient to convey the required message. Disloyalty was punishable by death. ''This is not a matter that is open to debate. The council has commanded you to cease. You may go.''

The lovely redhead stormed to the door, her cheeks blazing. The voice of the chairman arrested her, his tone cool once more. ''It is only because Gonzalo has a certain affection for you that the council allows you to live. Do not give us cause to regret our decision.''

Antonia slammed the door against the wall as she left.

"YOU CAN COME if you want to, Stone."

Bolan and Stone sat by a window overlooking the prison yard. Neither had spoken for a long while, each occupied with his thoughts, images of happier times far away from the ugliness of prison life. Bolan had revealed his escape plan to the ex-professor, feeling a measure of gratitude for the care the older man had given.

"I've thought of nothing else but escaping from here for years now," Stone said thoughtfully. "And yet, now that I have the chance, I wonder if I can do it. I'm not as strong or as brave as you are. And, I admit, I'm more frightened of the Shining Path than I am of Lurigancho prison.

"But I'll do it. Thank you for the chance. And if I die, it will be for a purpose, not just because I'm tired of living anymore."

A faint smile disturbed the stillness of Bolan's face. Stone was learning what living large meant. It wasn't dying or not dying that mattered, but whether you really lived at all that counted. And living meant a lot more to Bolan than just breathing foul prison air.

BOLAN AND STONE ENTERED the Path compound between two silent guards shortly before sundown the next day. There was no sign of any unusual activity among the inmates, who mostly sat stonily in corners or worked away at menial tasks. Libertad apparently had not yet informed his fellow prisoners of the impending breakout.

Libertad approached from inside the terrorist quarters, and did not appear happy to see Stone. "Listen, Blanski, I will not endanger my men to protect Stone. He is of no value to us. Is that clear?"

"You're all heart, buddy. But don't worry. I'll take care of both of us."

Libertad grunted in reply and stalked off to brief his lieutenants.

"What happens now?" Stone asked nervously.

"Now we wait," Bolan replied.

It was clear that the Path would have to breach the wall somehow. Unless the prisoners had explosives, which seemed unlikely, there would have to be plenty of outside help. There were three guard towers along the southern wall, which formed one side of the small exercise yard in the Path compound. Two of them directly overlooked the prison yard used by the Shining Path, while the third was farther down the wall and dominated the main yard. Each of them contained several heavily armed guards and a searchlight, ready to pick off anyone who made a move to go over the wall.

The terrorists began to move inside the main quarters individually, called in by their commanders for instructions. When they emerged, they resumed their former activities, trying to look nonchalant. The only change was that no one was venturing near the south wall.

Libertad beckoned to the Americans from a doorway. When they entered, he instructed them to stay close to him and ignore everything else that happened. He glanced repeatedly at his watch as they waited in silence.

"What will happen? What can we expect?" Stone's anxiety was getting the better of him.

The terrorist suppressed an urge to tell the man to shut up. It didn't matter now, and besides, Stone would be less likely to get anyone else killed if he could act on his own. The big American, Blanski, had already shown that he could look after himself very well.

"Last night our people planted dynamite along the wall. It will destroy the towers and blow a hole for our escape.

There will be a party waiting to take us to safety. That is all you need to know.''

"How much dynamite, and how soon?" Bolan asked.

"The dynamite?" Libertad shrugged expressively. "We will see. Perhaps too much, or maybe not enough. We will know in—" he paused briefly as he checked his black plastic watch "—less than two minutes."

Several more terrorists drifted inside, seeking shelter, leaving a few to take their chances in the yard in order to lend an air of normalcy to the area.

Two minutes passed, then three. At the end of ten minutes of watching the shadows deepen slowly in the yard, the Americans were becoming impatient.

"I thought you said—" Stone began.

And then the ground shook, followed by the rushing sound of crumbling masonry as a part of the wall disintegrated.

The terrorists and Americans rushed outside, just as several prison sirens began to wail.

Bolan breathed in a double lungful of concrete dust as he sprinted for the shattered wall after Libertad. Stone was behind, followed by more of the Path. Several of the terrorists were ahead, running interference.

A gap four feet wide had been blown in the base of the wall. There was no sign of the tower that had stood to the far left, while the tower in the middle of the wall had fallen into the Path's compound. To the right, the third guard post leaned drunkenly, but had not toppled.

The Path had taken casualties already. One torso lay in the middle of the yard, the head sheared away by flying masonry as completely as though struck by a cannonball. A second body was partly visible, only a pair of legs sticking from under the guard tower.

Bolan took a detour toward the ruined guard post that lay in the yard. Where there were watchmen there might still be usable weapons. It was worth a look.

There were two dead prison guards among the wreckage. One blood-covered body had been slashed a thousand times when he had fallen into the lens of the searchlight. The second looked as though it had been dropped from a third-story window, with splinters of broken bones sticking through the lacerated flesh. Bolan found the sharpshooter's rifle when he rolled the dead guard over, and he unbuckled a holster that contained a .357 Colt Python. He strapped it on quickly before drawing the weapon.

The entire search had taken only thirty seconds, but he was already late for the party.

Stone, Libertad and several of the terrorists waited on top of the rubble that formed a gentle slope by the breached wall. "Souvenir hunting, Blanski?" Libertad sneered as Bolan approached at a run.

Bolan ignored the remark and cast a quick glance at the terrain outside the wall. The ground was flat and featureless up to a ragged tree line more than three hundred yards away. To the left, less than a third of that distance from their position, was a low barracks. Riot-equipped guards poured from the building to join a line of at least a dozen men forming in front of the squat building.

Three bodies sprawled between the wall and the trees, while several more terrorists raced for the safety of the trees beyond. Night was falling rapidly, but not quickly enough to cloak their escape. As Bolan watched, a rifle chattered briefly from the teetering tower, stitching a line of bullets in the dust before climbing the back of the man who brought up the rear.

"If those guards set up, we're dead. Let's move." Bolan followed his own advice and scrambled over the broken concrete, taking a short drop to ground level and rolling.

He had attracted the attention of the remaining tower guard, and rounds slammed into the dirt beside him. The warrior was up and running, zigzagging toward the tree line while the gunner tried to line him in his sight. He hit the ground once more, rolling into a slight depression that he had spotted. The Executioner sighted his captured rifle and squeezed the trigger. The first round gouged chips from the tower wall; the second penetrated an inch below the guard's hairline, flinging the top of his skull over the side of the tower as the body sunk out of sight.

Bolan gave the thumbs-up sign to the others, who were now crouched by the base of the wall. They made their break, quickly stringing into a line with Stone—the oldest and least fit—puffing away at the rear.

The prison guards weren't about to let them escape without opposition, now that they had had time to gather their forces.

A sustained chattering began as the security force advanced in a strung-out skirmish line, firing their submachine guns in rapid bursts.

The first three terrorists through the wall were the first victims, falling like rag dolls in bloody heaps, little dots of white oozing red on the dusty plain.

The others went to ground immediately, recognizing that there was little chance of survival for anyone exposed to the merciless wall of flying lead pumped out by the massed guns of the advancing guards.

Their position was pretty grim. If they remained where they were, the line of advancing gunmen would overrun the escaping prisoners and they'd be slaughtered where they lay. Anyone who tried to flee would be chopped to bloody ribbons before they had gone ten feet.

Bolan knew that there was no chance of surrender, even if he was to consider that option for more than a flickering moment. The troops held a special hatred for the Path. The last time there had been an uprising at Lurigancho by the Shining Path the government had sent in the Republican Army. Every one of the terrorist inmates at Lurigancho had been killed. The army and local prison staff even killed two hundred more of the terrorists in other Lima jails, most of whom were already unarmed.

No quarter would be given in this war—on either side. For the moment, Bolan was stuck with the Path as his temporary allies until he could use their trust to blow them away.

He had no hesitation about dealing with the prison guards. In the short time he had been at the compound, he had observed firsthand that they were as corrupt and vicious as any of the prisoners. Rumor had spoken of murder and torture as common weapons in the guards' arsenal of repressive tactics, and Bolan had no doubt it was true.

The Executioner threw down his now-empty rifle and tracked onto an advancing gunner with the Colt. Accurate as the Python was, he had to be careful to make every shot count. His ammo supply was severely limited, and he hoped he could make the guards back off and give the escaping prisoners room to run before they were overwhelmed. One determined rush by the heavily armed troops would finish the small party, which now numbered less than ten.

Bolan focused chest high, the silhouette dim in the fading light. He squeezed once and shifted targets even as the big pistol bucked in his hand. The first victim had barely toppled to the ground before the Executioner picked his second mark, sending another heavy slug sprinting the short distance to smash ribs and tumble through soft organs.

The warrior cored one more gunner before the troops realized what was happening. Several turned in his direction, peppering the ground with a torrent of flying metal.

Bolan tried to ignore the manglers slamming all around him as he concentrated on reloading the swing-out cylinder of the Python. He could only keep his head down temporarily and count on the shallow pit he lay in to absorb the wave of death probing for him.

The guards were still trying to brazen it out, obviously poorly trained, content to hold their position and riddle the ground around Bolan's hiding place with random shots. They seemed to be ignoring the remaining prisoners for the moment.

Bullets kicked up spurts of dust in front of and beside the Executioner, clouding his vision as he sought his targets. Pretty warm work, Bolan thought, as beads of sweat crept down his forehead. Four slow shots ventilated four more guards before one of them turned to make a break for safety.

Two of the troops turned to watch him go.

An officer came from behind the wavering line of guards and stopped the fleeing man by swinging the barrel of his pistol into the running man's face. The wounded man crashed to all fours, hands clutched over his bleeding mouth, spitting remnants of his front teeth. The officer brandished his pistol at the remaining men, shouting commands.

Suddenly the gunner at the far end of the line vanished in a cloud of flame and smoke, his body catapulted into the air on the tips of a dynamite explosion.

A second guard disappeared, and small bits of burned flesh fell to the ground in a horrific rain.

Path reinforcements had arrived, flinging sticks of dynamite among the gunmen once they had crept unseen into range. Bolan's firing had distracted the security squad enough that the new arrivals had closed the distance undetected.

The shaky guardsmen gave up the fight and fled in panic toward their base, pursued by a creeping line of explosions as the Shining Path hurried them along their way.

Bolan and the rest made the best of the lull, sprinting the last few hundred yards at a pace that made their lungs ache. The Path rear guard followed, dynamite in hand.

The reduced band gathered among the trees. Many of the surviving terrorists had already left, beginning the long journey to rejoin their cells in various parts of the strife-torn country.

Two battered vans waited, large enough to hold about ten people each. The drivers didn't look any friendlier than the rest of the Shining Path terrorists.

Libertad motioned Bolan and Stone into the back of a dirty blue van. Half a dozen men climbed in with them, and they all sat silently on rough sacks as the truck bounced crazily along the poorly paved roads that led away from the prison. The first task was to clear the area before the police and army sealed the region to start an intensive search for the escapees.

Bolan had time to reconsider his strategy as the vehicle jumped over the potholed back road. He was sorely tempted to abort the mission, to give these guys the slip and head home. This wasn't his war. He had already accomplished the main part of his mission by icing McIntyre. Why not leave the rest of the action to the people most concerned? The Peruvian government had created most of this mess by the repression and poverty of its citizens. Let it solve the problem on its own.

But the idea just wouldn't go down.

Bolan was constitutionally unable to walk away and wash his hands once he had made a decision to get involved. The Shining Path had become his problem, too. And the Executioner had determined that he was going to be part of the solution.

He hadn't been imprisoned and beaten only to turn tail and run for cover. The Shining Path and he were locked together in a death grip, and Bolan would keep squeezing until something gave.

He knew that the bad feeling existed on both sides. In spite of anything the terrorists might say to ease his distrust, he knew they would kill him without hesitation when the time was right.

The warrior had to keep on top of the situation, stay one step ahead of his adversaries if he was going to make it out of Peru alive. The first objective was to get them to guide him to their base without giving up control of the arms shipment.

The weapons were his ace, and might be the only thing that would keep him breathing long enough to wreak havoc with the Shining Path operations. Like any kind of insurance, it was most valuable if it didn't have to be used. So Bolan had to use the guns as the bait to lead the Path along the course that he had set for them—until he could push them over the edge.

Bolan had a plan. He only had to make Libertad and his henchmen buy it.

After what seemed like an endless ride, the van shifted down and pulled slowly onto a secondary road, shaking brutally from side to side as the wheels climbed in and out of ruts in the dirt track. When the small truck drew to a halt the terrorist nearest the door swung it open, and everyone gratefully took the opportunity to stretch cramped and bruised limbs.

They were parked in front of a single-story house not much larger than a peasant's hut. The smoke curling from a crude chimney told him that the house was occupied. Bolan presumed that they had arrived at a rural safehouse.

Libertad was already waiting.

"Now it is time to talk again about our arrangement, Blanski. I think that you must tell us where the guns are hidden."

"You have a short memory, Libertad." Bolan was going to take a hard line. The only form of reasoning these people understood was simple power. Any concession would be assumed to be from weakness and would be followed by pressure for more and more compromises.

Bolan would make them play by his rules.

"You know that we agreed that I would lead you to the weapons when you sprung me. Only then do you get the goods, when I get my money, that is. Of course I'll give you a couple of freebies, as I promised. See what a sweet guy I am? You're lucky that I don't withdraw my offer as a reward for saving your miserable lives back at the prison."

This angered the terrorist, who snapped back, "You did us no favors back there! You were only protecting your own worthless life. Our lives belong to Gonzalo. We were of no value to him in prison and if we had died, it would have made no difference. Dead, at least we would have been martyrs, feeding the legend of the truth and justice of our righteous cause without harming our fighting strength. Our blood would come to haunt the guilty and serve to bring forth strong new fighters. So stick to your word!"

Bolan gained some valuable information from the tirade. This guy had a thin skin where his cause was concerned. A weakness to be filed away for later use. "Keep

your cool, amigo. I just want to know that you'll play fair
with me.''

Libertad was calm again, icily so. ''Gringo, why don'
you just tell us where the guns are and go about your busi
ness? Peru is not a safe place for you. We will arrange fo
payment, and then you will leave. You will hear from u
about the next order.''

''Man, you must take me for some kind of fool!'' Bola
laughed loudly for emphasis, maintaining his character a
a money-grubbing arms merchant. ''Do you really thin
that I'll walk and leave you the goods? I'll never see a penny
that way. If you're so trusting, give me my money, and
when I'm safely out of this rat hole I'll wire you the loca
tion of the arms. How about that for a deal?''

Libertad waved, and two of the terrorists grabbed Ston
by his arms and powered him over beside their leader. Lib
ertad drew a long knife and placed the point under the olde
man's chin. Stone looked as if he was about to faint, an
only the strong hands holding each arm prevented him from
crumpling to the ground.

''Unless you tell me now where the guns are, I will slit hi
throat and his blood will be at your feet.''

Bolan frowned. The terrorist had instinctively hit on on
of his few weaknesses, apparently knowing that Bola
would not let any harm come to the ex-professor if he coul
somehow prevent it. Or maybe Libertad was only bluff
ing.

''Go ahead. It still won't make me talk. But if you do
you'll be losing a valuable commodity—someone wh
could patch you or your men up if we get into a jam. Be
sides, he was of some help to me in prison, so I'll trade yo
a case of M-16s for his life, insignificant as it is. So there'
the deal. A case of guns if he lives, but absolutely nothin
gained if he dies.''

Libertad appeared to consider the offer. "Three cases," he responded.

"Two."

"All right, Blanski, two it is." He nodded to his men, who shoved Stone forward to sprawl at his feet. Without another word the terrorists marched toward the cabin.

"Are you okay, Stone?"

Stone spoke in a low voice, conscious of the half dozen men observing them. The terrorists weren't making any moves, but the two Americans were under a watchful guard. "I'll live. For a short while, that is. We have to make a break soon. Once you deliver the guns we'll be dead. The Path trusts no one, and you already know too much about them. They'll never let you live. Instead they'll find someone else to supply the arms, someone they can keep at arm's length. We have to get out of here!"

Bolan smiled grimly. "You're not telling me anything I don't already know. But we'll go when I'm ready. I have a surprise or two remaining."

A surprise, sure.

A nasty one.

15

The ancient truck chugged laboriously up the steep moun
tain slope, using every ounce of power remaining in it
often-repaired engine.

Bolan sat listlessly, watching the countryside pas
through the slats that ringed the bed. He rolled back an
forth in a double line with the other fifteen men, concen
trating on not being sick.

He was suffering the effects of *soroche*—altitude sick
ness—as the wheezing vehicle climbed the mountain pas
that would eventually lead them to the broad valley tha
held Ayacucho, their destination.

Illness was attacking on all fronts, including dizziness,
splitting headache, a fever and stomach-curdling nausea.

The sickness had been alleviated somewhat by a sooth
ing brew that Stone had made for him at the last stop. Th
tea had relieved his symptoms, yet had left him lethargic–
which was something of a blessing.

It would be quite easy to get excited over the travelin
conditions. The road was narrow and badly maintained. I
many spots it was barely as wide as the truck. The scener
was spectacular, a breathtaking series of chiseled peaks an
valleys of long, waving grass, viewed from a road that clun
to the side of the cliff like a ribbon spiraling up around
tree trunk. Sometimes a white-flecked mountain stream c
waterfall could be seen hundreds of feet below.

The Peruvians were very possessive of their trucks and cars, and habitually gave them fancy names. This one was no exception, and the driver had named it "The Friend of Death." He—and everyone else on the road—drove in a manner that lived up to the name. It was not uncommon for the vehicle to rush head-on at another car or truck, until one or the other swung to the outside and the two vehicles passed together, one hugging the edge of the precipice.

Small white crosses marked the route at points where some drivers hadn't been as careful—or lucky.

"This isn't as bad as it gets, Blanski," Stone had told him in an unsuccessful attempt to cheer him. "At some points on the other side of Ayacucho, the road is so narrow that the traffic passes in different directions depending on the day of the week. They use the same trails that were blazed in Inca times, narrow as they are."

Almost every roadside wall or smooth rock surface was defaced by some sort of political slogan, many of them by the local Communist party calling for an armed struggle. Most were by the Path, demanding death to the imperialists and their lackeys. Even among the deserted highlands between the scattered villages, grim reminders of the constant political battles remained, fading gradually in the harsh sunlight.

Libertad had been surprised when Bolan informed him that the arms had been moved into the mountainous Andean district.

"What are you complaining about?" Bolan had responded when Libertad queried him. "It's a lot more convenient for you there than it would be in Lima. I know the core in your little war. Besides, I didn't want to hang around in Lima any longer than I had to. Some people I know there wouldn't have been too happy to see me, if you know what I mean."

"I can certainly understand that, Blanski." The unexpected news that the weapons weren't in Lima had sparked the terrorist's suspicions once more. "Particularly since there's a rumor floating around the underground that you might have helped yourself to the arms."

Bolan couldn't help being startled by this news.

"Don't look so surprised—we have very accurate sources of information."

Bolan thought fast. He wasn't happy that the Peruvians had learned he was not exactly a well-established arms dealer. He also wondered at their source, since that information shouldn't have been available to anyone who wasn't familiar with the twisted relationship between McIntyre and Carrillo. And both of them were dead. So who was putting the pieces together, and how? It pointed once again to some outside source pulling the strings—a source with connections to the Shining Path.

"It doesn't matter how I got them. If I'm a thief, well, I'm your thief. I don't care about your politics, so don't you worry about my source of supply. All you have to know is that I can deliver what I promise and at a very competitive price."

"We'll see what you're capable of when we get to Ayacucho, won't we, Blanski?"

You don't know how right you are, pal, Bolan thought.

"Right on, hombre. But I've got one more piece of news for you. Before I give you so much as a rifle bullet, I want to see your boss."

"That is out of the question. No one sees Gonzalo. You will have to deliver the arms as we agreed."

"No way, buddy. I don't need to talk to the guy, but sure want to talk to someone more important than you. didn't come all this way to get turned off like a brush salesman. No way. I'll talk to your council, or somebod in charge, but I'm going to go away with another sale, a bigger and better one. You guys have got a lot of potential demand for my services, and I aim to make you good customers of mine." Bolan was playing his part to the hilt, since an aggressive pursuit of a dirty arms deal would provide a perfect cover to get a little closer to the heartland of the terrorist organization.

Libertad appeared to consider the proposition for a few moments and then relented. "It is highly unusual, but under the circumstances, I think an exception can be made. When we reach Ayacucho, I will make your request known to my superiors. Then we shall see."

When Bolan had departed to prepare for the long ride through the Andes, one of the terrorists accosted Libertad. "Are you mad? You would let an outsider into our secret enclave? What if he is a government agent or a CIA spy? What then?"

"It does not matter what he is, Pablo. Honest man, fool or traitor, he must die anyway. So let us do what we need to do to get the arms. Then we shall kill him. Very unpleasantly."

AYACUCHO STOOD 8,500 feet above Lima's dry coastline. Stone explained to Bolan some of the contrasts between the rich urban metropolis and the interior, where many impoverished peasants still worked on large, almost feudal estates that had survived since the time of the Spanish conquest.

The area was predominantly Indian, and the majority of the local population spoke nothing but the native Quechua. The majority lived as their forefathers had done. Their agricultural methods were primitive, relying on the ancient Inca foot plow. Nominally Catholic, the natives still mixed Inca practices with their ceremonies. Their staple diet was native potatoes and corn, and they drank *chicha*, a popular homemade beer considered especially delicious because women chew the corn before it is fermented.

The terrorists were poised now on the lip of the last pass before they would enter the regional capital. The city was spread before them, the most notable feature being the spires of nearly thirty churches.

Their entry into the city would be the most difficult part of the journey thus far. Ayacucho was the center of the main movement of the Shining Path, and consequently the military was present in force. It was likely that the truck would be checked at a roadblock before they would be allowed to proceed, as it was known that the escaped terrorists would eventually make for their mountain stronghold.

Bolan and Stone were ordered into a small box welded just below the high bed of the truck and each was given a pair of cracked goggles to shield his eyes. Barely able to squeeze in, the two Americans almost choked from the dust kicked up from the roadway as they rumbled down the mountainside.

The Indians would be safe enough. There was nothing to link them to the prison breakout, and police methods were too unsophisticated for there to be much chance that they would be identified. However, the Americans would be conspicuous in an area visited by only a few white tourists and might be shot on sight if they were captured.

Given the alternative, Bolan and Stone weren't about to complain too loudly about a little dust.

They were stopped for inspection at the foot of the slope just before the main highway into the city divided. The warrior saw heavy combat boots below jungle camouflage clothing circling the truck. To Bolan's relief, the trooper didn't bother with a search, and only asked the driver a few outine questions in a bored and disinterested tone before waving them through.

"That was pretty lax," Bolan shouted to Stone above the grinding of the engine.

"These soldiers are strictly amateurs, uneducated farm kids given a uniform and a gun. They are also highly unpredictable, so any checkpoint is a danger even for innocent travelers. The troops don't really care about finding the Path. If they are determined to kill someone, it makes no difference whether they are terrorists, or whether there is any evidence to link them to the Shining Path. The army has become a worse menace than the guerrillas they are trying to suppress. We're a long way from Lima here in the mountains, and the army treats the area like its private hunting preserve." Stone was bitter, having seen firsthand the destruction that the so-called protection forces had wrought among the native people he had come to like. In the years he had spent in prison, the situation had deteriorated considerably.

Violence by the left bred a more violent reaction by the right. Death squads from both sides roamed the hills, fighting for the hearts and minds of the ignorant villagers, and destroying everything in their path at the least suspicion of opposition or treachery.

The peasants were the losers no matter which way they turned. They either supported the Shining Path guerrillas in their demands for food and shelter, or they were killed. If they aided the guerrillas, then the army exacted a heavy price.

The escaped prisoners didn't linger in the city. The place was crawling with the drab uniforms of army and police units, many wandering the streets aimlessly in search of some excitement to relieve the boredom of garrison duty.

Many others stood alert in front of public buildings, submachine guns ready for instant action.

They paused briefly in a working class district for Libertad to call his superiors with Bolan's request for a meeting while Bolan and Stone stretched cramped limbs in the shelter of a Shining Path safehouse.

The warrior stewed as he waited for news. He knew that his cache was hidden somewhere within the city limits, the address committed to memory before he had left Los Angeles. At least he expected that it would be here now. His unplanned stop at Lurigancho had prevented him from contacting the shipping company with alternate instructions, so that his standing order should have resulted in the arms being shipped to this mountain town.

He had the bait. Now it was only a matter of building the trap.

Bolan was forming his game plan as he went along. Delivering the arms right here would have been a possibility, but with this many men around there was a good chance that he would be eliminated as soon as the terrorists had their hands on the weapons.

By getting into Shining Path territory, he could take advantage of any slip on their part to do some eliminating of his own. If nothing favorable transpired, he was no worse off than he was right now.

Bolan felt more at ease when Libertad informed him that a meeting had been agreed to. Things were finally falling into place.

Outside of Ayacucho, the hills began a remorseless climb once again. A short way beyond the town, Bolan and Stone took their seats in the truck, a welcome change from the dust-clogged hiding place.

Every dip to a shallow valley led to a steeper ascent on the other side. They were gaining hundreds of feet of altitude very hour. Each climb brought back the symptoms of *oroche* with increased severity. The Peruvian Andes soared up to more than twenty-two thousand feet, nearly two thousand feet higher than the loftiest peak in North America. And at the moment, Bolan was feeling every inch.

Stone assured him that he would feel better in about twenty-four hours—unless he was one of the unfortunate few that never adapted to the altitude. Bolan knew that this was not the case, having experienced high altitudes before. Still, the waiting time until he adapted was no more pleasant than it ever was.

After about five hours' travel, the engine started to emit clunking noise, which was completely different from the wheezing growls they had become accustomed to. Ten minutes later, the engine died completely. The truck coasted to a stop on a roadside shoulder above a small town that was huddled around a tiny church nine hundred feet below.

They got out and began to walk.

A half hour later, the group of men came to a dirt track that led to a collection of hovels hunched between a towering peak and the narrow road. Llamas roamed through the rough lanes of the village, cropping the rough *puna* grass. Outside one shanty, a boy played the haunting notes of the *guena*, a wooden flute whose origins could be traced to the days of the Inca empire.

The small mountain villages of the Andean altiplano presented the heartland of the Shining Path movement. Here the ancient Indian culture existed in an isolated community, remote, poor and primitive. Many of the Indians, inspired by the fantasies of the Shining Path, dreamed the irrational dream of a restored empire, of an ideal communism without want or exploitation.

Several of the decrepit huts still held washed-out remnants of the mark of the Path—the Communist red hammer and sickle with the slogan Shanghai Gang of Fouscrawled below it, harking back to the most radical days oRed China, when the Red Guards idolized the peasants andeclared the intellectuals their enemies.

But there were few friendly faces peering from the dooways of the scattered homes.

A movement that had been born of a will to freedom haturned into a vicious parody of the system that it proposeto overthrow. The road to freedom had become a twistepath to an early grave. Support for the Shining Path wanow achieved at the price of fear. Lack of cooperation wasavagely punished, and the Path replaced local leaders wittheir own supporters, defying the traditional Indian respect for their elders. Children were frequently kidnappefor indoctrination.

And yet to many the terrorists were preferable to thrandom violence of the army.

As the small band straggled into town, the attitude suspicion, pent-up oppression and fear was so strong thait was almost palpable to Bolan in the thin air of the smaAndean community. There was no way to predict whamight happen, or who might be friend or foe.

Trust or treachery; it was impossible to tell what the reaction would be from the closed and cautious expressionon the faces of the few natives who had shown themselve

The tense atmosphere didn't appear to bother Libertad

He took center stage behind a hand-operated water pumin the minuscule square of the village. He rang a solid irobell on a tripod repeatedly, the tocsin summoning the hiden villagers slowly. The terrorist leader called for attetion.

"My people, my brothers in arms and in our struggle for ustice and liberty, we have come to you in an hour of need cnowing that you will not fail us.

"As we aid and protect you at all times from the oppres-;ion of the capitalists and the imperialists, you shall now be ıble to assist your liberators in the great struggle against the 'panish conquerors.

"Remember, without power all is illusion. We must wage var without quarter against the money-loving city dwell-;rs. We are your sword and your shield, and together, :omrades, we will strike our enemies dead.

"So listen and hear our plea, and answer from your ıeart."

From the stolid looks of the watching natives, Bolan ;uessed they weren't too impressed with the oratory. Fancy vords and expressions of brotherhood sounded fine when he army was on the other side of the mountain. But every-•ne knew that the only reason why the soldiers didn't de-troy the Shining Path was that they couldn't find them. ıpart from the occasional hit-and-run attack, the Path voided the well-armed troops.

When the army returned on their next patrol, they would xact their revenge if the villagers gave any assistance to the uerrilla band. And the Shining Path would by then be long one.

A small man built like a fire hydrant spoke from the ·ont of the crowd. His clothes were a bit better than those f the rest of the villagers, who all wore rough homespun nd bright-hued cloth. Many of the men sported the *chullo*, knitted cap with earflaps. Often a felt hat perched on top f the *chullo*.

"Do not try to fool us with your banal and false prom-es. We know by now that your words are lies, that they are

traps for the unwary, as the crocodile lies in wait for th
man who steps thoughtlessly into a strange river.

"Leave us now and seek out some ignorant and back
ward village where they have never seen evil and do no
know you for who you are. You have the stench of deatl
about you, and you offend our noses. Begone!"

From the number of nods Bolan observed, he could tel
that the little man had his finger on the pulse of the com
munity. His words had hit home in a way that Libertad hac
completely missed.

The terrorist looked carefully at every face in the crowd
Most turned away, but the spokesman held the hardman'
gaze unflinchingly.

"You speak very bravely," Libertad remarked almos
conversationally. "Who are you?"

"I am Ferdinand Haya de la Torre, mayor of the villag
of Andahuaylas," he answered proudly and pugnaciously
If the mayor was intimidated by the unwashed and savage
looking group that had invaded his small town, he cer
tainly wasn't showing it.

Bolan could only admire the man's bravery without bein
in a position to render any assistance. The warrior had
bad feeling, looking at Libertad's closed and angry fac
that the small man was going to need all the help he coul
get.

"PCP?" Libertad asked, naming the Peruvian Con
munist Party. The Shining Path had marched far to the le
of the Communists, and the two groups had no love fo
each other. The mayor nodded assent.

"And a Spaniard?"

"Yes, I have that honor. And a true friend to the pe
ple, not a bloodsucker who will cast them to the dogs at th
first sign of trouble."

"Seize the traitor."

Two of Libertad's men responded, grabbing the small
man and hauling him in front of the crowd. None of the
villagers ventured forth to intervene in the face of the in-
timidation of the Path. De la Torre was temporarily struck
dumb, realizing that he had overplayed his hand badly.

Bolan knew that a tragedy was about to unfold, one that
he couldn't do anything to prevent.

The terrorist addressed the crowd. "Comrades, you have
been duped into becoming slaves of the unjust state. We
will now stage a popular trial to probe the errors of your
ways."

He turned to the captive mayor. "I suppose you were
elected?"

"Yes, by a free vote of these honest villagers," the mayor
responded.

"Guilty! He is guilty of parliamentary cretinism," Libertad shouted to the impassive gathering. "He believes that
a vote can determine the best interests of the people."

Then he addressed de la Torre again. "I suppose you are
an educated man?"

"I have finished high school in Ayacucho. I can read and
write. Can you say the same?"

"I do not need to justify anything. I am a warrior of the
republic of New Democracy, the only true representatives
of the people. What the great Gonzalo says is law, and I
must carry out his work of crushing counterrevolution
everywhere I find it." Libertad paused, examining the
community.

They had subsided into sullen acceptance, knowing that
their fate was to endure like the Andes, to suffer the shifting patterns of the undeclared war. "Don't think about tomorrow" had to be their watchword. "Just live through life
one day at a time." The Incas, the conquistadores, parlia-

ments, juntas, dictatorships had all come and gone with
out making much impression on their way of life.

The Shining Path was only one more natural disaster, lik
an epidemic among the sheep.

Libertad read acquiescence in the crowd. "This man
guilty once again, this time of being an intellectual plante
among you to lead you falsely from the road to the uto
pian Communist state.

"Where there is guilt, there must be punishment."

He moved slowly to the captive, drawing his knife. Th
late-afternoon sun caught the blade, sending shimmers o
orange fire crawling along the steel.

The mayor didn't protest, mesmerized by the flashir
weapon that would be his death.

The terrorist grabbed de la Torre roughly by the hai
pulling his head back. The mayor snapped out of his spe
and began to pray feverishly. Libertad silenced the pleas
heaven, drawing the sharp edge almost leisurely across th
man's throat.

The terrorists holding the body let go, allowing the corps
to collapse face first onto the blood-drenched square.

"Now you will aid us," Libertad told the gathered pea
ants in a commanding voice.

No one disagreed this time.

16

The Path left the little community the next morning after they had fed themselves from the locals' meager supplies. They traveled in a small convoy of four old cars commandeered from the villagers.

An hour's drive ahead was a small pass, one that alternated direction on a daily basis. Today they would be able to travel through it away from Ayacucho, which was the only reason the terrorists had remained overnight in the hostile town.

Bolan had been glad for the delay. Now he seemed to be over the worst of the *soroche*, although he still had a headache. However, he was careful not to let his well-being show. He didn't know what was coming and would rather save his renewed energy for a surprise.

Libertad paid Bolan no real attention, merely gesturing him to the third car in line, which was a battered Honda. The terrorist leader slid into the front passenger seat and stared stonily out the window, as did Bolan.

The Executioner could never hope to understand the terrorist mind. Their fanaticism was total, requiring a dedication that embraced their entire lives. They weren't in it for the money—they were after power pure and simple. If they ever achieved it, Bolan suspected that the bloody purges of Joseph Stalin would seem like a spring cleaning in comparison.

They killed easily and without conscience or regret; Libertad had demonstrated that yesterday, if Bolan had had any doubts. For the Shining Path, the world was a simple place. It divided evenly along the lines of good and evil, the good being their supporters. Evil embraced everyone else. In any situation there was only one course of action: do as their leader Gonzalo commanded through his writings, or die.

They were totally beyond rational thought. It was incredible to see how they had warped every perception around the distorted thoughts of some reclusive madman.

There was an ugly fascination in studying these men, much like watching cancer cells divide and multiply through the lens of a microscope.

The answer to their bizarre zealotry was equally clear to Bolan. He would crush the Shining Path and all they stood for at the first opportunity.

The convoy ran into trouble just as it left the ten-mile section of one-way road, no wider than one car, that crept along the edge of the deep mountain cleft. If the driver had sneezed and jogged the wheel, they would have dropped one mile into the swift mountain stream below.

The lead car eased around the first curve beyond the widening of the road and ran into a hornet's nest.

A line of troops was concealed behind a pair of tree trunks that had been toppled across the roadway. How the ambushers had known to expect the Path was a mystery. There might have been a radio hidden in the village, or possibly a peasant had trekked overland to the nearest government outpost. Any way it happened, the infantrymen spelled disaster. They opened fire with an array of automatic weapons, peppering the thin skin of the car with high-velocity slugs.

The driver slumped forward over the wheel, his brains sprayed over the three passengers behind. As he collapsed, he rode the wheel to the left, sending the car speeding over the cliff.

The four terrified survivors screamed every second of the long drop, before the plunging vehicle hit the ground below with the force of a dynamite explosion.

The second driver slammed on the brakes, screeching to a halt thirty yards from the roadblock. The gunman in the passenger seat, who was the only one armed with anything deadlier than a knife, provided covering fire from behind his door while the others made a break for the grassland and hills that edged the highway.

None of them made it to the edge of the grass before being chopped down by the flying parabellums.

Screened behind the door, the surviving terrorist screamed in anger, loosing off the last rounds in his captured SMG. A lucky shot caught one of the crouching troopers in the bridge of his nose, turning the face into an unrecognizable red mass.

Three steps from the car, as he made his break, the gunner paid his own price, dancing an awkward two-step under the impact of a dozen bullets.

Bolan and the others saw the carnage up ahead. The driver hesitated, slowing as though he were planning to stop. Bolan shouted instructions at him, telling him to veer to the right, up a low embankment and into the field beyond.

The driver looked at Libertad, who silently nodded.

There was a danger, of course—a good commander might have mined the shoulder or stationed more troops in the dead ground beyond the slight incline. But Bolan was betting that whoever was on the other side wasn't very smart. Certainly the execution and placement of the ambush didn't show a very high level of training in the Peruvian army.

The terrorist floored the gas pedal, and the light car shot up the embankment and came down hard on the other side. There was the sound of tortured metal, and the car lost power. Bolan guessed that they had popped the differential. The men piled out, clutching what guns they had.

The car behind them climbed the slope at an angle, and flipped onto its side as it rocketed over under full power. It slid twenty feet through the high grass before coming to rest, the right fender buried in the dirt. The two doors on the exposed side sprang open and three men climbed out, including Stone. The others weren't going anywhere but to a graveyard.

The terrorists began to run for the hills, pushing their way through the stringy, pale grass. There weren't any other places to hide.

Bolan ran up to Libertad. "I want a gun," he demanded. The terrorist leader had taken the Colt Python as soon as they had reached safety after the breakout. It was holstered around his waist now.

Libertad glared at him. "I don't think you can be trusted."

"You know I can use it. Or would you prefer the army to catch you?"

Libertad made a quick decision and stopped in his tracks. He unbuckled the holster and dangled it in front of Bolan. "So glad that you have recovered from the *soroche*. All right. Use it. Hold them off, and we'll meet you up ahead. Stone will be with us."

Bolan grabbed the belt. He had heard the mocking challenge in Libertad's voice, as well as the implied threat: run away and Stone dies. "Get the hell out of here. They're right behind."

Libertad ran off, leaving a trail as defined as though a herd of elephants had trampled through.

Bolan wasted no time. The warrior edged away from the trail and placed himself behind a scrawny tree thirty feet from the trail. From the shouts in the near distance, the Executioner knew he wouldn't have long to wait.

The Peruvian troops were advertising their presence by their poor discipline. The point man appeared, trotting slowly down the broad trail left by the fleeing terrorists. About twenty men were following single file, with an officer in the middle of the troops.

Bolan let the first man get twenty feet beyond the tree position before he began to fire as rapidly as he could. Given his limited amount of ammunition, he would have to hit hard and slip away before the soldiers could organize resistance. He was badly outnumbered and outgunned, and would be in grave danger in a protracted firefight.

The gun barked, and the point man toppled forward, a bullet lodged in the base of his skull. The second man, much too close to the leader, took a round in the upper spine and crashed onto the point's dirty boots.

The Executioner caught three more with hammer blows from the Python, the soldiers too stupid to take cover when the lead began to fly and men began to die. He sighted on the lieutenant, who was madly blowing his whistle and trying to rally his squad. At this point most of his men had wisely dived into the high grass and were scurrying back to the road.

Bolan stopped the annoying whistle sounds with a .357 stinger that caught the officer on the chin, crushing jaw and teeth before ripping into his larynx. The lieutenant breathed his last, a red foam soaking his drab uniform.

The remaining troops scattered. They pounded through the pampas to the safety of their vehicles, where they could form a defense perimeter and would be safe from attack by what seemed like a superior force.

Bolan paused to reload the Python, using the last of the bullets on the gun belt. Then he set to the grim task of stripping the dead Peruvians of anything useful.

Rifling dead bodies wasn't a task that Bolan enjoyed, but he always did what was necessary to survive. In this case, he wanted to form a small-arms cache for later use. He had no real plan on how to put the hit on the Path at present, and it would be wise to accumulate a stash of weapons in case he found himself in the vicinity again.

Two of the crumpled bodies held Walther 9 mm MP-K submachine guns. The ugly little brutes looked like machine pistols with a light stock added and fed on 32-round box magazines. The other three had held 5.56 mm SG-541 assault rifles. The transparent magazines on each showed full.

Bolan was surprised at the quality of the weapons. The Peruvians had had good tools, but they hadn't known how to use them. The dead soldiers had served as an example of a theory of Bolan's, that there were very few dangerous weapons, but there were dangerous men. And such a man, even completely unarmed, was still a force to be feared.

The warrior placed the guns in a hollow tree trunk that he discovered rotting away some fifty yards from the trail. It wasn't the best hiding spot, but it was the only one that presented itself under the circumstances. With luck, the guns and extra ammo would remain undisturbed until he was able to get back to them.

Bolan started up the trail, taking his time. He was conserving his energy in the high altitude, still not one hundred percent after his bout of *soroche*. He was certainly in no hurry to rejoin the terrorists.

After a half hour walk he was nearly at the base of a jagged cliff, a sheer rock face that rose two hundred feet before giving way to scrubby grass and stunted trees. The ground underfoot was rough and broken, with patches of rock poking through the thin topsoil.

There was no sign of Stone or the terrorists.

Bolan retraced his steps, looking for a fork in the trail that he might have missed. He spent twenty minutes searching, going back to the last visible remnants of the trail and then casting outward. It was as though the terrorists had sprouted wings and flown off. They had vanished without a trace.

He took a seat on a flat rock for a moment to consider his next move. Then he went back to the area where the trail ended and searched once more, carefully examining every inch of dirt and each blade of the stringy grass. He spotted a three-inch rusted iron T-bar barely above ground level. He reached down and heaved. Nothing happened. Bolan walked around to the T-bar and tried again.

A section of grass covering a trapdoor swung back. He found himself staring into the barrel of Libertad's Walther.

"Good morning, Blanski. I wondered if I would see you again." From his tone, it was hard to tell if Libertad was disappointed or pleased that Bolan had made it back.

Bolan grimaced as Libertad motioned for him to climb down the rickety ladder that led to an underground tunnel system. The Path had taken a page from the Vietcong combat manual, going subsoil like moles, like rats in a sewer.

Bolan wasn't fond of tunnels.

ANTONIA DE VINCENZO was slowly working herself into a frenzy, raw nerves rubbing on one another as every hour ticked slowly past.

It was an effort to keep the strain from registering on her face. But any sign of nervousness would be sure to invite questions.

Questions that she would not like to answer.

Carrillo's former secretary waited at the Path base camp for word on the progress of Libertad and his men. They were bringing Michael Blanski with them.

She felt trapped, like a weary fox pursued by a pack to her last hiding place. And it wasn't her fault.

In spite of her long association with the movement, she had always felt like an outsider, as though she were tolerated rather than respected. The distrust from the other terrorists arose from a number of sources: her Spanish heritage, her intellect and education, her gender. Even her good looks were more of a hindrance than a help among the dour Indians. They recognized her value, but kept her in positions of little importance and no influence.

Maybe that was part of the reason why she had felt it necessary to strike in a new direction, to make a statement of her independent ideas and methods. She wanted to lead, to be responsible for turning the whole Shining Path onto a new and more violent course of action.

She wanted to make a difference in the movement.

Instead, she was in a more precarious position than ever. To her superiors, her political radicalism smacked of rebellion. And although the Path claimed to be egalitarian and open, a sign of internal revolt or factioning of the movement would be mercilessly crushed. She knew any further questioning of her loyalty or obedience could be fatal for her.

If Michael Blanski arrived, there would be all the more reason for her actions to be suspect. If Blanski got here alive and saw her, he would start making damaging accusations. If her superiors believed his story, or even had a suspicion that he might be telling the truth, they would want to know the answers to the mystery behind Carrillo's murder.

And if they had any doubts about her honesty, they wouldn't stop at just asking polite questions.

Antonia had seen prisoners interrogated by the Shining Path before; she had helped ask the questions on occasion. The redheaded beauty would rather kill herself than face the ordeal.

News traveled slowly this far into the mountains. It was only a day ago that she had learned of the breakout from Lurigancho prison, and had heard that a large-scale arms dealer had got out, as well. That had to be Blanski.

Antonia was both surprised and chilled by the unexpected development. She had believed he would never make it from Lurigancho alive. If the other inmates didn't kill him, she'd been sure the foul, disease-ridden conditions would.

Now he had been delivered from prison by the Shining Path, had risen like a vampire from his coffin, to torment her thoughts and bring disaster to her plans and her future.

Only a few hours after the first word about Blanski, Libertad had phoned for permission to bring the arms merchant to their secret encampment. Alarm bells had trilled in her head, warning of the consequences to her if Blanski was brought to the hidden installation. Antonia had urged the governing council not to grant the request and not to let an outsider into their secure fortress. Unfortunately for her, she had been dismissed out of hand.

She was afraid she had run out of alternatives. It was she or Blanski. Only one of them could live.

The irony of the situation struck her. If it hadn't been for the efforts of the Shining Path, Blanski would still be rotting in a bug-infested wormhole in Lima. Now her confederates had brought the man to within a few miles.

Until the day Blanski had arrived in Peru, Antonia had never even heard his name. Now his very existence was driving her to desperate measures that she never could have contemplated if she had not been placed in a vise of pressure. Every minute that crawled tortoiselike along her watch face tightened the noose around her neck.

There was one escape from the trap. She would have to prevent Blanski from ever reaching the base. And there couldn't be any witnesses left to point the finger of accusation in her direction.

She couldn't do the job herself. In her present position, she couldn't leave the base even for a few minutes. It was too likely that her absence would be noticed, and that risk was unacceptable. The solution she had in mind would take care of any loose ends, yet not require her presence.

There were only two people in the base that she could rely on to carry out her instructions.

She had known Federico and Paulo since childhood. Unlike most of the Indians, they both liked her and obeyed her. And lusted after her, if the way that they watched her was any guide to their desires.

When one or both of them were in Lima, they conducted clandestine missions together, small and secretive things. They had planted bombs in elevators, gas stations, fancy stores. Where the bombs exploded or how much destruction they achieved was unimportant. All that mattered was that the authorities were surprised and that the citizens were fearful that the next place they visited might be the site of the next blast.

Fear was the object and the body count only a by-product of their tactics.

The two Indians had fallen under her sway gradually and now looked to her for instruction and reward, as a well-trained dog looks to its mistress.

She took them to a deserted rest area where they would not be overheard. "Listen carefully," she began. "You must do something very, very important for me. I want you to kill an American."

The two men broke into smiles. Neither had killed an American before, at least not knowingly. This would be something to look forward to.

"He will be coming down the trail from the highway. You must kill him and make sure that the body is never found." Antonia could not be sure that Libertad would take that route into the headquarters, since there were several entrances. However, she could only cover one way in, and that trail was the most likely choice for someone traveling by truck from Ayacucho.

"But there is one more thing. There can't be any witnesses. No one must be left alive to tell about you killing the American. Is that clear?"

Apparently not, from the puzzled expressions. "Who will these witnesses be?" Paulo asked.

"They are brothers, but they are traitors. I give you my word on it."

Both of the young men looked aghast. They had killed often, but never before their own men.

"Traitors?"

"Yes, they are." Antonia was exerting all her charisma to sway them and banish the doubt in their tiny minds. "But only I know it. You must not tell the others about this. Not now. Not ever. Do you promise?"

They both promised, although reluctantly. Antonia decided that she had better watch them carefully until this particular incident had blown over. They had agreed for now, but she wasn't sure they could keep silent about the executions over the long run.

It was a terrible world when you couldn't trust anyone anymore, she reflected as she watched them walk toward the highway tunnel.

Later, she would have to kill them both.

17

The going was tough in the underground tunnel. Bolan crawled along on bruised hands and knees, a slow, tedious journey only faintly illuminated by a miner's helmet perched on Libertad's head. The terrorist leader was far ahead, and at times Bolan was plunged into absolute blackness when the small lamp that was the only source of light disappeared around a corner of the twisting horizontal shaft.

The ground below him was hard and uneven. At times a rock, invisible in the gloom, would score his face or limbs. The darkness was oppressive, as forbidding as midnight in a graveyard, the silence broken only by the labored breathing of the gang members in the thin air. There was a foul smell to the tunnel, wet and sickly, like the air trapped in a long-disused crypt. Occasionally something would crunch under his palm, a squashed bug dying stickily on his fingers. Sweat dripped into his eyes, already sore and strained from peering into the murk.

He had no way to estimate the length of time he had been traveling underground. His watch had disappeared long ago into the slippery hands of one of the policemen in Carrillo's office. He only knew that the monotonous motion had made his legs feel like lead bars and his arms like jelly.

At last a faint light shimmered an indeterminate distance in front, growing more distinct with every passing minute.

After another hundred yards of laborious creeping, the dirt passage ended. The warrior found, when he emerged from the shaft, that he was in an underground passageway six feet wide and eight feet high, edged with stone. Bolan noticed that the stones were so exactly cut that they fit together without mortar. The passage ran ruler-straight as far as he could see in both directions.

He began to stretch, working out the kinks that had numbed every muscle that hadn't been overworked to the point of collapse.

Bolan knew without a moment's hesitation that this superbly constructed passage hadn't been built by the Shining Path. An aura of age emanated from the walls, as nearly perfect as when the stones were carefully fitted together. He couldn't guess how long ago that had been.

"You see, American, that we Indians have not always been ignorant savages." Libertad was anxious to boast to him of the accomplishments of his forefathers. "Hundreds of years ago, maybe thousands, my ancestors built this. If it had not been for the coming of the European monsters, those savages who destroyed our homes and our civilization, who knows what heights we would have achieved! And one day, there will be a new Inca empire to amaze an admiring world. Yes, the Republic of New Democracy will provide a shining example of justice to the masses, a model of a new and better life."

"Yeah, a nice place to visit, but I wouldn't want to live here. All I know, amigo, is that you're going to need lots of guns to bring the other side around to your way of thinking. So how about getting us out of here so I can do some dealing? I don't like running around underground like some kind of South American gopher.''

That shut up Libertad, and the Peruvian stalked off, muttering to himself. A ferocious glare in the man's eye told Bolan how much Libertad was looking forward to executing him.

The labyrinth explained a lot to Bolan. It told him how the Path was able to operate with relative impunity in an area overrun with combat troops. Somehow, they had discovered a network of tunnels that might honeycomb the whole region, allowing them to come and go unseen. And as had just been demonstrated to Bolan, the shafts provided a ready escape route, allowing the revolutionaries to vanish when the pursuit got too hot. The terrorists had evidently dug a few crude exits from the ancient and more elaborate Inca passageways to give them some alternate escape routes.

When Libertad gave the light to an underling and set the small group on their way after a short rest, Bolan sought out Stone. They conversed in low voices as they walked down the straight corridor, their boot heels echoing on the granite floor.

"I'm surprised to find this here," Bolan began. "I would have thought that something this extensive would be well-known."

"It's not so astonishing as you might think," Stone explained. "The locals aren't very responsive to outsiders, as you may have guessed. And this area isn't really that well explored. The army is lazy and won't venture far from the highway or its base camps. So, if no one suspects these tunnels are here, then no one is going to look for them."

"What about archaeologists or treasure hunters?"

"In the first place, this is a big country, almost the size of Alaska, with about a quarter of it covered by the Andes.

There are a lot of sights that are very well-known and easy to get to that have yet to be explored because of lack of funds. Most of the current work is going on near Cuzco, the Inca capital. And second, this has become a very dangerous place to work—which you already know. Neither the army nor the Shining Path care much for gringos. And finally, if a treasure hunter had found this place, he wouldn't be too likely to tell anyone else. So, the terrorists are pretty safe.''

One of the guards overheard them talking and came over to force them apart, leaving Bolan alone with his thoughts once again.

Bolan knew that Stone was probably right. The ancient Inca city of Machu Picchu had sat undiscovered on the top of a mountain until 1911. It was quite possible that other fortresses and refuges were yet to be found, particularly since it was rumored that the Incas had hidden huge amounts of gold and silver from the Spanish invaders. A large room had been filled from floor to ceiling with gold to ransom the last emperor's life before the Spaniards strangled him.

And yet that gold was said to represent only a fraction of the Inca hoard. What had happened to the bulk of the incalculable wealth, including a golden fish bigger than a man's arm and a gold-hung chain so heavy that two hundred men were needed to carry it, remained a mystery after more than four hundred years of patient searching.

The Incas were master builders and were certainly capable of undertaking a project as large as the tunnel system. The great citadel of Sacsahuaman in the imperial capital of Cuzco had required twenty thousand men toiling for ninety years to finish. Building these miles of rock-lined corridors would have seemed like an afternoon nap by comparison.

At various points in the long walk, they passed apertures in the walls, leading off to unknown destinations. Some might lead to storerooms, guardhouses or other exits. One might even lead to the fabled treasure of the Incas. It would take years of continuous searching to explore every side tunnel and blind alley in the complex. Bolan had been walking for more than two hours and had bypassed dozens of alternate routes, the rock walls marked in fading paint with some colorful identifying symbols.

The warrior wasn't much of a mole. He preferred his enemies aboveground, not burrowing in the middle of some anthill.

Right now, he was certainly glad to have a guide in the maze. Occasionally Libertad directed the lead man carrying the lamp left or right into a crossing corridor, seemingly identical to the one they had just traversed.

Even if the army found their way to the underground complex, the Path could hide undetected for months before an exploring soldier stumbled on them.

From time to time they circumvented ancient booby traps, pits dug in the floor to catch a careless enemy. They edged past on narrow ledges at the side. A defending force on the other side could hold up an attacker indefinitely, since only one person at a time could possibly slide past the pit.

Once, the terrorists stopped and clustered around something along the path, talking animatedly. When Bolan caught up, he found the Peruvians assembled around a shrunken and wrinkled body facedown on the stones. A dusty felt hat had rolled away from the corpse. Apparently a comrade who had lost his way.

The march resumed, after Libertad had stripped the desiccated body of anything of value.

After a very long period, which Bolan guessed was at least four hours of solid movement, he was fading into a haze. A powerful combination of days of monotony, exhaustion, poor food in minuscule quantities and lack of sleep were making the warrior almost dead on his feet. He placed one foot mechanically in front of the other, stumbling along followed by two of the terrorists, hardly conscious of himself or his surroundings.

Suddenly he came very much awake.

The Executioner's heart was pounding, blood flowing into adrenaline-energized muscles. His senses reached to a combat high as his body kicked almost instantaneously into a fighting mode.

His ears had detected a metallic noise that had sounded very familiar to his trained ear.

It was the harsh click of the safety popping on a gun.

Bolan was down and rolling even as a gunner stepped from a narrow rat hole that the Executioner had passed moments before. The intruder opened fire, blasting controlled 3-round bursts down the corridor. The orange muzzle-flame cast transient shadows, like the flare of a camera flash.

Screams answered the gunfire as the panicked terrorists began to run forward, trying to escape the hurtling lead.

The gunman placed a burst between the shoulder blades of the man who brought up the rear, and got lucky with the Indian immediately in front. Three rounds cored the Peruvian's head, splattering a red-and-gray pattern on the ancient walls.

The lead man raced for safety, legs pumping as he guided himself down the passage by the faint light of the one lamp the group possessed.

A darker shadow loomed from the blackness. The ambusher hurled the fleeing man into his own lightless void with a single shot that carved through the runner's heart.

The two machine gunners fired sporadically but methodically, a cross fire that picked victims carefully. Each bandit took refuge in a side corridor, poking his muzzle around the edge to reduce the possibility of being cored by friendly fire from his opposite number.

A couple of the armed terrorists replied with death streams of their own, but the bullets cascaded harmlessly from the sheltering rock corners.

Bolan's party wasn't as lucky, caught in the open. The terrorists' gunfire died away to a chorus of agonized shrieks, as the ambushers raked the Peruvians with a steady stream of hellfire.

Bolan remained where he lay spread-eagled, trying to blend into the shadows as he assessed his next move. His stomach and side were wet, as a thin stream of blood trickled his way from two corpses heaped three feet away.

The ambushers had the small party trapped in a narrow corridor with both ends sealed with hot lead, like beetles trapped in a jar, waiting for the sun to fry them. The only good thing about the precarious situation was that the attackers didn't have grenades.

Bolan's choices were limited.

If he stayed still, there was the chance that he'd catch a stray round. Flying metal was ricocheting from the hard stone, filling the air with tumbling rock chips.

After a while, when all movement ceased, the gunmen would probably move in to finish the job, put an insurance round through the head of everybody, moving or not.

Just to make sure the "dead" stayed dead.

That might be the Executioner's best opportunity, but it was a risky strategy.

A momentary silence fell, the stammering of the machine guns falling away in echoes reverberating down the long corridor.

Someone began screaming in Quechua, frantically calling to the hidden gunmen. The only answer was a swarm of stingers from both directions. The screaming faded to a soft gurgle, which collapsed into a faint wheeze and died away.

Someone besides Bolan had figured out that the assassins were members of the Path, ruthlessly killing their own comrades. No one else could have been waiting in the close confines of the passage.

The who and why would have to wait. Now the only important question was how to stay alive.

The only answer he could think of stood out like burning letters etched in his brain.

Move.

Bolan tensed, coiling his muscles. His target was only twenty-five feet away. He could do three hundred feet in just about thirteen seconds, so he should be able to reach the gunner in just over a second.

But a bullet from the barrel of the submachine gun could hit home before he'd taken his first step.

The Executioner didn't think about it. He was up and running.

The gunner didn't notice Bolan until the warrior was almost upon him. Whether he was slightly dazzled by the muzzle-flashes or had gotten too cocky imagining that no one would actually charge him, it didn't matter. The gun fired wild.

Bolan grunted as one round nicked his left ear. The others whistled away harmlessly above his shoulder, the wind of their passing fanning his cheek.

The Executioner clipped the gunner in the knee as he raced into the side passage, the shooter falling to the floor as Bolan slid headfirst into the wall. The warrior spun and flailed out in the darkness, catching the other guy a hard backhand in the jaw. Then he sprang, one knee coming down heavily on something soft and vital.

The Peruvian screamed and jerked up, trying to double over. Bolan grabbed the guy's head in both hands. One hand gripped under the chin and the other fisted his opponent's dark hair, propelling the head back with all his adrenaline-fired strength. The spine popped like a scrawny chicken's.

The body shuddered once and lay still.

Bolan wasn't wasting any time. He searched out the fallen gun in the blackness and pulled out the clip to check the weight. It wasn't quite empty.

He edged along the wall toward the other ambusher's position. The only light was a faint glow ahead from the fallen lamp.

Would the other guy make a break or hold out and try to finish the job alone? Bolan was betting on the shooter sticking around. If he was a member of the Shining Path, he would most likely be fanatical about a mission to the point of being suicidal.

The assassin was getting nervous. He had obviously heard the sound of the fight and knew that something was amiss. Several times the man called "Federico," hoping that his comrade would answer.

Bolan silently encouraged the hitter to keep shouting. It made it a lot easier for him to zero in on his target, and the lack of response would be making the assassin jittery.

Bolan held the weapon at arm's length, not wanting to take a chance on being surprised. In the dark he couldn't tell what type of gun he was holding, but it was light, like an Ingram or an Uzi machine pistol.

He held a small advantage, since the fallen light pointed slightly toward the hidden gunner, making it a little more difficult for Bolan to be seen as he silently crept forward for the showdown.

He didn't hear any other sounds and wondered briefly if he was the only one of the group still alive.

A muzzle poked around a corner ahead, swinging in Bolan's direction. The warrior squeezed off a burst, and the SMG went flying into the dark. Those were the last shots fired. Bolan's gun registered empty.

The hitter took to his heels. Bolan had apparently hit the gun but missed anything vital on the ambusher. The impact of Bolan's rounds on the terrorist's weapon must have numbed his hands at the very least. The guy certainly wasn't hanging around for a hand-to-hand encounter.

Bolan dropped the useless weapon and pursued, one hand on the wall for guidance as he ran in complete darkness, guided only by the ringing sound of footsteps leading him by a few feet.

For a moment, the warrior considered giving up the chase and allowing his quarry to escape but abandoned the thought. It was in his best interest to catch the guy and keep him alive, if possible. This shadowy fleeing figure might be the warrior's only way out of the maze if everyone else had been killed in the attack.

His hands told him that the pathway veered sharply to the right. He powered around the bend, listening for the footsteps. The cadence changed, as though the man in front did a dance step, followed by a slight pause, then a thump.

Even as the significance registered, Bolan jumped, arms outstretched. His legs came down on air, but his arms fell heavily on stone, scrambling madly for a purchase. He had almost fallen into a yawning chasm in the center of the passageway.

The man in front had guts, Bolan admitted grudgingly, even as his fingers scratched for a hold in the smooth rock floor. It took nerve to run the corridor in the dark and time a jump like that. He had to know the place the way his socks knew his shoes.

His adversary hadn't given up yet. Bolan could hear him breathing just inches away.

A fan of air brushed Bolan's right ear—the killer was trying to kick Bolan off his precarious perch and send him for a long jump into nothingness.

The heavy boot sailed by Bolan's ear once more, but this time the warrior was ready. He shot his hand forward, gripping the ankle in a viselike grip, and yanked hard.

With an unintelligible curse, the overbalanced terrorist toppled into the pit. At the last second the guy made a desperate move, grabbing Bolan around the knees and holding on for dear life.

Bolan shook himself as hard as he dared. He rocked back and forth, trying to bang the guy into the wall or scrape him off against the side.

But the desperate man clung to Bolan like a barnacle attached to a ship. And the Executioner's arms were getting tired. Already his shoulders were screaming, the joints stretched by the double weight on the sockets. His ribs, injured only a few days ago, were sending jets of agony coursing through his body.

He couldn't swing a leg up as long as the terrified hitter below gripped them like a living rope. Carefully Bolan removed his right arm from the edge and powered a rocklike fist repeatedly onto the top of the Peruvian's head.

The gunner's death grip didn't loosen—he completely ignored the hammer blows raining on him, too terrified to fight back or make any move to protect himself. Bolan's fist rocketed down once more.

One time too many. Bolan's arm slipped from the edge. His hands searched frantically for a crevice, for the smallest finger hold to halt his slide.

He fell into the pit.

Screeching, the Peruvian finally let go.

The two men tumbled through the blackness, heading for the bottom.

18

fter he had listened to the pounding footsteps fade away
the distance, Libertad lifted himself carefully from the
one, assured that all danger was now passed.

"Up, you cowards," he shouted, moving to retrieve the
llen light.

Three men responded, two of his men and Stone, as he
w by shining the light in their faces.

Libertad began to examine the bodies crumpled on the
d-pooled, sticky floor. Most of them were clearly dead,
ith massive injuries caused by the high-velocity rounds.

One was unconscious but still breathing, although with
very breath bright red blood bubbled from a large hole in
s right side, adding to the splotchy stain creeping over his
irt.

The terrorist leader called Stone over, but the American
st shook his head and turned away.

Libertad grunted with frustration. This was hardly going
be the triumphant return that he had planned. Instead of
inging back a sizable force along with a useful Yankee,
would go creeping back with two men and Stone. What
plague of bad luck had befallen him.

He moved to where the assassin lay. He had heard the
ght between Blanski and the hidden gunman, but had not
terfered. What would have been the point? He would
ave only succeeded in getting himself shot.

Even now, either Blanski was alive, in which case h
would be found wandering in the underground complex, c
he was dead. Then he would be no further trouble. Eith
way, he wasn't worth worrying about right now. There wei
more pressing matters for Libertad's attention, such a
figuring out who had planned to have him killed.

More specifically, what member of the Shining Path ha
sought to have him obliterated and left to be forgotte
somewhere in the underground caverns?

He directed the light onto the twisted face of the assa
sin. The neck jutted at an odd angle, and the mouth wa
open in a final snarl, the tongue sticking out of one sid
Libertad wasn't bothered by the sight; he had had too muc
combat experience to be disturbed by death.

He kicked the body in the side several times, the dea
man sliding along the smooth stones with every impact. H
stopped when his foot became sore, some of his ange
vented on the unresisting corpse.

"Does anyone recognize him?" he demanded of his mer

Each shook his head in denial. "He looks slightly fami
iar, but I couldn't tell you his name," commented one mar

Useless offal, Libertad thought. There was only one wa
to find out who this creature had been. He reached for h
knife.

The terrorists prepared to leave, gathering the weapon
scattered among the bodies. At least now they had thre
lights, since each of the assassins had brought a powerf
flashlight.

"What about the wounded man?" Stone asked as the
prepared to leave.

"What about him?" Libertad answered.

"You're not going to leave him here, are you? He's st
alive, you know."

"Yes, he's alive. But he will be dead soon, and we both now it. Should we carry him along? For what purpose would we tire ourselves, since he will either die as we travel or at our camp? When we arrive at our base, we would not expend any of our few and precious medicines on someone who will not recover. As it is, he is a brave martyr for our cause and will die a happy man."

Stone was astonished at the cold-blooded analysis of the value of the fallen man. "But...but he is still alive!" Stone couldn't think of an argument to use, although he knew that Libertad must be wrong.

Libertad didn't answer immediately and appeared to be thinking. Abruptly he took two long steps to the injured man. With a swift motion, he unsheathed his knife and plunged it into the prone man's ribs below the heart. The body shuddered once and lay still.

Libertad wiped his knife on the dead man's pants and sheathed the knife. "Now he's not. Are you satisfied? Let's go."

Stone followed, casting a backward glance at the fallen men, already vanished in the shadows.

In a few minutes they came to a pit in the corridor floor. One of the men pointed to some drying red streaks at the edge of the hole.

The four men gathered at the edge of the vertical shaft, shining the lights far down the rock walls. No bottom appeared in the beams.

"I don't think we will be seeing Blanski again," Libertad commented, as each mentally reconstructed what must have happened here—the unseen pit, a frantic last effort and a final fall. Very final.

"Why don't we throw this other American after him?" suggested one of the terrorists. "Let all Yankees rot in the darkness, I say."

Libertad shook his head, although the prospect was a[t]tractive. He was in a black mood, having lost the maj[or] prize, the reason why they had been brought from Lu[ri]gancho. He felt like killing something, and Stone would [be] a satisfying sacrifice. But duty was more important tha[n] pleasure. And anyway, he might still have an opportuni[ty] to cut out Stone's heart at some later date.

"No. He may still have some value to us as a healer, u[n]trained though he is. He does have some small skill wi[th] plants and herbs. We will keep him alive until we are to[ld] otherwise."

"And I hope that it is soon," said one, a dull-looki[ng] squat lump of a man, waving his knife under Stone's chi[n.]

Stone suddenly felt a wave of nostalgia for Lurigancho.

That's when he realized how much he missed Blanski.

BOLAN AWOKE. At least he thought he was awake. [He] couldn't see, even though his eyes were open.

Gradually, as though he were waking from a long a[nd] horrible dream, the past few hours came back to him. [He] remembered the fall, the Peruvian shrieking, the helple[ss] fear of falling washing over him as he dropped in the a[b]solute blackness.

Then he hit, landing directly onto the Peruvian's che[st] before rolling to the granite floor.

He must have smashed his head, for the hair on the le[ft] side of his scalp was matted and caked with dried blood.

As awareness returned, he felt racked with pain: his hea[d] hurt, his muscles ached as though he had had a close e[n]counter with a steamroller, and his throat felt as if he ha[d] swallowed a sandbox.

And to top it off, he was stuck in the middle of a sto[ne] Chinese puzzle, left to himself to wander around in the da[rk] without any food or water until he somehow found his way out of this trap. Or died of thirst or starvation first.

He was beginning to hate Peru.

Well, no point in putting it off. It was time to get moving. He began by feeling around on all fours for the Peruvian, ignoring the insistent protests of bruised muscles. At least nothing felt cracked or broken, so he had better consider himself fortunate.

He found the body after a few moments of groping. The chest was a funny concave shape; Bolan could almost discern the impression his knees had made when he had dropped on the already smashed corpse of the gunner. Lucky for Bolan that they hadn't fallen in the opposite order.

What a run of tremendously good luck he was having, he thought ironically.

The body was warm but cooling. He didn't know how to estimate the time of death, but guessed that it had been no more than an hour ago.

He continued to explore the body by touch, not knowing what to expect. He discovered a pouch, the string wrapped around the dead man's neck.

Bolan reached in to see if there was anything edible and found several smaller pouches inside. By the smell, one contained tobacco. He couldn't identify the contents of the rest of the pouches. He opened one of them, placed a small amount of its contents on his right forefinger and tasted it. A ball of fire formed on his tongue and burned a trail down his throat. It was some fierce spice, like chili pepper or hot curry, and it seared his mouth like a branding iron.

He threw the small pouch somewhere into the darkness, and decided not to experiment anymore.

Bolan ran his hands over the corpse again, searching for water flask. No sign of one, although he did find a knife

in a sheath, which he added to the pouch of foodstuffs. H
searched around the body with fading hope, but at last hi
hands encountered a tough hide pouch that sloshed faintly

He found the top and drank deeply before he caugh
control of himself. There was no way of telling how lon
this tiny water supply might have to last, so he decided t
drink no more now.

He had no reason to remain where he was any longer. H
began to walk, going right because it rhymed with light—
there was no rational basis for choosing a direction, sinc
he had no way of judging even where north or south were

Bolan proceeded cautiously. With one hand on a wall, h
slid his feet forward slowly in case he came upon anothe
pit in the floor. It was a tiring and slow way to cove
ground. Whenever he came to a side tunnel, he bypassed it
preferring to keep going in a straight line, if possible. H
had no idea where he would end up, but he figured if h
went far enough in one direction, he would finally arriv
somewhere. At least he hoped so.

The experience was disorienting, like being placed in
sensory deprivation tank. Bolan could move and hear th
sound of his own voice and steps, but there was no stimu
lus apart from what he produced for himself. When h
stopped, there was complete silence other than the sound
of his own body.

His eyes were sore, strained from the effort of trying t
see when vision was impossible. His legs were tired, h
arms protesting from reaching out to the wall. He couldn
tell if his limbs were revolting because he had been walkin
for hours or because he ached from the combination c
falls, fights and fevers he had endured over the past fe
days.

He tried counting paces, but found his mind drifting. H
lost the numbers so often that he gave up the effort. He wa

)o weary to keep on walking. It was obvious that he
eeded rest.

The big man lay down on the cold stone and slept.

IBERTAD WAS ANGRY as he approached the base camp, a
ghteous feeling directed at whoever had tried to kill him.
Ie was more than a little nervous, too, since it could have
een anyone in the complex who had known that he was
oming. Who would want him dead? And why?

He was going to get the answers, for leaving the puzzle
nsolved might mean his eventual death. It wasn't a pleas-
nt feeling, returning to a place he had always thought of
s a refuge and finding a worm in the apple. Actually the
eeling was more like finding a poisonous snake in one's
ed. If there was a traitor to the organization planning his
emise, he must be found and eliminated before he could
o any more damage.

But only after he had been made to tell everything he
new.

A minor commissar greeted Libertad when he arrived,
nd tried to send him off to the dormitory for rest. Liber-
d would have none of it.

"I demand a meeting with the Revolutionary Council,"
e stormed, refusing to be placated.

"That is impossible," the other man answered coldly. "If
ey wish to see you, they will send for you. Something that
very much doubt will happen." The commissar glared at
ibertad as though he were some lower form of life.

Libertad kept his temper in check, telling himself that it
as not for the likes of this headquarters parasite that he
ad killed and risked being killed. However, at this mo-
ent he would gladly have added the sniveling bureaucrat
• his list of victims.

"Tell the council that I have evidence of treason, of counterrevolutionary plot within these very walls. If I mus break up their meeting myself, I will do so. Then I will b forced to name you among those I suspect of obstruction ism, revisionism and sentiments contrary to the well-bein of the party."

Libertad sneered as the functionary ran off to pass alon his message. He knew it took very little suspicion to mak the council decide someone was a liability to the move ment. The next step was a Revolutionary Tribunal, fo lowed by execution by the People's Justice Squad. An inevitably, a cold, lonely grave.

Libertad sat on a rough bench, prepared to wait. wouldn't be a long stay.

BOLAN AWOKE REFRESHED although stiff from sleeping o the rough and unyielding stone, the details of the pa events flooding his mind. His plan was clear: get the he out of here. It was the "how" that was kind of hazy.

He drank a little water before moving off, ignoring th rumblings of his stomach. He could live for a long tim without food, but without water he would have lasted on a day or two before he collapsed, able only to wait for a unpleasant death.

He must move slowly, conserve his strength and, abov all, ration his water rigidly. Then he might have a chance

He had taken the precaution of placing his food sack few feet farther down the corridor in the direction that had been traveling before he went to sleep. That way could be sure not to retrace his steps.

Bolan began to walk, continuing the monotonous tre straight ahead. This time he counted the paces, stepping o the distance at as rapid a tempo as he could maintain wit out beginning to sweat.

He had almost reached twelve thousand paces when the corridor ended. Feeling in front of him, Bolan touched raw earth. Apparently the Incas hadn't advanced any farther along this route. He had marched down a dead end.

The big man fought off a wave of depression. Instead of resting, he drank a little water from his dwindling supply and started back the way he had come, turning at the first left he came to.

Bolan walked on along the smooth-walled passageway, skipping over occasional breaks in the regular stonework. He was curious about the purpose of the underground maze. Surely some of these openings must be for quarters, armories, treasure houses, kitchens or stairways, any of the thousands of kinds of activities that took place in an ancient fortress. But he knew that if he began to explore, the chances were great that he would never find his way out.

As he walked, nagging doubts began to come to mind. Maybe the whole lower level was only air ducts or for flood control. Maybe it was a punishment, a sadistic torture chamber for enemies who were thrown down here to starve to death. What if there really was no way out?

Bolan slumped to the floor, exhausted. He took a short swallow of water, shook the bag and discovered it was almost empty.

The warrior fought a desperate struggle with a black depression that threatened to creep over him, sap his spirit and immobilize him where he lay.

It wasn't purely muscle that powered the big man on. It was his indomitable spirit that drove him, and if that cracked, he knew he was as good as dead.

Once he had wrestled down the black waves lapping at his soul, he sat back to take stock of his situation.

Somewhere in the far distance, just at the edge of perception, Bolan heard the first natural sound that he had detected since he had entered the tunnels—the tinkling noise of running water.

LIBERTAD WAS USHERED IN to see the Revolutionary Council after a short wait. Stone was pushed in behind him. Nine impassive men sat quietly around an ordinary kitchen table, dressed no differently than he was.

"What is this news of treason that you bring us?" demanded one whom Libertad knew as the council chairman, a middle-aged man with a beak nose who reminded Libertad of a predatory bird.

"First, comrades, before I discuss our confidential business, what do you wish done with this American? He was a companion to the arms dealer, Blanski, and I did not wish to kill him without your permission."

Stone, trapped between two guards, blanched as he realized that he might not leave the room alive.

"Is the Yankee devil of any value?" one of the councilmen asked in a bored voice, not in the least interested in whether Stone lived or died.

"I think he may be of use, since he is familiar with many herbs and their medicinal properties. He sometimes treated our people in prison. I think he should be kept alive for a while to judge his usefulness."

A councillor who gave a strong impression of authority glanced from one face to another around the table. "Make it so, then. Just let him be guarded well. If he escapes, Libertad . . . Let me just say that it will be held against you."

The terrorist knew all too well what that meant—a bullet in the brain.

Stone was removed, finally daring to breathe again.

"Now, tell us about these serious charges you have brought against some unknown party. But remember, causing internal strife among our brotherhood is a serious crime and will be punished. So speak, but know that we will judge you, as well as your words.''

Libertad told the story of the underground ambush, feeling carefully for the right words, conscious of the cold eyes fixed on him. He relayed how the other prisoner had escaped and had apparently been lost in the pit.

''Did you find the body?'' one of the listeners interrupted.

''No, we did not. Our lights could not illuminate the bottom of the shaft, and we had no rope to climb down.''

''This is worrisome,'' the questioner said to the other councillors. ''What if he is alive and roaming through our complex? He might escape and take word of our base to the government troops.''

''Relax,'' said the chairman. ''You know that no one who has fallen into the pits has ever been seen alive again. Continue, Libertad.''

Libertad finished quickly, emphasizing that the death of his men had been the result of treachery, possibly of a spy.

''Strong words, Libertad, and a very dramatic story. But how do we know that any of this is true? Maybe this lost American killed your men and escaped, and to cover your incompetence from our just wrath you have concocted this fable. Where is your proof?''

Libertad licked his lips, relieved that he had prepared for this eventuality. He gestured to one of his men.

The man reached into his sack and withdrew a crudely severed head by the hair. He placed it on the table, where the protruding tongue appeared to mock the solemn council.

''This is one of the two gunmen I told you about.''

The councillors contemplated the grisly trophy in silence, as though a head on the table were a daily occurrence.

"I believe I recognize this man," one commented. "It is Federico."

"But why would he do such a thing? He was a loyal soldier, if not very smart."

"Loyal to whom?" the chairman rumbled, his hawk eyes blazing. "There is only one person who might have swayed him from the true path of the movement. A childhood friend who held great influence over him and his friend Paulo. Summon Antonia!"

He shouted this last command at a guard, who then disappeared. The chairman gestured to Libertad to hide the head.

Libertad held the evidence behind his back, as they waited for the woman to be brought.

Antonia was not particularly concerned to be brought before the council. She had been working on several projects since her recent arrival, and it was natural that the council would wish a report. Federico and Paulo were not likely to return for several hours, so this meeting couldn't be about their activities. She certainly hoped not.

When she entered the council chamber there were three men in the room whom she didn't recognize. Each looked dirty and dusty, as though recently arrived from a long journey. She didn't find their presence comforting.

"Antonia, when did you last see Federico? He appears to be missing." The chairman began without preamble, watching her face for a reaction to the name.

"I have not seen him since yesterday, comrade. I have no idea where he might be." Antonia believed that her voice had remained level, although she had been disconcerted at the mention of the name. She knew that she was fighting for her life now, and the least mistake would cost her dearly.

The chairman paused for a few seconds, lengthening the silence between them. When he was sure that she had no more to say, he resumed. "In that case, I don't suppose that you can explain how Federico has come to be at this meeting."

He looked at Libertad, who immediately drew the blood-streaked head from behind his back. The dead eyes stared accusingly at the beautiful Spanish woman.

Antonia's hands flew to her eyes to hide the grisly sight. From the look of the painful grimace etched into his face she had sent her childhood playmate to a horrible death.

Looking between her fingers, she searched the faces of the others. From their grim expressions, she was convinced that they knew who was responsible for the attack that had killed Federico.

She had to escape. Now.

Antonia bolted for the door, but was intercepted by two guards. In a desperate move she wrenched an arm free and pulled a knife from one man. She slashed him across the midriff, and he collapsed shrieking, his guts leaking from the wound.

She drove the knife toward the second man's throat, but he reacted faster than his dying companion, catching Antonia's wrist in a powerful grip and backhanding her across the temple.

The red-haired woman collapsed like an ivory doll thrown to the floor by an angry child.

The chairman gazed angrily at the fallen woman. "Take her to the interrogation room. Make sure that she tells everything she knows."

Stupid woman, he thought to himself as Antonia was carried from the room. She should have used the knife on herself while she could.

Soon she would be begging for a chance to cut her own throat.

19

Bolan hiked along with renewed energy, knowing that his immediate problem, a water supply, was almost solved.

He searched for another hour, guiding himself by his acute sense of hearing. Occasionally he had to retrace his steps when the soft gurgling sound grew fainter, before he found his way to the small stream that had beckoned him.

The tinkling came from a small drainage ditch, a narrow channel beside a broad corridor, as Bolan discovered when he put his foot into it. He dropped to his knees and cautiously sampled the water, relieved to find it sweet and pure.

The big man drank his fill and started on his way again, this time following the small rivulet upstream. He guessed that if he found the source of the water, he might very well find a way out of the labyrinth.

Bolan walked a seemingly endless distance, his feet aching in his poorly constructed prison shoes. He didn't notice any incline at all. The slope upward had to have been very shallow, with only a gradual rise to ground level.

Suddenly the stream dipped underground into a hole too narrow to accommodate more than Bolan's head, leaving him without a guide. The path forked at this point, as he determined by groping a narrow column of rock that divided the tunnel. He paced a short way up each corridor before trying his luck. The left trail appeared to climb, while the track to the right continued straight ahead.

After filling his water pouch Bolan chose the left fork, preferring to continue to climb. He wanted out as soon as possible, and the passageway to the right might continue for another hundred miles, for all he knew.

He began to regret his decision when the corridor began to shrink. Soon he was ducking his head to avoid a low ceiling, while the width had narrowed to the point where the sides brushed his shoulders.

A few minutes later, Bolan ran into another dead end. However, as he determined from feeling the area ahead of him, this was a very different tunnel end. The other corridor had simply stopped, unfinished, as though the workmen had quit for the day once upon a time, and had never returned to complete their tasks. This path ended in a flat, smooth-finished surface.

Bolan hammered a clenched fist on the wall. The vibrations didn't feel as though there were solid rock ahead. He shoved, hard. Nothing happened. He moved to the extreme left and tried again.

With a groan from a hinge that probably hadn't budged in five hundred years, the rock moved two inches, swinging back like a door. He could see a faint light through the crack, although to his dilated pupils it seemed so dazzling that he had to shut them. Another energized push opened the rock wall a foot more, and Bolan squeezed through.

He opened his eyes gradually, peering through narrow slits until he became accustomed to the light. Bolan observed that he was in the lower level of some tall structure, with a large opening like an atrium extending far above him. A stairway angled upward, folding back and forth on itself as it headed for an opening above. A soft amber-

inged light streamed down, catching motes of dust and
small flying insects in its beam.

The ground was covered with pots of various sizes, some
intact and some reduced to shards, which probably had
contained gifts of some kind to the gods. Bolan tried to remember if the Incas had practiced human sacrifice the way
the Aztecs to the north commonly had.

For a brief moment he imagined this as the site of an ancient and barbaric ritual, captives stretched on an altar at
the top of the pyramid, while priests cut open the victims'
chests and ripped out the still beating hearts. Possibly the
hearts had rested in those decayed jars.

Bolan began to climb, anxious to reach the sunlight,
careful of his footing on the disused stairway. He breathed
deeply, savoring the fresh air after the stale and uncircu-
lated air of the maze.

The stairs turned several times before Bolan reached the
final landing, where he found himself in a small rectangu-
lar structure open on one long side. Flaking paintings
adorned each wall. He poked his head out cautiously.

He was on the top of a high temple in the middle of a
ruined city. A steep set of stairs led to the ground, with the
top step flanked by two snarling stone jaguar heads. Several hundred yards away, another pyramid faced him, almost completely hidden beneath a green mantle of vines
and mold. A level area between the two large structures was
dotted with fallen columns and altars. All around the temple, stone houses stood open to the sky, thatched roofs long
since withered into dust.

Beyond the ruined village, a high ring of jagged hills en-
circled the valley. At one time, a road must have mean-
dered over one of the clefts between the peaks, but the trail
was invisible beneath the underbrush that had overgrown
the site.

The sun was setting to his left, but the rays were still strong enough to show several men standing by a cave mouth half a mile away. Several more openings pock marked the hills in the same vicinity.

Bolan had just found the lair of the Shining Path.

It wouldn't be long before the scorpions hiding among the rocks got a surprise visit from the Executioner.

It was going to be quite a party.

LIBERTAD HURRIED from the interrogation chamber to report to the council on the latest information he had obtained from his victim. With the assistance of skilled torturers, he had been able to break Antonia's will.

He felt a momentary pang for Antonia. Like any woman she had been vain about her beauty. She had been the kind of woman who made heads turn, even among the brother hood.

No one would ever call her beautiful again.

Marxist doctrine taught that torture was undignified both for the questioner, as well as the victim and that it should be done only as a last resort against the most unrepentant enemies of the people.

But Libertad had to admit that he enjoyed it, and that every scream reinforced his own sense of power and strength. The more helpless the victim, the more savage the punishment, the greater the terror and pain, the more pleasure he felt.

Antonia had given him immense satisfaction. He wondered if he had finally found his true calling.

Libertad was ushered in immediately to see the council. He had the impression that none of them ever moved, since each time he had made a progress report, they were seated exactly as he had left them the time before.

"Report," the chairman commanded.

"Comrade, she has broken completely. She has already onfessed that the ambush was set up to prevent the American, Blanski, from informing us that she had murdered her mployer, Carrillo. We have now learned the motive be-ind the murder."

Libertad paused theatrically, waiting to be prompted. nstead the councillors simply stared at him.

"She has stated that she has been in contact with a high overnment official—General Arturo Palma, chief com-nander of the Peruvian Military Police!"

The council members exchanged puzzled glances. It was nown that Palma was an avowed enemy of the Shining *ath. If Antonia had been passing secrets to him, why was his base still in operation?

"Has she explained why?" the chairman inquired.

"She claims that Palma's goals are the same as the Shin-ng Path's—in the short run. He wishes to destabilize the tate so that he can seize power with a military coup. Only hen will the General hunt us down. For now, he is content ɔ aid our struggle through access to armaments and infor-nation."

"And how much has she told him about our opera-ons? How much has she revealed?"

Libertad shrugged. "Nothing, she says. Supposedly the eneral was not interested in pumping her for informa-on, since he had no intention of aiding his colleagues in mashing the movement."

"She was questioned thoroughly?" another member sked.

"Yes. Very thoroughly." Libertad smiled to himself at e memories.

"Question her some more," the chairman decided. "Do ot hurry, but make sure that you learn everything there is ɔ know. And if she is still alive when you are finished, then

kill her. Slowly. The Shining Path has no room for trai
tors.''

Libertad hurried away, anxious to obey.

WHEN THE SUN had finally dipped below the hills, and the
last traces of red were fading from the sky, Bolan began to
move out. He crept cautiously down the back of the Inca
pyramid, using hands and feet to keep from sliding down
the slippery incline. He intended to start the action shortly
after sunset, during the early evening hours when the
guards would be relaxed.

The warrior edged through the low underbrush that
covered the ruined city, not pausing to look at any of the
ancient stones—covered with images of gods and de
mons—that poked from among the weeds. It was eerie
knowing that he was probably the first North American to
walk through these forgotten monuments.

Bolan chose an observation post in a ravaged home at the
edge of the desolate city. There seemed to be activity at only
one cave entrance. Possibly all the others were sealed. From
here he could clearly see the guards talking and smoking on
the cavern ledges. Each carried a rifle or machine gun
which made them the initial targets for the Executioner.

As an uninvited guest, he didn't want to join the party
empty-handed.

He began his stalk when the sun was down, and the stars
shone overhead. The thin mountain air made them glow
with a brightness he had never seen in the grimy urban
battlegrounds he often frequented. A chorus of soft ani
mal sounds echoed all around him as he brushed stealthily
through the tall grass covering the valley floor.

Soon he lay near the mouth of the cave guarded by the
terrorists. No light filtered from the cavern.

Although the Shining Path had taken some precautions against discovery, the two guards weren't expecting any trouble. They chatted away noisily, undoubtedly bored with a routine assignment often repeated. Bolan suspected it was a rare occurrence for anyone to wander into the valley, given the size of the cliffs surrounding it.

The warrior crawled undetected to within twenty feet of the two men. With a knife as his only weapon, Bolan decided to wait for a break. At some point, one of the guards would make a mistake, perhaps fall asleep, and then the Executioner would strike. He was in no hurry, since he wasn't following a timetable and had no specific plan of action once he got inside. He just planned to make things happen and cause maximum damage before he got the hell out of there.

Bolan had to wait a long time before he got his chance. A half moon had climbed a handbreadth above a craggy pinnacle. A large army of small but hungry insects had discovered Bolan as he crouched in the grass, and he tried to ignore their stinging bites as he concentrated on the guards.

One of them finally left, heading back inside.

The door had barely closed before Bolan rose and drew back his knife. The blade flew straight and true at the man outlined in the moonlight, stabbing directly through the base of the throat.

The terrorist dropped, his hands clutching at the knife hilt flush against his skin. His death throes gradually subsided until he lay still.

Bolan sprinted to the cave mouth, ripping the AK-47 from the dead guard's hands.

The warrior froze by the door, listening for sounds of activity beyond. The other guard would eventually return and if he came back to find his partner dead, the alarm would be given instantly. It would be better to hang tough for a while and eliminate this particular nest of vipers. Not only would he buy himself some time, but he would clear an escape route behind him.

The waiting paid off. The second terrorist barreled through the door, shouting something incomprehensible to his watch mate.

The words forewarned Bolan of the guy's arrival. As the hardman stepped through the doorframe, Bolan rocketed the butt of the assault rifle head high, connecting on the man's jaw. The newcomer dropped backward through the doorway, and the Executioner stepped after the falling body. One hard slam with the rifle finished the job, cracking the skull like a soft-shelled crab.

He dragged the corpse into the brush and returned for the other body. When it, too, was concealed Bolan took the time to scuff away the signs of the struggle. It might only buy him a few seconds of grace, but in combat seconds were more precious than jewels.

The Executioner slung the AK over his shoulder and grabbed the Uzi the other guy had toted, stuffing extra clips in his pockets. Then he eased the door back, his finger on the trigger of the Uzi.

LIBERTAD LEFT the interrogation chamber in search of fresh amusement. Antonia was beginning to wane as an attraction, remaining unconscious for longer periods of time. She wasn't responding to the questioning as well, either, seeming to be in a state of shock most of the time that protected her from realizing what was being done to her.

He was afraid that the red-haired traitor was going to die on him. But it was much too soon for that. She had not yet come close to paying for the fear he had felt when crouched in the dark tunnel with bullets whining all around him.

The coldhearted sadist had many more vicious experiments in mind.

It was not at all satisfying. He supposed the woman would have to rest until she was able to be aware of what was being done to her. In the meantime, he decided to pay a visit to Stone.

The American crouched in a cleverly designed cell. The ceiling wasn't high enough to permit a prisoner to stand upright, nor was the cell wide enough at any point for the prisoner to sit with any degree of comfort. There was no water, there were no sanitary facilities, and the only light and air came through a small grate in the iron door.

Libertad watched Stone for a moment. He looked perfectly miserable. It had been the squad leader's idea to subject the American to this indignity and discomfort until his spirit was broken. Only then would he be a reliable captive.

"Stone, do you hear me?"

The American stirred, rousing himself from a pain-filled stupor.

"Are you ready to be given your parole, American? Will you become a loyal servant of the great Republic of New Democracy? Will you renounce the capitalist lies and embrace the teachings of the wise Gonzalo?"

Stone was fully awake now and full of vinegar. "You miserable son of a slug. What makes you think I would ever become part of what Gonzalo plans for Peru? I hope that he rots in hell!"

Libertad was tempted to shoot Stone on the spot. The barrel of his Uzi was jammed through the grate before he realized through a hate-filled haze that Stone was goading him into doing just that. He lowered the subgun.

"It is not wise to insult your captors. Very foolish in deed, Stone. If you wish to die of starvation, be our guest Or be wise and join us. Live or die, it's your choice."

Libertad stalked off while he still had the last word, no at all pleased by the encounter.

As the footsteps faded into the distance, Stone won dered why he was being so stubborn. It was not at all like him. But every time he thought of giving in, Blanski came to mind. Somehow, he knew instinctively that the big man would rather die than surrender, and he felt inadequate doing anything less. But still, he felt sorry for himself.

Sometimes dying was a lot easier than living.

BOLAN CREPT DOWN a broad corridor. Now that he was inside, he had three objectives: to find some weakness in the organization and exploit it, to find Stone if he was still living and rescue him and to make it out alive.

He had been traveling down deserted halls, peering into each room he passed. He had checked several dozen store rooms and thus far had seen nothing of interest, just heaps of innocuous boxes, sacks of tobacco and mounds of other things necessary to keep a guerrilla force fighting. Every thing except weapons and dynamite, the two things he sought.

The corridors were similar to those he had traversed underground, relics of the ancient Incas. This complex appeared to be primarily a storehouse for the town beyond with lots of small rooms off a web of passages. The main difference was that the halls were lit by crude strings of electric lights powered by some hidden generator.

The next room had a wooden door, which immediately aroused the warrior's suspicions, as none of the others had been secured. Apparently the Incas and the Path usually didn't believe in doors. He opened it silently and found himself in a large, shadow-filled room, staring at the back of a man who was tending what looked to be a small forge. This would be an excellent opportunity to gather some intelligence.

The Executioner slipped inside, closing the door softly behind him. The terrorist by the fire was so intent on his work that it was easy for Bolan to creep up behind him unnoticed.

The warrior lashed out with his forearm, catching the hardguy around the neck. He squeezed, but not hard enough to cut off the air supply.

The man's hands clawed at Bolan's arm. "Stop it," Bolan commanded in Spanish, his mouth near the guy's ear. "Any more trouble and I'll break your neck." The resistance stopped instantly.

"Now tell me, where is Gonzalo? Is he here?"

The terrorist shook his head as hard as he was able. The big man eased off a little at the throat. "No, he is not here. He has never been here. I have never seen him. It is true!"

As the warrior digested the words he admitted to himself that it jibed with what Brognola had told him. Gonzalo was more of a legend than a leader. Unless this guy was completely ignorant—or a better actor than Bolan gave him credit for—the Executioner wouldn't be able to settle any score with the big boss in this valley.

As Bolan considered his next move, his gaze moved around the room and fastened on an object in a far corner.

Someone was tied to a rack, the signs of torture visible even across the chamber. And now that Bolan looked more closely, what he had taken for a forge for working metal was a small furnace, with an array of irons and pincers glowing red-hot on the burning coals.

It reminded Bolan of some of the worst times in his Mafia hunts, the times when he had come across the tortured remnants of what had once been men and women.

Bolan's rage reached fever pitch and erupted, a fierce volcano that washed over the man in his grasp, a red tide of anger that flowed through his body. He jerked his muscled forearm, cutting off the hapless man's wind. When the warrior's wrath abated, he dropped the lifeless corpse to the ground. He wasn't going to get any more information from the guy, but at the moment Bolan didn't care.

He walked over to the rack, and with a shock, Bolan recognized its occupant as the radiant beauty who had approached and spoken to him in the restaurant, Carrillo's secretary.

His stomach churned as he looked at the damage, and he had to turn away, bile rising in his throat. His eyes fixed on an array of rusty, blood-stained knives and other implements heaped on a low table. He picked up the sharpest looking one.

He would do what had to be done.

20

Bolan left the chamber, a shiver of disgust running down his spine. People died, that was inevitable. He had been behind the gun often enough himself. But the mentality that was required to perform such brutal acts, to do things to another human that were rooted in sick nightmares, was beyond his comprehension.

He didn't want to understand.

Bolan forced himself to become calm, to concentrate on staying alive, rather than on his revenge. Anything else risked disaster—such as being gunned down by someone who had stayed frosty and had not let his emotions run wild.

The big man would have liked to ask Antonia some questions himself, since much of what he had endured since coming to Peru was the direct result of his visit to her boss's office. Now he might never know the answers.

Tough. He was just going to have to play out his hand the way it had been dealt to him. But that didn't mean that he couldn't try to stack the deck in his favor.

Bolan eased down the corridor, every sense attuned to his surroundings. Through an effort of will, he turned his mind from the bloody lump of flesh he had left, and tried to imagine where the best spot for a weapons depot would be.

He checked each room as he passed, not at all sure what
he was looking for. Most were simply large empty squares.

The warrior was somewhat surprised that he hadn't seen
much of the opposition so far. He guessed that the complex
was probably lightly manned at the best of times, serving
as a headquarters and a transit station for the terrorists.

Bolan kept moving forward. Since he didn't know where
he was going, the safest route was straight ahead, making
it easy for him to retrace his steps to the exit. As he moved
farther into the complex, the fresh air and starlight of the
outdoors seemed more like a distant and elusive memory.

A couple of doors down, he found a small man with a
thin mustache scribbling at a desk made from boards piled
on crates. This was definitely a low-budget revolution, Bolan thought. The man didn't notice the Executioner's
stealthy approach until the big man's shadow eclipsed the
terrorist's writing pad. The Peruvian looked up with a start
and gaped at the stranger.

Bolan reached over the narrow desk, wrapped a callused
hand around the other man's throat and jerked him out of
his hard-backed chair.

"You've got two seconds to tell me where your leaders
are before I crush your windpipe."

He eased up the pressure a bit to let the other guy choke
out an answer. "Capitalist pig!" was all the response he
listened to before he clamped down again.

"You don't hear very well, do you? I'll ask you one last
time. Where are your leaders?"

"Yankee bastard! I will never tell—"

"You're right. You'll never tell anyone anything again."
Bolan gripped the hardman's neck with both hands and
pressed. The warrior released his hold and the dead man fell
to the floor, his eyes glassing over.

Bolan pulled the body behind the desk. He was about to leave when an idea twigged in the back of his mind. The warrior paced across the room, picked up a small alarm clock and stuffed it in the sack he carried. He also stripped the dead terrorist of his cheap wristwatch.

Bolan continued his investigation, moving slowly and at all times trying to determine his location relative to the main exit. Getting lost in the rock-lined web would be all too easy and a potentially fatal mistake.

He wandered up and down corridors methodically, and passed more storerooms and an occasional empty office or bunk room before he found what he was searching for.

A large iron door signaled that something valuable was protected in the room behind. Fortunately the terrorists didn't believe in locking doors. He pushed the heavy portal back and found himself in another storeroom.

The dim light from the bulb outside the entrance showed dozens of cases of dynamite piled floor to ceiling, leaving barely enough room to walk in the chamber.

Bolan gave a low whistle. It was hard to estimate the total stock—kind of like guessing the number of jelly beans crammed into a jar—but he figured there had to be at least a hundred thousand sticks jammed into the room.

Enough to reduce the fortress to smoking rubble.

He checked to make sure there were some blasting caps among the explosives, then went looking for more supplies. He had a plan in mind, but there were a couple of pieces that he still had to fit together.

Bolan padded along more dim corridors, avoiding those that were completely dark. He concentrated on constructing a mental map of the area, with the exit and the dynamite room firmly in mind.

As he moved forward in the shadows, a sound from an intersection up ahead stopped him in his tracks. He listened more closely. To his left, he heard the crackle of static and snatches of conversation.

He followed the racket, and in moments he was outside a radio room. The operator was writing a transmitted message and was oblivious to the Executioner's entry.

The butt of the AK-47 rocketed down on the radioman's spine with killing force. The technician dropped over his pad as his pen rolled onto the floor. The deadly blow was the last message he would ever receive.

The radio gave an outraged squeal as Bolan drove the butt of the Kalashnikov into the delicate machinery, cutting off the monotonous voice coming from the speaker. Then the warrior picked up a powerful battery and some wire from among the wreckage and began to retrace his steps to the explosives.

After a few minutes, he began to think that he had missed a turn. The empty rooms and featureless corridors suddenly all looked the same. Bolan had had a lifetime dose of being lost underground already. He had no desire to repeat the experience.

He told himself resolutely that he knew where he was going. Soon, he believed, since the areas he passed began to look familiar. Bolan thought grimly that he might be falling victim to his own imagination, to his growing sense of unease at being stuck underground.

But those were emotions that had to take a back seat to what he had set out to accomplish. He didn't have time to lose his cool.

When Bolan finally reached the dynamite storerooms, he hurriedly assembled a bomb trigger with the wire and alarm clock. He hesitated over setting the timer. If he allowed himself only an hour, that wouldn't give him much time to find Stone. If he left it much longer, there was the danger that someone might find his surprise and disarm it. He compromised on a two-hour delay, noting the time as he set the clock.

Minutes were precious now, as the seconds ticked down to destruction.

LIBERTAD COULDN'T SLEEP. He lay alone on his hard bed, his mind juggling various factors as he wondered how he could turn them to his advantage. The council, General Palma, Antonia, the missing arms cache...all of these tumbled through his mind in myriad combinations.

The fighters of the Shining Path were not supposed to have any personal ambition. That might be true for the distant and almost mythical Gonzalo, but it apparently didn't apply to the present council members. Even in prison rumors had reached Libertad of factions and struggles for control within the senior ranks. The penalty for being on the wrong side of these rivalries might be death when one group finally gained the upper hand and began to purge opponents of the new terrorist regime.

Power was the elusive goal of every man in the higher echelons. Not only did power bring a measure of safety from the periodic waves of suspicion-fueled purges within the organization, but whoever ruled the Shining Path could rule all of Peru when the group finally gained control of the country.

Libertad believed that Gonzalo was dead and that the council used the fiction of their founder's continued existence as a convenient rallying point. And to justify their own actions, of course.

Libertad was young and ambitious. He had once been a rising star within the organization, propelled upward by his competence and his ruthlessness. Then for two years he had rotted in prison, ever since he was wounded in a bloody assault on a police barracks. He had had a lot of time to think and plan for the day when he was free. Almost unexpectedly, that day had actually arrived.

Now that he had returned, he intended to gain a place in the hierarchy and, eventually, take control of the council. He could certainly be more effective than the useless old men who were now mishandling the Shining Path's campaign against the government.

In the meantime, he needed to distract himself. Libertad decided to visit Antonia one more time. He had left her in the company of the inquisitor, who was just finishing up in preparation for tomorrow's session. The terrorist didn't intend to brutalize the woman any further tonight. He planned only to disturb her sleep with stories of the exquisite tortures he had planned for the next day.

Psychological pain could be as frightful as physical pain, although in a very different way, and he would do his utmost to bring her any suffering he could.

Libertad opened the door to the interrogation room and snapped on a light. His eyes fixed on the shoes of the inquisitor, who looked as though he had fallen drunk in front of his furnace.

On closer inspection the squad leader was taken aback to discover that someone had beaten the man's head in, leaving only a seeping ruin flooding the ancient bricks.

Libertad rushed to the rack, wondering if Antonia could possibly have rallied and escaped her bonds. But she was still there, her feet bound and her arms stretched above her head, which was tilted to the side, resting on a shoulder.

The terrorist sensed that something was wrong. When he examined the scarred body, he could tell that his victim was no longer breathing. A small wound above the heart, hardly visible on her marred flesh, told him that a single thrust from a sharp blade had robbed him of any more pleasure from the former terrorist.

Libertad ran from the room, shouting an alarm at the top of his lungs. There was an intruder in the complex.

BOLAN FADED into the doorway as he heard the approaching men. He poked his head out slightly until he could see what was happening. Farther down the corridor four men were coming his way, carrying flashlights to supplement the dim bulbs strung intermittently throughout the gloom. Each man toted a rifle.

They were moving cautiously, shining their beams into each area they passed. From their wariness, Bolan guessed that this wasn't some routine security patrol making the rounds. Obviously someone had become aware of his presence.

He was faced with a difficult choice. For thirty yards behind him there was nothing but a few more rooms similar to the one he was in right now, stone boxes that offered nowhere to hide.

And there was no way that he could leave his niche without risking a bullet in the back. Yet if he remained where he was, he would have to rely on not being spotted by the searchers—a poor bet at best.

Since he couldn't hide and he couldn't run away, there was no option.

The Executioner slid the assault rifle from his shoulder, poked the barrel of the AK-47 through the doorway and squeezed off a series of 3-round bursts.

Two of the terrorists crumpled to the ground, cored b
the tumbling slugs. The remaining two found cover in op
posite rooms and returned fire, bullets chipping away at th
stone near Bolan's face.

The warrior snapped at several bursts, conscious that b
didn't have many spare clips. The hammering of the gur
reverberated like nearby thunder in the confined space. F
wondered how long it would be before the sounds of th
firefight attracted reinforcements.

The Executioner had made up his mind to change po
tion and zigzag toward the two gunners. That way he cou
force the action and improve his angle on the conceal
men. He could also get himself killed, but there weren't ar
options. Time was against him. He glanced at his watch.
one hour and fifty-one minutes, the headquarters would b
history.

As would Bolan unless he escaped by then.

The terrorists made their move first. One man charg
Bolan, spraying a wall of flying metal ahead of him, wh
the second man sprinted in the opposite direction to sur
mon more troops.

Bolan dropped the messenger first, then tracked onto t
other rifleman and walked a line of parabellums from b
chest up to his throat.

Bolan paused momentarily to strip one of the bodies
a couple of spare clips. He slung the rifle and held the l
in a large hand as he trotted down the corridor. The b
man had abandoned stealth in favor of speed, knowing th
his priority was to hit hard. Then to get the hell out.

He knew more or less where he was headed, so he e
cided to take some time to look for Stone. However, th
was no point in wasting too much time in the search, a
was likely that Libertad had murdered Stone long ago. T

ofessor's body was probably lying at the bottom of some
rk shaft in the labyrinth.

Bolan spotted more men in the near distance, intent on
mbing the underground passages. He took a right, plan-
ng to circle around them quickly.

"Blanski! Wait! Get me out of here!"

Bolan started in surprise. "Stone. I'm glad you made it
s far." Bolan peered through the grate in the door of a
y cell. "I see that you and Libertad have become great
ends in my absence."

"So it really is you. I thought I might be hallucinating
en I saw you go by. I was sure you were dead, fallen into
e pit."

"We're not dead yet, Stone. Just let me take care of some
siness, and then I'll get you out. Hang in there."

"Where does he think I'll go?" Stone muttered to him-
f as Bolan returned the way he had come.

The warrior got the drop on the terrorists again and ex-
ded from the side corridor, firing into the closely packed
oup of three moving down the passage. The Uzi spit
nd after round into the surprised troopers. When the
rrior released the trigger, three ventilated bodies lay
aped together in the corridor.

He trotted back to Stone and concentrated on freeing the
er man. There was no way of picking the lock, so Bolan
dered Stone to stand back as far as he could. After two
rsts from the Uzi the door swung free.

Stone stumbled from the cell and fell on his face, groan-
, as his muscles spasmed. "Just leave me here, Blanski.
t yourself out. I can't move."

'We'll both get out," Bolan said, bending over to reach
Stone. The other man looked quite light, and the war-

rior wouldn't have any difficulty in carrying the small ma
the short distance to freedom.

A shot rang out, but Bolan didn't hear it as he pitche
over on top of Stone.

LIBERTAD LOWERED THE RIFLE, thinking how lucky it wa
that he had been trailing his team. They were dead and
had single-handedly killed the Yankee dog.

Stone was screaming hysterically, almost complete
covered by the body of his companion. Libertad walked
to him and kicked him heavily in the side. Stone shut up

Bolan was still bleeding, a rivulet oozing from his scal
The terrorist could see the arteries pulsing in the Ame
can's neck. So he wasn't dead yet.

Another patrol arrived attracted by the metallic soun
of gunshots. "Two live Americans? Let us kill them rig
now before they can cause any further trouble," the patr
leader said. He swung his rifle toward the two prone me

"No!" Libertad commanded, pushing the barrel of t
assault gun aside. "They are my prisoners. I intend to ke
them alive until the council orders otherwise. So do not
terfere unless you want the council to wonder why you
stroyed prisoners before they could be questioned."

The other squad leader got the point and clicked
safety on. "Then let us get them somewhere safe for no
This cell can no longer be used."

"I know just the place," Libertad replied with a smil

WHEN BOLAN AWOKE, his head throbbed as though
NFL linebacker were inside trying to smash his way o
His hair was matted with dried blood, and more coated
cheek.

With a start, he realized where he was. His feet were
ound and his hands were tied above him. An orange glow
t the room from the opposite end, while various imple-
ents of torture were scattered on tables around him.

He was naked and tied to a rack, the same one that An-
nia de Vincenzo had occupied a short while ago.

Stone was roped to a chair across the room, a gag stuffed
his mouth.

"Ah, Blanski, you are awake. I see that you recognize
here you are." Libertad advanced from beside the fur-
ace until he stood beside his prisoner. "I know that you
ere here not long ago. And so you recognize full well what
es on here, and you understand just what you can expect.
or Antonia. She was so beautiful. No one would call you
eautiful, Blanski, but if you ever escape from here you will
ighten small children with your ugliness."

Bolan spoke, his voice sounding harsh and dry. His
outh felt as though it had been stuffed with cotton. "No
atter what you do to me, you'll always be a damn sight
glier than me. Your ugliness comes from within."

Libertad struck Bolan across the cheek repeatedly.
Brave words, American. But I will see you whimpering for
ercy soon. You will plead with me to kill you, but I won't.
e will enjoy ourselves with you for a very long time. And
en maybe, just maybe we will let you go, so that for the
st of your miserable life you will hate mirrors. But you
ill see yourself in the disgusted, pitying looks of every-
e who turns away from the sight of you. And you will
member Libertad and the power of the Shining Path."

The terrorist strode toward the door and paused. "My
sistant here will acquaint you with some of our tools.
ch has a different purpose and creates a new sensation.
st a sampling of what is to come over the next few days,

when you will learn about their uses in great detail. Stor
will keep you company. I'm sure that what he sees will pe
suade him of where his true loyalties should lie. In th
meantime I shall tell our council about my brave recaptu
of the capitalist animals. You have done me a great f.
vor.''

As Libertad turned to leave, Bolan noticed a second ma
in the chamber, who advanced toward him, a wide gr
plastered across his face, a poker extended in front of hir

The tip was glowing white-hot and driving like a rock
directly at Bolan's right eye.

21

.bertad walked down the corridor, considering what he
ould tell the council. He realized that his success in cap-
ring the intruder was tempered with a certain element of
sponsibility for the American's actions.

His concern was to distance himself from the damage this
ingerous Yankee had caused. He was shown in to the
volutionary Council immediately.

The atmosphere in the room was electric. The glances
rected his way by the council members were baleful and
ll of suspicion. Libertad realized that he was in for a
ugh ride.

"Tell us, comrade, how this has come to be. An Ameri-
n, whom you claim to be dead, shows up in our most se-
t complex, killing many of our people." The chairman
oke in a low voice, barely above a whisper. Libertad had
strain to pick up the words above the minute noises the
er members made. The terrorist knew that the quiet tone
s a sign of extreme anger.

"Comrade, I truly thought that the American was dead.
s appearance here is as much a surprise to me as it is to
u. Fortunately I recaptured him and he is now being held
questioning. I will soon find out everything we need to
ow." Libertad tried to keep his voice from quavering.

"Yes, find out how he was able to make his way una
sisted through the tunnels and what his purpose was
coming here. Maybe he was guided by another traito
Maybe he has come to destroy the council. What do y
think, Libertad?"

The ambitious young man was sweating now. He cou
see where this line of questioning might lead him—in fro
of a Revolutionary Tribunal or, worse, the inquisitor.

"I had nothing to do with his escape from the pits or l
coming here. Nothing at all."

"Why so defensive, Libertad?" The chairman's ey
sparkled with the evil light of a cobra ready to strike. "I
because it was your idea to bring this Blanski here?"

"It was with your approval," Libertad protested.

"Yes, on your recommendation," the chairman sl
back.

"Soon I will have all the answers you require." Libert
had run out of comebacks. The facts, twisted as they we
made him look pretty bad. Blanski would have to sing
other song, and sing it loud.

Libertad would make sure the Yankee sang any song
terrorist requested.

The chairman seemed to sense what Libertad was thi
ing. "Come, comrades," he said, as he pushed back
chair. "Let us see what this American has to say for hi
self."

The council left for the interrogation room, with Lib
tad reluctantly following. Who knew what the Americ
would say just to exact his revenge against the man w
captured him?

THE HOT POKER HALTED two inches from Bolan's eye.
could feel the searing heat of the metal tickling the orb.

The sadist threw back his head and laughed, his noxious breath washing over Bolan. "Capitalist pig! We will not begin so quickly. One day we will poke your eyes out with a burning rod, but until then, you will have that to look forward to. Today will be just a small sample of everything we have planned for the days to come. Where shall we begin?"

Bolan's tormentor began to slowly wave the hot rod over the length of his prisoner's body, letting his victim anticipate the moment when the white-hot tip would come to rest on his skin.

A tremor coursed down the big man's spine—he was angry. He exerted every last ounce of strength he could on the manacles binding his hands. His head throbbed and a red mist swam in front of his eyes as his muscles strained the iron chains.

The terrorist chuckled as he saw the muscles bulging. "Save your energy for screaming, American dog. No one has ever escaped."

The bolts popped from the wall with a screech of torn metal. The startled terrorist reacted quickly, swinging the poker like a bat at Bolan's forehead.

Although his arms felt as if they were on fire, the warrior reached up to grab the bar, keeping his hands well away from the glowing tip. He seized it with both fists and pulled.

The terrorist didn't let go. Instead he dropped on the prisoner, shifting his grip so that he now grasped the branding iron near each end. The torturer pushed down with his weight behind him, slowly forcing the tip toward Bolan's cheek.

The Executioner took a deep breath and exerted a pulsing surge of power through his right arm. The iron bar pivoted back and caught the terrorist in the left side. Bolan thought he heard the crack of breaking bone.

The man fell away, dropping the hot poker. He got up again with a snarl, his left arm grasping his side. He grabbed a long pole off the wall, a metal spear that tapered in a fine point. It was more than long enough to spit Bolan where he sat, trapped by the chains securing his ankles.

Bolan wound up and threw the poker just as the terrorist began his charge. The rod sailed through the air like an iron arrow and buried itself in the guy's belly.

The man began to scream hysterically as the hot metal burned his flesh, giving him a taste of the agony that he had eagerly dealt his helpless victims.

He stumbled a few more steps and crumpled to the floor beside the rack, his hands working feebly at the heated rod. Bolan reached over and extracted a set a keys from the guy's belt, and in a moment he was free from his shackles.

He moved quickly to Stone and cut his bonds. "Let's get the hell out of here. We don't have much time." Less than fifteen minutes remained until zero hour.

Before they quit the chamber the warrior dressed himself with his torn clothes and picked up the Uzi and the AK-47, which Libertad had conveniently dumped in a corner. He handed the assault rifle to Stone. "Use this."

"How?" the academic protested. "I've never fired a gun in my life."

"Simple. The safety's off. Point at the bad guys and pull the trigger. Stop when they all fall down. Now let's move."

Bolan fisted the Uzi and pushed the door open. The way to the exit was clear. But twenty yards ahead a dozen men filled the passage and were marching toward the interrogation room.

The Executioner opened fire with the SMG, concentrating on the two point men. A stream of 9 mm death punched the men to the ground, jets of blood spurting onto the uniforms of their surprised comrades.

The survivors began a stampede to the rear, kicking and clawing on the now slippery stones in an effort to escape.

Bolan dropped one last man, practically tearing the terrorist's head from his body with a burst to the neck before the lucky few survivors vanished out of sight around a corner.

LIBERTAD SLUNK BACK around the corner after a long wait, when he was sure the coast was clear. The rest of the council members were still running, heading for the deep underground refuges.

He examined the heaped bodies of the Path's leaders, looking for survivors. There were none. He found the chairman near the front of the pack. The hawk eyes that had pinned Libertad minutes earlier were no longer there. They, along with the rest of his features, had been smashed by the force of several bullets that had scrambled the chairman's keen brain before bursting through his face.

Well, that was one less rival. Still, Libertad thought, in spite of the chaos, perhaps he could turn this disaster to his advantage.

He grabbed a rifle and walked cautiously down the passage leading to the exit. It was an M-16. How appropriate that he should kill the American with a weapon manufactured by his own countrymen. In the distance, he heard the hammering sound of a firefight in progress. The terrorist flattened himself in a shadow, waiting for the telltale signs of violence to fade away. The American was a very dangerous man.

This time Libertad wasn't taking prisoners.

THERE WASN'T TIME to mop up, so Bolan headed for the exit at a trot, reloading on the run. Stone brought up the rear. The warrior was certain that the guards at the gate would have been replaced, and he was right. Two men stood by the inner gates, facing down the corridor, weapons drawn.

They made the fatal mistake of shouting a challenge at the approaching men.

Bolan fired first, spraying the guards chest high, knocking them back against the heavy wooden door as he stitched a lengthwise figure eight back and forth over the gunners. Blotchy red patches peppered the wood behind them, like a scarlet abstract painting.

The warrior traded weapons with Stone. He gripped the Kalashnikov, commanding the professor to watch their back. He stepped over one of the leaking bodies and shoved the door inward. The space between the two sets of doors was empty. Bolan could almost visualize the gunmen crouched outside, rifles trained on the exit, waiting for him to step through.

The Executioner dropped to the floor, aimed the assault rifle and fired low, tracking a line of heavy metal through the thin wood and back again, sighting just above ground level on the second pass. Splinters flew as the slugs bored through to the darkness beyond.

Bolan released the trigger and listened. Nothing seemed to be moving outside. He stood and opened the rear door and motioned Stone inside, instructing him in what he wanted done.

At his signal, Stone flung the door wide and Bolan popped through, landing in a roll from the tumble.

He found himself eyeball to eyeball with a dead man, a small hole in his forehead leaking a trickle of blood into the heavy eyebrows. The second ambusher sprawled motionless at the side of the exit.

"Get out here, Stone," Bolan called. "Let's head for the hills."

"It seems like weeks since I was last in the fresh air. You lose all sense of time underground."

"Speaking of time, we don't have much of it to waste. Let's get moving."

"Why? Is something going on that I should know about?"

"You'll know when it happens."

They trudged over the broken ground, stumbling among the protruding stones and ancient ruins that poked through the dust. The moon had moved halfway across the sky. Bolan found it difficult to believe that only a few hours had passed since he'd entered the Shining Path headquarters.

They had trekked a few hundred yards and were about to enter the desolate village when they heard a dull roar behind them. A faint tremor vibrated beneath their feet.

The cave mouth exploded with a spout of flame, spewing a mixture of pulverized rock and dust. The mountain above appeared to settle, as a portion was sucked down to fill the collapsing interior chambers.

Bolan paused a moment, thinking about the men trapped inside the mountain. A fitting end for murderers who ruthlessly butchered their fellow man.

TWO BODIES LITTERED the ground near the exit. Libertad cursed. Idiots, all of them. They had had a perfect opportunity to destroy the invaders and had let them get away.

They had paid for their stupidity, and their failure would only make his success the more brilliant by comparison.

He stepped into the underbrush, confident of his ability to track and kill the American monsters. This was a game that he had practiced for years, hunting the government pigs in the wilds of the mountains. He had always been victorious. Soon Blanski's head would be in his sights.

Libertad had moved only a few dozen yards from the exit when he was knocked to the ground by a gale-force wind. He felt the ground heave under him, and heard a grinding rumble from behind.

He knew immediately what had happened. "The dynamite," he moaned. Libertad hated to think what a blow this was to the organization. Most of their supplies—including weapons, dynamite, food and money—had been scattered in underground chambers. The terrorist doubted that even a bent nail could be recovered now.

Many of the movement's great leaders had died this day.

He had lost his torture chamber, but he would still make the American pay.

He moved out, noticing for the first time how much his back hurt. The explosion had peppered him with rock chips—it was almost like being blasted with a load of buckshot.

Libertad would attend to that later, after he had destroyed the Americans.

He crept forward in the darkness, and it was almost as if his feet remembered the ground beneath him from the many times he had walked it in the past. Ahead, he heard the jabbering of the foolish academic, Stone.

The terrorist gave a guttural snarl and picked up his pace.

BOLAN AND STONE WERE in the middle of the plaza between the temples. The former professor was indulging his interest in the ruins and was explaining his theories to Bolan.

"Listen, Stone, if you want to stay and explore, fine. I'm leaving." Bolan stalked off across the square.

Stone hurried to catch up. "All right. But I don't see why you are being so objectionable. With the Shining Path destroyed, there probably isn't another human being within ten miles. So what's the hurry?"

Bolan wasn't sure. His finely honed combat sense told him they weren't alone. There was someone on their trail, and he meant to find out who it was.

He signaled to Stone to go to ground at the base of a statue of an ancient reclining god and shifted off to the left, doubling back.

He waited behind a tumbled column, hardly breathing, until a faint shadow appeared and disappeared between two monuments. From the way the shadow moved, Bolan had been spotted, and the hunter was trying to turn his flank.

Bolan had learned that trick years ago. He watched the shadow weave and duck one more time. The guy was good, not giving Bolan a clear shot as he moved.

The next time the invader shifted position, Bolan moved stealthily to a stone obelisk farther left. When the hunter moved again, it was evident that he hadn't seen Bolan change cover.

The mystery man didn't know it, but the hunter had become the hunted. His next move would be his last.

When the shadow broke cover again, Bolan cut loose with the AK-47. The tracker screamed and toppled, thrashing, to the ground.

The Executioner stepped warily forward, the barrel pointed at the wounded man's chest. He stopped three feet away from the sprawled figure, who was moaning in the moonlight.

"Ah, Libertad. How nice to meet again." The terrorist had a slug in the shoulder and another in the belly. Stone came charging up, anxious to see what had happened.

"Blanski, you dog..." Libertad found it hard to choke the words from between pain-stretched lips.

"If I really was an animal, I'd leave you here to fry."

"You mean you will save me?"

"In a manner of speaking." A gunshot rang out, followed by dead silence. Then, gradually, the faint night sounds resumed.

EPILOGUE

As his chauffeur drove him across the city in a limousine, General Arturo Palma raised his head from the report he had been reading and wondered for perhaps the thousandth time what had become of Blanski and the de Vinenzo woman. He knew that he should have killed both of them earlier when he had the chance. That way he would at least know now where they were.

Palma hadn't heard from Antonia since she had fled Lima. She represented a danger, particularly when out of his sight, for if word of his tenuous connection to the Shining Path ever surfaced it would ruin his political career.

His plan to use the Shining Path to further his ambitions was a good one, and Antonia had proved to be the perfect link.

He must keep his eyes open now to spot another likely contact among the prisoners he captured.

The limousine halted at a traffic light. A foolish waste of his time, the general thought. He made a mental note to arrange for a police escort in future to save himself from these bothersome delays.

As he stared uninterestedly out the window, he noticed a man fifty yards away raise an object to shoulder height and aim in his direction.

Realization hit Palma with a wave of shock.

His hand fumbled for the door handle just as the rocket was launched.

The limousine and Arturo Palma exploded in a fireball of scorched metal and charred flesh.

Phoenix Force—bonded in secrecy to avenge the acts of terrorists everywhere.

Super Phoenix Force #2

American ''killer'' mercenaries are involved in a KGB plot to overthrow the government of a South Pacific island. The American President, anxious to preserve his country's image and not disturb the precarious position of the island nation's government, sends in the experts—Phoenix Force—to prevent a coup.

**The struggle continues
in a land of death . . .**

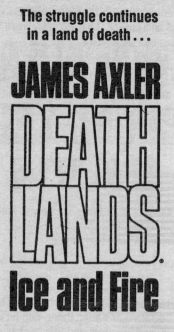

JAMES AXLER
DEATH LANDS®
Ice and Fire

A startling discovery that will alter the lives of Ryan Cawdor and his band of postholocaust survivors is made when the group finds several cryogenically preserved bodies and encounters renegade bikers who call themselves "Hell's Angels."

More than action adventure...
books written by the men who were there

VIETNAM: GROUND ZERO T.M.

ERIC HELM

Told through the eyes of an American Special Forces squad, an elite jungle fighting group of strike-and-hide specialists fight a dirty war half a world away from home.

These books cut close to the bone, telling it the way it really was.

"Vietnam at Ground Zero is where this book is written. The author has been there, and he knows. I salute him and I recommend this book to my friends."

—Don Pendleton
creator of *The Executioner*

"Helm writes in an evocative style that gives us Nam as it most likely was, without prettying up or undue bitterness."

—*Cedar Rapids Gazette*

"Eric Helm's Vietnam series embodies a literary standard of excellence. These books linger in the mind long after their reading."

—*Midwest Book Review*

Available wherever paperbacks are sold.

VIE-1

TAKE 'EM NOW